# More Legends & Stories of Ireland

Here's the best o' good spirits.

# More Legends & Stories of Ireland

*Samuel Lover*

NONSUCH

First published 1837


Nonsuch Publishing Limited
The Mill, Brimscombe Port, Stroud, Gloucestershire, GL5 2QG
www.nonsuch-publishing.com

Nonsuch Publishing is an imprint of Tempus Publishing Group

For comments or suggestions, please email the editor of this series at:
classics@tempus-publishing.com



British Library Cataloguing in Publication Data.
A catalogue record for this book is available from the British Library.

ISBN 1-84588-201-6
ISBN-13 (from January 2007) 978-1-84588-201-3

Typesetting and origination by Nonsuch Publishing Limited
Printed in Great Britain by Oaklands Book Services Limited

# CONTENTS

# Introduction to the Modern Edition

In 1800, three years after the birth of Samuel Lover, the British and Irish parliaments passed the Act of Union which, on 1 January 1801, would lead to the creation of the United Kingdom of Great Britain and Ireland. Since the twelfth century Ireland had been under English and, later, British rule (even if, at times, their writ ran only as far as the bounds of the Pale, twenty miles from Dublin), and Poyning's Law of 1494 had made the parliament in Dublin effectively subservient to that in London. The Constitution of 1782 had given unprecedented legislative freedom to the Parliament of Ireland, which not all of its members wanted to surrender, but the political situation following the bloody Irish Rebellion of 1798 and the favourable terms proposed by the British meant that the Act was eventually passed with large majorities in both houses.

The Union of Britain and Ireland was, though, only a political union. Ireland retained its cultural identity, which was strengthened by the fact that, unlike the populations of England, Wales and Scotland, the majority of the Irish were (and are) Roman Catholics (most of Ireland's Protestants descended from those 'planted' there by the British in the sixteenth and seventeenth centuries). Also, unlike Wales and Scotland, Ireland had a Lord Lieutenant with viceregal powers and a Chief Secretary imposed by the Prime Minister in London. But, in common with the Scots and the Welsh, although the Irish were ruled by the English, they always remained Irish.

The Society of United Irishmen, led by Protestants inspired by the French Revolution, had risen against the British in 1798 and been brutally put down. The subsequent abolition of the Irish parliament led to the emergence of two forms of Irish nationalism: the more radical, violent branch had only a small following in the early nineteenth century, whereas the more moderate, non-violent movement had the support of a larger number of people as well as the Roman Catholic Church. The Catholic Association and the Repeal Association campaigned for Catholic Emancipation (which was achieved in 1829) and the repeal of the Act of Union, rather than the overthrow of British rule through force of arms (which did not come about until 1922). Both were led by Daniel O'Connell, known as 'The Emancipator' and 'The Liberator,' Ireland's foremost politician during the early nineteenth century.

In these circumstances, it is hardly surprising that there was considerable interest in Irish legends and stories: a common heritage unites the people of a country against outsiders. One writer to cater for this taste was William Carleton (1794–1869). His *Traits and Stories of the Irish Peasantry* first appeared in 1830 in two volumes, with a further three volumes being published in 1833 and *Tales of Ireland* in 1834; the five volumes of *Traits and Stories* went through more than fifty editions before his death. Brought up amongst the peasantry of rural Ireland, Carleton was able to describe their lives and their stories with authority and affection.

Samuel Lover, however, came from a very different background. The son of a stockbroker, he was born in Dublin in 1797 and began his career as a painter, being elected to the Royal Hibernian Academy in 1828, at the age of thirty-one. His peculiar talent was for miniature portraits, and he painted a number of the Irish aristocracy; one of his best-known portraits was of Niccolò Paganini, the celebrated virtuoso violinist, painted during his visit to Dublin, which was exhibited at the Royal Academy in London. He was one of the first writers for the *Dublin University Magazine* but it was with *Legends and Stories of Ireland*, published in two parts, in 1831 and 1834, and illustrated by himself, that he made his name as an author. *More Legends and Stories* is the second of those volumes.

As well as a painter and a writer, Lover was a musician and, after he moved to London in 1835, he was well received in society, often appearing at the fashionable receptions of the Countess of Blessington, where he sang a number of his songs. They proved so popular that he published them, as *Songs and Ballads*, in 1839. Lady Blessington's receptions were not only an opportunity for Lover to display his musical prowess, they were also a way for him to meet influential people. Amongst his fellow guests was Charles Dickens, with whom Lover founded *Bentley's Miscellany*, the magazine in which Dickens would serialise *Oliver Twist*. Through moving in the right circles, he was asked to paint the ambassador of the Nawab of Awadh, who was visiting London, and Lord Brougham, the Lord Chancellor, in his official robes.

Irish folklore was a recurrent theme of Lover's ballads, and one of them, 'Rory O'More,' about the principal organiser of the Irish Rebellion of 1641, proved so popular that he later developed it into a novel, *Rory O'More: a National Romance*, which was first published in 1837 and later dramatised for the Adelphi Theatre, the first of several plays to be written by him. *Handy Andy: an Irish Tale,* followed in 1842 and *Treasure Trove* in 1884; *The Lyrics of Ireland*, which he edited, appeared in 1858 and *Metrical Tales and Other Poems* in 1860. He returned to Dublin some years before his death, but died in St Helier, on the island of Jersey, where he had gone for his health, in 1860.

# NOTICE

A BOOK, ENTITLED "POPULAR STORIES and Legends of the Peasantry of Ireland, with Illustrations, by Samuel Lover," &c. &c. has lately been published in Dublin, with the authorship of which book I am totally unconnected.

Six illustrations for the volume were supplied by me, and those who are answerable for the work should have let the public distinctly understand that *so far only* was I concerned, and not have imputed to me, by a questionable use of my name, an authorship which I feel it necessary to disavow.

From the duplicity of this title, many have been induced to imagine that the work, to which it is prefixed, is *my* Second Series of Legends and Stories; and this very name, too, has been assumed, with a mere transposition, the book being entitled "Stories and Legends," although *there is not a single legend in its pages*.

I leave the Public to call such conduct by its right name.

The very great popularity with which BARNY O'REIRDON, THE NAVIGATOR, was favoured on its appearance in the *Dublin University Magazine*, has induced me to add it, along with LITTLE FAIRLY, from the same quarter, to the following Collection of Tales, which, with these exceptions, I place, for the first time, before the Public, in hope of their continued indulgence.

# ADDRESS

GENTLE READER, I SEND UP my card, and I hope you will not say you are "not at home."

It is some time since I paid you a visit, and you received me then so well, though quite a stranger, that I am tempted to hope you will not drop my acquaintance, now that you know who I am.

It is no easy matter to have a card presented to you, seated as you are in the Temple of Public Favour:—Critics are the lacqueys that line the hall leading to the sanctuary, and it is not every one's card they will send in; while, sometimes an unfortunate name gets so roughly handled amongst them, as to be rendered quite illegible.

However, they were extremely obliging to me, the last time I needed their good offices, and as I have done nothing since to offend them, I hope they won't keep me standing at the door, in these Easterly winds, till I catch a Spring cough, though, I dare say, my friends in the Row would be well pleased if I were driven into a *rapid consumption*.

Be that as it may, I trust they will know me again as I stand in the crowd, although a slight alteration has taken place in my costume since last I appeared before them. I then wore a *caubeen*, being only a raw recruit, but as I was permitted at once, to rise from the awkward squad, and since then have been promoted, on the strength of my first exercise, to the rank of *third edition*, I gratefully carry the honor that has been conferred upon me, and hope I may, for the future, be permitted to wear the feather in my cap.

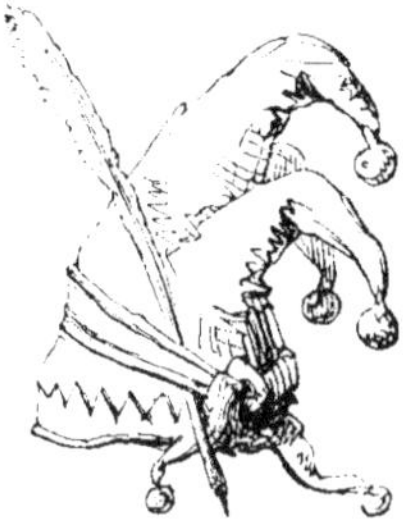

# BARNY O'REIRDON,

## THE NAVIGATOR

### CHAP. I.—OUTWARD-BOUND

"Well, he went farther and farther than I can tell."

NURSERY TALE.

A VERY STRIKING CHARACTERISTIC OF an Irishman is his unwillingness to be outdone. Some have asserted that this arises from vanity, but I have ever been unwilling to attribute an unamiable motive to my countrymen where a better may be found, and one equally tending to produce a similar result, and I consider a deep-seated spirit of emulation to originate this peculiarity. Phrenologists might resolve it by supposing the organ of the love of approbation to predominate in our Irish craniums, and it may be so; but as I am not in the least a metaphysician, and very little of a phrenologist, I leave those who choose, to settle the point in question, quite content with the knowledge of the fact with which I started, viz. the unwillingness of an Irishman to be outdone. This spirit, it is likely, may sometimes lead men into ridiculous positions; but it is equally probable, that the desire of surpassing one another has given birth to many of the noblest actions, and some of the most valuable inventions; let us, therefore, not fall out with it.

Now, having vindicated the *motive* of my countrymen, I will prove the total absence of national prejudice in so doing, by giving an illustration of the ridiculous consequences attendant upon this Hibernian peculiarity.

Barny O'Reirdon was a fisherman of Kinsale, and a heartier fellow never hauled a net nor cast a line into deep water: indeed Barny, independently of being a merry boy among his companions, a lover of good fun and good whiskey, was looked up to, rather, by his brother fishermen, as an intelligent fellow, and few boats brought more fish to market than Barny O'Reirdon's; his opinion on certain points in the craft was considered law, and in short, in his own little community, Barny was what is commonly called a leading man. Now, your leading man is always jealous in an inverse ratio to the sphere of his influence, and the leader of a nation is less incensed at a rival's triumph, than the great man of a village. If we pursue this descending scale, what a desperately jealous person the oracle of oyster-dredgers and cockle-women must be! Such was Barny O'Reirdon.

Seated one night at a public house, the common resort of

Barny and other marine curiosities, our hero got entangled in debate with what he called a strange sail—that is to say, a man he had never met before, and whom he was inclined to treat rather magisterially upon nautical subjects; at the same time that the stranger was equally inclined to assume the high hand over him, till at last the new-comer made a regular out-break by exclaiming, "Ah, tare-an-ouns, lave aff your balderdash, Mr O'Reirdon, by the powdhers o'war its enough, so it is, to make a dog bate his father, to hear you goin' an as if you war Curlumberus or Sir Crustyphiz Wran, when ivery one knows the divil a farther you ivir wor, nor ketchin' crabs or drudgin' oysters."

"Who towld you that, my Watherford Wondher?" rejoined Barny; "what the dickins do you know about sayfarin' farther nor fishin' for sprats in a bowl wid your grandmother?"

"Oh, baithershin," says the stranger.

"And who made you so bowld with my name?" demanded O'Reirdon.

"No matther for that," said the stranger; "but if you'd like for to know, shure its your cousin Molly Mullins knows me well, and maybe I don't know you and your's as well as the mother that bore you, aye, in throth; and shure I know the very thoughts o' you as well as if I was inside o' you, Barny O'Reirdon."

"By my soul thin you know betther thoughts than your own, Mr Whippersnapper, if that's the name you go by."

"No, it's not the name I go by; I've as good a name as your own, Mr O'Reirdon, for want of a betther, and that's O'Sullivan."

"Throth there's more than there's good o' them," said Barny.

"Good or bad, I'm a cousin o' your own twice removed by the mother's side."

"And is it the Widda O'Sullivan's boy you'd be that left this come Candlemas four years?"

"The same."

"Throth thin you might know betther manners to your eldhers, though I'm glad to see you, any how, agin; but a little thravellin' puts us beyant ourselves sometimes," said Barny, rather contemptuously.

"Throth, I nivir bragged out o' myself yit, and it's what I say, that a man that's only a fishin' aff the land all his life has no business to compare in the regard o' thracthericks wid a man that has sailed to Fingal."

This silenced any further argument on Barny's part. Where Fingal lay was all Greek to him; but, unwilling to admit his ignorance, he covered his retreat with the usual address of his countrymen, and turned the bitterness of debate into the cordial flow of congratulation at seeing his cousin again.

The liquor was freely circulated, and the conversation began to take a different turn, in order to lead from that which had nearly ended in a quarrel between O'Reirdon and his relation.

The state of the crops, county cess, road jobs, &c. became topics, and various strictures as to the utility of the latter were indulged in, while the merits of the neighbouring farmers were canvassed.

"Why thin," said one, "that field o' whate o' Michael Coghlan, is the finest field o' whate mortial eyes was ever set upon—divil the likes iv it myself ever seen far or near."

"Throth thin sure enough," said another, "it promises to be a fine crap anyhow, and myself can't help thinkin' it quare that Mickee Coghlan, that's a plain spoken, quite (quiet) man, and simple like, should have finer craps than Pether Kelly o' the big farm beyant, that knows all about the great saycrets o' the airth, and is knowledgeable to a degree, and has all the hard words that iver was coined at his fingers' ends."

"Faith, he has a power o' *blasthogue* about him sure enough," said the former speaker, "if that could do him any good, but he isn't fit to hould a candle to Michael Coghlan in the regard o' farmin'."

"Why, blur an agers," rejoined the upholder of science, "sure he met the Scotch steward that the Lord beyant has, one day, that I hear is a wondherful edicated man, and was brought over here to show us all a patthern—well, Pether Kelly met him one day, and, by gor, he discoorsed him to that degree that the Scotch chap hadn't a word left in his jaw."

"Well, and what was he the betther o' having more prate than a Scotchman?" asked the other.

"Why," answered Kelly's friend, "I think it stands to rayson that the man that done out the Scotch steward ought to know somethin' more about farmin' than Mickee Coghlan."

"Augh! don't talk to me about knowing," said the other, rather contemptuously. "Sure I gev in to you that he has a power o' prate, and the gift o' the gab, and all to that. I own to you that he has *the-o-ry* and the *che-mis-thery*, but he hasn't the *craps*. Now, the man that has the craps, is the man for my money."

"You're right, my boy," said O'Reirdon, with an approving thump of his brawny fist on the table, "it's a little talk goes far—*doin'* is the thing."

"Ah, yiz may run down larnin' if yiz like," said the undismayed stickler for theory versus practice, "but larnin' is a fine thing, and sure where would the world be at all only for it, sure where would the staymers (steam boats) be, only for larnin?"

"Well," said O'Reirdon, "and the divil may care if we never seen them; I'd rather dipind an wind and canvass any day than the likes o' them. What are they good for, but to turn good sailors into kitchen-maids, all as one, bilin' a big pot o' wather and oilin' their fire-irons, and throwin' coals an the fire? Augh! thim staymers is a disgrace to the say; they're for all the world like ould fogies, smokin' from mornin' till night, and doin' no good."

"Do you call it doin' no good to go fasther nor ships ivir wint before?"

"Pooh; sure Solomon, queen o' Sheba, said there was time enough for all things."

"Thrue for you," said O'Sullivan, "*fair and aisy goes far in a day*, is a good ould sayin'."

"Well, maybe you'll own to the improvemint they're makin' in the harbour o' Howth, beyant in Dublin, is some good."

"We'll see whether it 'ill be an improvemint first," said the obdurate O'Reirdon.

"Why, man alive, sure you'll own it's the greatest o' good it is, takin' up the big rocks out o' the bottom o' the harbour."

"Well, an' where's the wondher o' that? sure we done the same here."

"Oh yis, but it was whin the tide was out and the rocks was bare; but up in Howth, they cut away the big rocks from undher the say intirely."

"Oh, be aisy; why, how could they do that?"

"Aye, there's the matther, that's what larnin' can do; and wondherful it is intirely! and the way it is, is this, as I hear it, for I never seen it, but hard it described by the lord to some gintlemin and ladies one day in his garden where I was helpin' the gardener to land some salary (celery). You see the ingineer goes down undher the wather intirely, and can stay there as long as he plazes."

"Whoo! and what o' that? Sure I heerd the long sailor say, that come from the Aysthern Ingees, that the Ingineers there can a'most live undher wather; and goes down lookin' for dimonds, and has a sledge-hammer in their hand, brakein' the dimonds when they're too big to take them up whole, all as one as men brakein' stones an the road."

"Well, I don't wan to go beyant that; but the way the lord's ingineer goes down is, he has a little bell wid him, and while he has that little bell to ring, hurt nor harm can't come to him."

"Arrah be aisy."

"Divil a lie in it."

"Maybe it's a blessed bell," said O'Reirdon, crossing himself[1].

"No, it is not a blessed bell."

"Why thin now do you think me sitch a born nat'hral as to give into that; as if the ringin' iv a bell, barrin' it was a blessed bell, could do the like. I tell you it's unpossible."

"Ah, nothin's unpossible to God."

"Sure I wasn't denyin' that; but I say the bell is unpossible."

"Why," said O'Sullivan, "you see he's not altogether complate in the demonstheration o' the mashine; it is not by the ringin' o' the bell it is done, but——"

"But what?" broke in O'Reirdon impatiently. "Do you mane for to say there is a bell in it at all at all?"

"Yes, I do," said O'Sullivan.

"I towld you so," said the promulgator of the story.

"Aye," said O'Sullivan, "but it is not by the ringin' iv the bell it is done."

"Well, how is it done, then?" said the other, with a half

offended, half supercilious air.

"It is done," said O'Sullivan, as he returned the look with interest, "it is done intirely be jommethry."

"Oh! I undherstan' it now," said O'Reirdon, with an inimitable affectation of comprehension in the Oh!—"but to talk of the ringin' iv a bell doin' the like is beyant the beyants intirely, barrin', as I said before, it was a blessed bell, glory be to God!"

"And so you tell me, sir, it is jommethry," said the twice discomfited man of science.

"Yes, sir," said O'Sullivan, with an air of triumph, which rose in proportion as he saw he carried the listeners along with him—"jommethry."

"Well, have it your own way. There's them that won't hear rayson sometimes, nor have belief in larnin'; and you may say it's jommethry if you plaze; but I heerd them that knows betther than iver you knew say——"

"Whisht, whisht! and bad cess to you both," said O'Reirdon, "what the dickens are yiz goin' to fight about now, and sitch good liquor before yiz? Hillo! there, Mrs Quigley, bring uz another quart i' you plaze; aye, that's the chat, another quart. Augh! yiz may talk till you're black in the face about your invintions, and your staymers, and bell ringin', and gash, and rail-roads; but here's long life and success to the man that invinted the impairil (imperial) quart[2]; that was the rail beautiful invintion,"—and he took a long pull at the replenished vessel, which strongly indicated that the increase of its dimensions was a very agreeable *measure* to such as Barny.

After the introduction of this and other quarts, it would not be an easy matter to pursue the conversation that followed. Let us, therefore, transfer our story to the succeeding morning, when Barny O'Reirdon strolled forth from his cottage, rather later than usual, with his eyes bearing *eye*-witness to the carouse of the preceding night. He had not a head-ache, however; whether it was that Barny was too experienced a campaigner under the banners of Bacchus, or that Mrs Quigley's boast was a just one, namely, "that of all the drink in her house, there wasn't a head-ache in a hogshead of it," is hard to determine, but I rather incline to the strength of Barny's head.

The above-quoted declaration of Mrs Quigley is the favourite inducement held out by every boon companion in Ireland at the head of his own table. "Don't be afraid of it, my boys! it's the right sort. There's not a head-ache in a hogshead of it."

This sentiment has been very seductively rendered by Moore, with the most perfect unconsciousness on his part of the likeness he was instituting. Who does not remember—

"Friend of my soul, this goblet sip,
'Twill chase the pensive tear;
'Tis not so sweet as woman's lip,
But, oh, 'tis more sincere:
Like her delusive beam,
'Twill steal away the mind;
But, like affection's dream,
It leaves no sting behind."

Is not this very elegantly saying, "there's not a head-ache in a hogshead of it?" But I am forgetting my story all this time.

Barny sauntered about in the sun, at which he often looked up, under the shelter of compressed bushy brows and long-lashed eyelids, and a shadowing hand across his forehead, to see "what time o' day" it was; and, from the frequency of this action, it was evident the day was hanging heavily with Barny. He retired at last to a sunny nook in a neighbouring field, and stretching himself at full length, basked in the sun, and began "to chew the cud of sweet and bitter thought." He first reflected on his own undoubted weight in his little community, but still he could not get over the annoyance of the preceding night, arising from his being silenced by O'Sullivan; "a chap," as he said himself; "that lift the place four years agon a brat iv a boy, and to think iv his comin' back and outdoin' his elders, that saw him runnin' about the place, a gassoon, that one could tache a few months before;" 'twas too bad. Barny saw his reputation was in a ticklish position, and began to consider how his disgrace could be retrieved. The very name of Fingal was hateful to him; it was a plague spot on his peace that festered there incurably. He first thought of leaving Kinsale altogether; but flight implied so much of defeat, that he did not long indulge in that notion. No; he *would* stay, "in spite of all the O'Sullivans, kith and kin, breed, seed, and generation." But at the same time he knew he should never hear the end of that hateful place, Fingal; and if Barny had had the power, he would have enacted a penal statute, making it death to name the accursed spot, wherever it was; but not being gifted with such legislative authority, he felt Kinsale was no place for him, if he would not submit to be flouted every hour out of the four-and-twenty, by man, woman, and child, that wished to annoy him. What was to be done? He was in the perplexing situation, to use his own words, "of the cat in the thripe shop," he didn't know which way to choose. At last, after turning himself over in the sun several times, a new idea struck him. Couldn't he go to Fingal himself? and then he'd be equal to that upstart, O'Sullivan. No sooner was the thought engendered, than

Barny sprang to his feet a new man; his eye brightened, his step became once more elastic,—he walked erect, and felt himself to be all over Barny O'Reirdon once more. "Richard was himself again."

But where was Fingal?—there was the rub. That was a profound mystery to Barny, which, until discovered, must hold him in the vile bondage of inferiority. The plain-dealing reader will say, "couldn't he ask?" No, no; that would never do for Barny,—that would be an open admission of ignorance his soul was above, and, consequently, Barny set his brains to work to devise measures of coming at the hidden knowledge by some circuitous route, that would not betray the end he was working for. To this purpose, fifty stratagems were raised, and demolished in half as many minutes, in the fertile brain of Barny, as he strided along the shore, and as he was working hard at the fifty-first, it was knocked all to pieces by his jostling against some one whom he never perceived he was approaching, so immersed was he in his speculations, and on looking up, who should it prove to be but his friend "the long sailor from the Aysthern Injees." This was quite a godsend to Barny, and much beyond what he could have hoped for. Of all the men under the sun, the long sailor was the man in a million for Barney's net at that minute, and accordingly he made a haul of him, and thought it the greatest catch he ever made in his life.

Barny and the long sailor were in close companionship for the remainder of the day, which was closed, as the preceding one, in a carouse; but on this occasion, there was only a duet performance in honour of the jolly god, and the treat was at Barny's expense. What the nature of their conversation during the period was, I will not dilate on, but keep it as profound a secret as Barny himself did, and content myself with saying, that Barny looked a much happier man the next day. Instead of wearing his hat slouched, and casting his eyes on the ground, he walked about with his usual unconcern, and gave his nod and passing word of "*civilitude*" to every friend he met; he rolled his quid of tobacco about in his jaw with an air of superior enjoyment, and if disturbed in his narcotic amusement by a question, he took his own good time to eject "the leperous distilment" before he answered the querist, with a happy composure, that bespoke a man quite at ease with himself. It was in this agreeable spirit that Barny bent his course to the house of Peter Kelly, the owner of the "big farm beyant," before alluded to, in order to put in practice a plan he had formed for the fulfilment of his determination of rivalling O'Sullivan.

He thought it probable that Peter Kelly, being one of the "snuggest" men in the neighbourhood, would be a likely person to join him in a "spec," as he called it, (a favourite abbreviation of his for the word speculation), and, accordingly, when he reached the "big farm-house," he accosted its owner with the usual "God save you." "God save you kindly, Barny," returned Peter Kelly, "an' what is it brings you here, Barny," asked Peter, "this fine day, instead o' bein' out in the boat?"—"Oh, I'll be out in the boat soon enough, and it's far enough too I'll be in her; an' indeed it's partly that same is bringin' me here to yourself."

"Why, do you want me to go along wid you, Barny?"

"Troth an' I don't, Mr Kelly. You're a knowledgeable man an land, but I'm afeard it's a bad bargain you'd be at say."

"And what wor you talking about me and your boat for?"

"Why, you see, sir, it was in the regard of a little bit o' business, an' if you'd come wid me and take a turn in the praty field, I'll be behouldin' to you, and may be you'll hear somethin' that won't be displazin' to you."

"An' welkim, Barny," paid Peter Kelly.

When Barny and Peter were in the "praty field," Barny opened the trenches (I don't mean the potato trenches), but, in military parlance, he opened the trenches and laid siege to Peter Kelly, setting forth the extensive profits that had been realized by various "specs" that had been made by his neighbours in exporting potatoes. "And sure," said Barny, "why shouldn't *you* do the same, and they here ready to your hand? as much as to say, *why don't you profit by me, Peter Kelly?* And the boat is below there in the harbour, and, I'll say this much, the divil a betther boat is betune this and herself."

"Indeed, I b'lieve so, Barny," said Peter, "for, considhering where we stand, at this present, there's no boat at all at all betune us," and Peter laughed with infinite pleasure at his own hit.

"Oh! well, you know what I mane, any how, an', as I said before, the boat is a darlint boat, and as for him that commands her—I b'lieve I need say nothin' about that," and Barny gave a toss of his head and a sweep of his open hand, more than doubling the laudatory nature of his comment on himself.

But, as the Irish saying is, "to make a long story short," Barny prevailed on Peter Kelly to make an export; but in the nature of the venture they did not agree. Barny had proposed potatoes; Peter said there were enough of them already where he was going; and Barny rejoined, that "praties were so good in themselves there never could be too much o' thim any where." But Peter being a knowledgeable man, and up to all the "saycrets o' the airth, and understanding the the-o-ry and the che-mis-thery," overruled Barny's proposition, and determined upon a cargo of *scalpeens* (which name they give to pickled mackerel), as a preferable merchandise, quite forgetting that

Dublin Bay herrings were a much better and as cheap a commodity, at the command of the Fingalians. But in many similar mistakes the ingenious Mr Kelly has been paralleled, by other speculators. But that is neither here nor there, and it was all one to Barny whether his boat was freighted with potatoes or *scalpeens*, so long as he had the honour and glory of becoming a navigator, and being as good as O'Sullivan.

Accordingly the boat was laden and all got in readiness for putting to sea, and nothing was now wanting but Barny's orders to haul up the gaff and shake out the jib of his hooker.

But this order Barny refrained to give, and for the first time in his life exhibited a disinclination to leave the shore. One of his fellow-boatmen, at last, said to him, " Why thin, Barny O'Reirdon, what the divil is come over you, at all at all? What's the maynin' of your loitherin' about here, and the boat ready and a lovely fine breeze aff o' the land?"

"Oh! never you mind; I b'lieve I know my own business any how, an' it's hard, so it is, if a man can't ordher his own boat to sail when he plazes."

"Oh! I was only thinkin' it quare—and a pity more betoken, as I said before, to lose the beautiful breeze, and——"

"Well, just keep your thoughts to yourself, i' you plaze, and stay in the boat as I bid you, and don't be out of her on your apperl, by no manner o' manes, for one minit, for you see I don't know when it may be plazin' to me to go aboord an' set sail."

"Well, all I can say is, I never seen you afeard to go to say before."

"Who says I'm afeard?" said O'Reirdon; "you'd betther not say that agin, or in throth I'll give you a leatherin' that won't be for the good o' your health—throth, for three sthraws this minit I'd lave you that your own mother wouldn't know you with the lickin' I'd give you; but I scorn your dirty insinuation; no man ever seen Barny O'Reirdon afeard yet, any how. Howld your prate, I tell you, and look up to your betthers. What do you know iv navigation? may be you think it's as aisy for to sail an a voyage as to go a start fishin'," and Barny turned on his heel and left the shore.

The next day passed without the hooker sailing, and Barny gave a most sufficient reason for the delay, by declaring that he had a warnin' given him in a dhrame, (Glory be to God,) and that it was given to him to understand (under Heaven) that it wouldn't be looky that day.

Well, the next day was Friday, and Barny, of course, would not sail any more than any other sailor who could help it, on this unpropitious day. On Saturday, however, he came, running in a great hurry down to the shore, and, jumping aboard, he gave orders to make all sail, and taking the helm of the hooker, he turned her head to the sea, and soon the boat was cleaving the blue waters with a velocity seldom witnessed in so small a craft, and scarcely conceivable to those who have not seen the speed of a Kinsale hooker.

"Why, thin, you tuk the notion mighty suddint, Barny," said the fisherman next in authority to O'Reirdon, as soon as the bustle of getting the boat under way had subsided.

"Well, I hope it's plazin' to you at last," said Barny, "throth one 'ud think you were never at say before, you wor in such a hurry to be off; as newfangled a'most as a child with a play-toy."

"Well," said the other of Barny's companions, for there were but two with him in the boat, "I was thinkin' myself, as well as Jimmy, that we lost two fine days for nothin', and we'd be there a'most, may be, now, if we sail'd three days agon."

"Don't b'lieve it," said Barny, emphatically. "Now, don't you know yourself that there is some days that the fish won't come near the lines at all, and that we might as well be castin' our nets an the dhry land as in the say for all we'll catch if we start an an unlooky day; and sure I towld you I was waitin' only till I had it given to me to undherstan' that it was looky to sail, and I go bail we'll be there sooner than if we started three days agon, for if you don't start, with good look before you, faix maybe it's never at all to the end o' your thrip you'll come."

"Well, there's no use in talkin' about it now, any how; but when do you expec' to be there?"

"Why, you see we must wait antil I can tell how the wind is like, to howld an, before I can make up my mind to that.'

"But you're sure now, Barny, that you re up to the coorse you have to run."

"See now, lay me alone and don't be crass-questionin the tare an ouns, do you think me sitch a bladdherang as for to shuperinscribe a thing I wasn't aiquil to?"

"No; I was only gum to ax you what coorse you wor gum to steer."

"You'll find out soon enough when we git there—and so I bid you agin lay me alone—just keep your toe in your pump. Sure I'm here at the helm, and a woight an my mind, and its fitter for you, Jim, to mind your own business and lay me to mind mine; away wid you there and be handy, haul taught that foresheet there, we must run close an the wind; be handy boys; make everything dhraw."

These orders were obeyed, and the hooker soon passed to windward of a ship that left the harbor before her, but could not hold on a wind with the same tenacity as the honker, whose qualities, in this peculiarity, render them particularly suitable for the purpose to which they are applied, namely pilot and fishing boats.

We have said a ship left the harbor before the hooker had set sail, and it is now fitting to inform the reader that Barny had contrived, in the course of his last meeting with the long sailor, to ascertain that this ship, then lying in the harbor, was guing to the very place Barny wanted to reach. Barny's plan of action was decided upon in a moment; he had now nothing to do but to watch the sailing of the ship and follow in her course.

Here was, at once, a new mode of navigation discovered.

The stars, twinkling in mysterious brightness, through the silent gloom of night, were the first encouraging, because visible, guides to the adventurous mariners of antiquity. Since then, the sailor, encouraged by a bolder science, relies on the unseen agency of nature, depending on the fidelity of an atom of iron to the mystic law that claims its homage in the north. This is one refinement of science upon another. But the beautiful simplicity of Barny O'Reirdon's philosophy cannot be too much admired. To follow the ship that is going to the same place. Is not this navigation made easy?

But Barny, like many a great man before him, seemed not to be aware of how much credit he was entitled to for his invention, for he did not divulge to his companions the originality of his proceeding; he wished them to believe he was only proceeding in the commonplace manner, and had no ambition to be distinguished as the happy projector of so simple a practice.

For this purpose he went to windward of the ship and then fell off again, allowing her to pass him, as he did not wish even those on board the ship to suppose he was following in their wake; for Barny, like all people that are quite full of one scheme, and fancy every body is watching them, dreaded lest any one should fathom his motives. All that day Barny held on the same course as his leader, keeping at a respectful distance, however, "for fear 'twould look like dodging her," as he said to himself; but as night closed in, so closed in Barny with the ship, and kept a sharp look-out that she should not give him the slip in the dark. The next morning dawned, and found the hooker, and ship companions still; and thus matters proceeded for four days, during the entire of which time they had not seen land since their first losing sight of it, although the weather was clear.

"By my sowl," thought Barny, "the channel must be mighty wide in these parts, and for the last day or so we've been goin' purty free with a flowin' sheet, and I wondher we aren't closin' in wid the shore by this time; or maybe it's farther off than I thought it was." His companions, too, began to question Barny on the subject, but to their queries he presented an impenetrable front of composure, and said, "it was always the best plan to keep a good bowld offin'."In two days more, however, the weather began to be sensibly warmer, and Barny and his companions remarked that it was "goin' to be the finest sayson—God bless it—that ever kem out o' the skies for many a long year, and maybe it's the whate wouldn't be beautiful, and a great plenty of it." It was at the end of a week that the ship which Barny had hitherto kept a-head of him, showed symptoms of bearing down upon him, as he thought, and, sure enough, she did; and Barny began to conjecture what the deuce the ship could want with him, and commenced inventing answers to the questions he thought it possible might be put to him in case the ship spoke him. He was soon put out of suspense by being hailed and ordered to run under her lee, and the captain, looking over the quarter, asked Barny where he was going.

"Faith then, I'm goin' an my business," said Barny.

"But where?" said the captain.

"Why, sure, an it's no matther where a poor man like me id be goin'," said Barny.

"Only I'm curious to know what the deuce you've been following my ship for, for the last week?"

"Follyin' your ship!—Why thin, blur an agers, do you think it's follyin' yi I am?"

"It's very like it," said the captain.

"Why, did two people niver thravel the same road before?"

"I don't say they didn't; but there's a great difference between a ship of seven hundred tons and a hooker."

"Oh, as for that matther," said Barny, "the same high road sarves a coach and four, and a low-back car; the thravellin' tinker an' a lord a' horseback."

"That's very true," said the captain, "but the cases are not the same, Paddy, and I can't conceive what the devil brings *you* here."

"And who ax'd you to consayve any thing about it?" asked Barny, somewhat sturdily.

"D—n me, if I can imagine what you're about, my fine fellow," said the captain, "and my own notion is, that you don't know where the d—l you're going yourself."

"*O baithershin!*" said Barny, with a laugh of derision.

"Why then do you object to tell?" said the captain.

"Arrah sure, captain, an' don't you know that sometimes vessels is bound to sail undher *saycret ordhers*?" said Barny, endeavouring to foil the question by badinage.

There was a universal laugh from the deck of the ship, at the idea of a fishing-boat sailing under secret orders; for, by his time, the whole broadside of the vessel was crowded with grinning mouths and wondering eyes at Barny and his boat.

"Oh, it's a thrifle makes fools laugh," said Barny.

"Take care, my fine fellow, that you don't be laughing at the wrong side of your mouth before long, for I've a notion that you're cursedly in the wrong box, as cunning a fellow as you think yourself. D—n your stupid head, can't you tell what brings you here?"

"Why thin, by gor, one id think the whole say belonged to you, you're so mighty bowld in axin questions an it. Why tare-an-ouns, sure I've as much right to be here as you, though I haven't as big a ship nor as fine a coat—but maybe I can take as good sailin' out o' the one, and has as bowld a heart under th' other."

"Very well," said the captain, "I see there's no use in talking to you, so go to the d—l your own way." And away bore the ship, leaving Barny in indignation and his companions in wonder.

"An' why wouldn't you tell him?" said they to Barny.

"Why don't you see," said Barny, whose object was now to blind them, "don't you see, how do I know but maybe he might be goin' to the same place himself, and maybe he has a cargo of *scalpeens* as well as uz, and wants to get before us there."

"Thrue for you, Barny," said they. "By dad you're right." And their inquiries being satisfied, the day passed as former ones had done, in pursuing the course of the ship.

In four days more, however, the provisions in the hooker began to fail, and they were obliged to have recourse to the *scalpeens* for sustenance, and Barny then got seriously uneasy at the length of the voyage, and the likely greater length, for any thing he could see to the contrary, and, urged at last by his own alarms and those of his companions, he was enabled, as the wind was light, to gain on the ship, and when he found himself alongside he demanded a parley with the captain.

The captain, on hearing that the "hardy hooker," as she got christened, was under his lee, came on deck, and as soon as he appeared Barny cried out—

"Why, thin, blur an agers, captain dear, do you expec' to be there soon?"

"Where?" said the captain.

"Oh, you know yourself," said Barny.

"It's well for me I do," said the captain.

"Thrue for you, indeed, your honor," said Barny, in his most insinuating tone; "but whin will you be at the ind o' your voyage, captain jewel?"

"I dare say in about three months," said the captain.

"Oh, Holy Mother!" ejaculated Barny; "three months!—arrah, it's jokin' you are, captain dear, and only want to freken me.'

"How should I frighten you?" asked the captain.

"Why, thin, your honor, to tell God's thruth, I heerd you were goin' *there*, an' as I wanted to go there too, I thought I couldn't do better nor to folly a knowledgable gintleman like yourself, and save myself the throuble iv findin' it out."

"And where do you think I *am* going?" said the captain.

"Why, thin," said Barny, "isn't it to Fingal?"

"No," said the captain "'tis to *Bengal*."

"Oh! Gog's blakey!" said Barny, "what'll I do now at all at all?"

1. There is a relic in the possession of the Macnamara family, in the county Clare, called the "blessed bell of the Macnamara's;"

sometimes used to swear upon in cases of extreme urgency, in preference to the Testament: for a violation of truth, when sworn upon the blessed bell, is looked upon by the peasantry as a sacrilege, placing the offender beyond the pale of salvation.

2. Until the assimilation of currency, weights, and measures between England and Ireland, the Irish quart was a much smaller measure than the English. This part of the assimilation pleased Pat exceedingly, and he has no anxiety to have *that* repealed.

## CHAP. II.—HOMEWARD-BOUND

"'Tis an ill wind that blows nobody good."

OLD SAYING.

THE CAPTAIN ORDERED BARNY ON deck, as he wished to have some conversation with him on what he, very naturally, considered a most extraordinary adventure. Heaven help the captain! he knew little of Irishmen, or he would not have been so astonished. Barny made his appearance. Puzzling question, and more puzzling answer, followed in quick succession between the commander and Barny, who, in the midst of his dilemma, stamped about, thumped his head, squeezed his caubeen into all manner of shapes, and vented his despair anathematically—

"Oh! my heavy hathred to you, you tarnal thief iv a long sailor, it's a purty scrape yiv led me into. By gor, I thought it was *Fin*gal he said, and now I hear it is *Bin*gal. Oh! the divil sweep you for navigation, why did I meddle or make wid you at all at all! And my curse light on you, Terry O'Sullivan, why did I iver come acrass you, you onlooky vagabone, to put sitch thoughts in my head? An so its *Bin*gal, and not *Fin*gal, you're goin' to, captain."

"Yes, indeed, Paddy."

"An' might I be so bowld to ax, captain, is Bingal much farther nor Fingal?"

"A trifle or so, Paddy."

"Och, thin, millia murther, weirasthru, how 'ill I iver get there, at all at all" roared out poor Barny.

"By turning about, and getting back the road you've come, as fast as you can."

"Is it back? Oh! Queen iv Heaven! an how will I iver get back?" said the bewildered Barny.

"Then you don't know your course it appears?"

"Oh faix I knew it, iligant, as long as your honor was before me."

"But you don't know your course back?"

"Why, indeed, not to say rightly all out, your honor."

"Can't you steer?" said the captain.

"The divil a betther hand at the tiller in all Kinsale," said Barny, with his usual brag.

"Well, so far so good," said the captain. "And you know the points of the compass—you have a compass, I suppose?"

"A compass! by my sowl an it's not let alone a compass, but a *pair* a compasses I have, that my brother the carpinthir, left me for a keepsake whin he wint abroad; but, indeed, as for the points o' thim I can't say much, for the childher spylt thim intirely, rootin' holes in the flure."

"What the plague are you talking about?" asked the captain.

"Wasn't your honor discoorsin' me about the points o' the compasses?"

"Confound your thick head!" said the captain. "Why, what an ignoramus you must be, not to know what a compass is, and you at sea all your life? Do you even know the cardinal points?"

"The cardinals! faix an its a great respect I have for them, your honor. Sure, ar'n't they belongin' to the Pope?"

"Confound you, you blockhead!" roared the captain in a rage—"'twould take the patience of the Pope and the cardinals, and the cardinal virtues into the bargain, to keep one's temper with you. Do you know the four points of the wind?"

"By my sowl I do, and more."

"Well, never mind more, but let us stick to four. You're sure you know the four points of the wind?"

"By dad it would be a quare thing if a sayfarin' man didn't know somethin' about the wind any how. Why, captain dear, you must take me for a nath'ral intirely to suspect me o' the like o' not knowin' all about the wind. By gor, I know as much o' the wind a'most as a pig."

"Indeed I believe so," laughed out the captain.

"Oh, you may laugh if you plaze, and I see by the same that you don't know about the pig, with all your edication, captain."

"Well, what about the pig?"

"Why, sir, did you never hear a pig can see the wind?"

"I can't say that I did."

"Oh thin he does, and for that rayson who has a right to know more about it?"

"You don't for one, I dare say, Paddy; and maybe you have a pig aboard to give you information."

"Sorra taste your honor, not as much as a rasher o' bacon;

but it's maybe your honor never seen a pig tossin' up his snout, consaited like, and running like mad afore a storm."

"Well, what if I have?"

"Well, sir, that is when they see the wind a comin'."

"Maybe so, Paddy, but all this knowledge in piggery won't find you your way home; and, if you take my advice, you will give up all thoughts of endeavouring to find your way back, and come on board. You and your messmates, I dare say, will be useful hands, with some teaching; but, at all events, I cannot leave you here on the open sea, with every chance of being lost."

"Why thin, indeed, and I'm behowlden to your honor; and its the hoighth o' kindness, so it is, your offer; and its nothin' else but a gentleman you are, every inch o' you; but I hope it's not so bad wid us yet, as to do the likes o' that."

"I think it's bad enough," said the captain, "when you are without a compass, and knowing nothing of your course, and nearly a hundred and eighty leagues from land."

"An' how many miles would that be, captain?"

"Three times as many."

"I never larned the rule o' three, captain, and maybe your honor id tell me yourself."

"That is rather more than five hundred miles."

"Five hundred miles!" shouted Barny. "Oh! the Lord look down on us! how 'ill we iver get back!!"

"That's what I say," said the captain; "and, therefore, I recommend you come aboard with me."

"And where 'ud the hooker be all the time?" said Barny.

"Let her go adrift," was the answer.

"Is it the darlint boat? Oh, by dad, I'll never hear o' that at all."

"Well, then, stay in her and be lost. Decide upon the matter at once, either come on board or cast off;" and the captain was turning away as he spoke, when Barny called after him, "Arrah, thin, your honor, don't go jist for one minit antil I ax you one word more. If I wint wid you, whin would I be home agin?"

"In about seven months."

"Oh, thin, that puts the wig an it at wanst. I dar'n't go at all."

"Why, seven months are not long passing."

"Thrue for you, in throth," said Bamny, with a shrug of his shoulders. "Faix it's myself knows, to my sorrow, the half-year comes round mighty suddint, and the Lord's agint comes for the thrifle o' rint; and faix I know, by Molly, that nine mouths is not long in goin' over either," added Barny with a grin.

"Then what's your objection, as to the time?" asked the captain.

"Arrah, sure, sir, what would the woman that owns me do while I was away? and maybe its break her heart the craythur would, thinkin' I was lost intirely and who'd be at home to take care o' the childher, and airn thim the bit and the sup, whin I'd be away? and who knows but it's all dead they'd be afore I got back? Och hone! sure the heart id fairly break in my body, if hurt or harm kem to them, through me. So, say no more, captain dear, only give me a thrifle o' directions how I'm to make an offer at gettin' home, and its myself that will pray for you night, noon, and mornin' for that same."

"Well, Paddy," said the captain, "as you are determined to go back, in spite of all I can say, you must attend to me well while I give you as simple instructions as I can. You say you know the four points of the wind, north, south, east, and west."

"Yis, sir."

"How do you know them? for I must see that you are not likely to make a mistake. How do you know the points?"

"Why, you see, sir, the sun, God bless it, rises in the aist, and sets in the west, which stands to raison; and whin you stand bechuxt the aist and the west, the north is forninst you."

"And when the north is forninst you, as you say, is the east on your right or your left hand?"

"On the right hand, your honor."

"Well, I see you know that much however. Now," said the captain, "the moment you leave the ship, you must steer a north-east course, and you will make some land near home in about a week, if the wind holds as it is now, and it is likely to do so; but, mind me, if you turn out of your course in the smallest degree, you are a lost man."

"Many thanks to your honor!"

"And how are you off for provisions?"

"Why thin indeed in the regard o' that same we are in the hoighth o' distress, for exceptin' the scalpeens, sorra taste passed our lips for these four days."

"Oh! you poor devils!" said the commander, in a tone of sincere commiseration, "I'll order you some provisions on board before you start."

"Long life to your honor! and *I'd like to drink the health of* so noble a jintleman."

"I understand you, Paddy, you shall have grog too."

"Musha, the heavens shower blessins an you, I pray the Virgin Mary and the twelve apostles, Matthew, Mark, Luke, and John, not forgettin' Saint Pathrick."

"Thank you, Paddy; but keep all your prayers for yourself, for you need them all to help you home again."

"Oh! never fear, whin thing is to be done, I'll do it, by dad, wid a heart and a half. And sure, your honor, God is good, an' will mind dissolute craythurs like uz, on the wild oceant as well as ashore."

While some of the ship's crew were putting the captain's benevolent intentions to Barny and his companions into practice, by transferring some provisions to the hooker, the commander entertained himself by further conversation with Barny, who was the greatest original he had ever met. In the course of their colloquy, Barny drove many hard queries at the captain, respecting the wonders of the nautical profession, and at last put the question to him plump.

"Oh! thin captain dear, and how is it at all at all, that you make your way over the wide says intirely to them furrin parts?"

"You would not understand, Paddy, if I attempted to explain to you."

"Sure enough indeed, your honor, and I ask your pardon, only I was curious to know, and sure no wonder."

"It requires various branches of knowledge to make a navigator."

"Branches," said Barny, "by gor I think it id take *the whole three o' knowledge* to make it out. And that place you are going to, sir, that *Bin*gal (oh bad luck to it for a *Bin*gal, it's the sore *Bin*gal to me), is it so far off as you say?"

"Yes, Paddy, half round the world."

"Is it round in airnest, captain dear? Round about?"

"Aye indeed."

"Oh thin ar'nt you afeard that whin you come to the top and that you're obleeged to go down, that you'd go sliddherin away intirely, and never be able to stop maybe. It's bad enough, so it is, goin' down-hill by land, but it must be the dickens all out by wather."

"But there is no hill, Paddy, don't you know that water is always level?"

"By dad it's very *flat* any how, and by the same token it's seldom I throuble it; but sure, your honor, if the wather is level, how do you make out that it is *round* you go?"

"That is a part of the knowledge I was speaking to you about," said the captain.

"Musha, bad luck to you, knowledge, but you're a quare thing! and where is it Bingal, bad cess to it, would be at all at all?"

"In the East Indies."

"Oh that is where they make the *tay*, isn't it, sir?"

"No, where the tea grows is farther still."

"Farther! why that must be the ind of the world intirely. And they don't make it, then, sir, but it grows, you tell me."

"Yes, Paddy."

"Is it like hay, your honor?"

"Not exactly, Paddy; what puts hay in your head?"

"Oh! only bekase I hear them call it Bo*hay*."

"A most logical deduction, Paddy."

"And is it a great deal farther, your honor, the *tay* country is?"

"Yes, Paddy, China it is called."

"That's, I suppose, what we call Chaynee, sir?"

"Exactly, Paddy."

"By dad I never could come at it rightly before, why it was nath'ral to dhrink tay out o' chaynee. I ax your honor's pardin for bein' throublesome, but I hard tell from the long sailor, iv a place they call Japan, in thim furrin parts, and is it there, your honor?"

"Quite true, Paddy."

"And I suppose it's there the blackin' comes from."

"No, Paddy, you're out there."

"Oh well, I thought it stood to rayson, as I heerd of japan

blackin', sir, that it would be there it kem from, besides as the blacks themselves—the naygurs I mane, is in thim parts."

"The negroes are in Africa, Paddy, much nearer to us."

"God betune uz and harm. I hope I would not be too near them," said Barny.

"Why, what's your objection?"

"Arrah sure, sir, they're hardly mortials at all, but has the mark o' the bastes an thim."

"How do you make out that, Paddy?"

"Why sure, sir, and didn't Nathur make thim wid wool on their heads, plainly makin' it undherstood to chrishthans, that they wur little more nor cattle."

"I think your head is a wool-gathering now, Paddy," said the captain, laughing.

"Faix maybe so, indeed," answered Barny, goodhumouredly, "but it's seldom I ever went out to look for wool and kem home shorn, any how," said he, with a look of triumph.

"Well, you won't have that to say for the future, Paddy," said the captain laughing again.

"My name's not Paddy, your honor," said Barny returning the laugh, but seizing the opportunity to turn the joke aside, that was going against him, "my name isn't Paddy sir, but Barny."

"Oh, if it was Solomon, you'll be bare enough when you go home this time; you have not gathered much this trip, Barny."

"Sure I've been gathering knowledge, any how, your honor," said Barny, with a significant look at the captain, and a complimentary tip of his hand to his caubeen, "and God bless you for being so good to me."

"And what's your name besides Barny?" asked the captain.

"O'Reirdon, your honor—Barny O'Reirdon's my name."

"Well, Barny O' Reirdon, I won't forget your name nor yourself in a hurry, for you are certainly the most original navigator I ever had the honor of being acquainted with."

"Well," said Barny, with a triumphant toss of his head, "I have done out Terry O'Sullivan, at any rate, the devil a half so far he ever was, and that's a comfort. I have muzzled his clack for the rest iv his life, and he won't be comin' over us wid the pride iv his *Fin*gal, while I'm to the fore, that was a'most at *Bin*gal."

"Terry O'Sullivan—who is he pray?" said the captain.

"Oh, he's a scut iv a chap that's not worth your axin for—he's not worth your honor's notice—a braggin' poor craythur. Oh wait till I get home, and the devil a more braggin' they'll hear out of his jaw."

"Indeed then, Barny, the sooner you turn your face towards home the better," said the captain, "since you will go, there is no need in losing more time."

"Thrue for you, your honor—and sure it's well for me had the luck to meet with the likes o' your honor, that explained the ins and the outs iv it, to me, and laid it all down as plain as prent."

"Are you sure you remember my directions?" said the captain.

"Throth an I'll niver forget them to the day o' my death, and is bound to pray, more betoken, for you and yours."

"Don't mind praying for me till you get home, Barny; but answer me, how are you to steer when you shall leave me?"

"The Nor-Aist coorse, your honor, that's the coorse agin the world."

"Remember that! never alter that course till you see

land—let nothing make you turn out of a North-East course."

"Throth an' that id be the dirty turn, seein' that it was yourself that ordered it. Oh no, I'll depend my life an the *Nor-Aist coorse*, and God help any one that comes betune me an' it—I'd run him down if he was my father."

"Well, good bye, Barny."

"Good bye, and God bless you, your honor, and send you safe."

"That's a wish you want more for yourself, Barny—never fear for me, but mind yourself well."

"Oh sure, I'm as good as at home wanst I know the way, barrin the wind is conthrary; sure the Nor-Aist coorse 'ill do the business complate. Good bye, your honor, and long life to you, and more power to your elbow, and a light heart and a heavy purse to you evermore, I pray the blessed Virgin and all the saints, amin!" and so saying, Barny descended the ship's side, and once more assumed the helm of the "hardy hooker."

The two vessels now separated on their opposite courses. What a contrast their relative situations afforded! Proudly the ship bore away under her lofty and spreading canvass, cleaving the billows before her, manned by an able crew, and under the guidance of experienced officers. The finger of science to point the course of her progress, the faithful chart to warn of the hidden rock and the shoal, the log line and the quadrant to measure her march and prove her position. The poor little hooker cleft not the billows, each wave lifted her on its crest like a seabird; but three inexperienced fishermen to manage her; no certain means to guide them over the vast ocean they had to traverse, and the holding of the "fickle wind" the only *chance* of their escape from perishing in the wilderness of waters. By the one, the feeling excited is supremely that of man's power. By the other, of his utter helplessness. To the one, the expanse of ocean could scarcely be considered "trackless." To the other, it was a waste indeed.

Yet the cheer that burst from the ship, at parting, was answered as gaily from the hooker as though the odds had not been so fearfully against her, and no blither heart beat on board the ship than that of Barny O'Reirdon.

Happy light-heartedness of my poor countrymen! they have often need of all their buoyant spirits! How kindly have they been fortified by Nature against the assaults of adversity; and if they blindly rush into dangers, they cannot be denied the possession of gallant hearts to fight their way out of them.

But each hurra became less audible; by degrees the cheers dwindled into and finally were lost in the eddies of the breeze.

The first feeling of loneliness that poor Barny experienced was when he could no longer hear the exhilarating sound. The plash of the surge, as it broke on the bows of his little boat, was uninterrupted by the kindred sound of human voice; and, as it fell upon his ear, it smote upon his heart. But he rallied, waved his hat, and the silent signal was answered from the ship.

"Well, Barny," said Jemmy, "what was the captain sayin' to you alı the time you wor wid him?"

"Lay me alone," said Barny, "I'll talk to you when I see her out o'sight, but not a word till thin. I'll look afther him, the rale gintleman that he is, while there's a topsail of his ship to be seen, and then I'll send my blessin' afther him, and pray for his good fortune wherever he goes, for he's the right sort and nothin' else." And Barny kept his word, and when his straining eye could no longer trace a line of the ship, the captain certainly had the benefit of "a poor man's blessing."

The sense of utter loneliness and desolation had not come upon Barny until now; but he put his trust in the goodness of Providence, and in a fervent mental outpouring of prayer, resigned himself to the care of his Creator. With an admirable fortitude, too, he assumed a composure to his companions that was a stranger to his heart; and we all know how the burden of anxiety is increased when we have none with whom to sympathise. And this was not all. He had to affect ease and confidence, for Barny not only had no dependence on the firmness of his companions to go through the undertaking before them, but dreaded to betray to them how he had imposed on them in the affair. Barny was equal to all this. He had a stout heart, and was an admirable actor; yet, for the first hour after the ship was out of sight, he could not quite recover himself, and every now and then, unconsciously, he would look back with a wistful eye to the point where last he saw her. Poor Barny had lost his leader.

The night fell, and Barny stuck to the helm as long as nature could sustain want of rest, and then left it in charge of one of his companions, with particular directions how to steer, and ordered, if any change in the wind occurred, that they should instantly awake him. He could not sleep long however, the fever of anxiety was upon him, and the morning had not long dawned when he awoke. He had not well rubbed his eyes and looked about him, when he thought he saw a ship in the distance approaching them. As the haze cleared away, she showed distinctly bearing down towards the hooker. On board the ship, the hooker, in such a sea, caused surprise as before, and in about an hour she was so close as to hail, and order the hooker to run under her lee.

"The divil a taste," said Barny, "I'll not quit my *Nor-Aist coorse* for the king of Ingland, nor Bonyparty into the bargain. Bad cess to you, do you think I've nothin' to do but to plaze you?"

Again he was hailed.

"Oh! bad luck to the toe I'll go to you."

Another hail.

"Spake loudher you'd betther," said Barny, jeeringly, still holding on his course.

A gun was fired ahead of him.

"By my sowl you spoke loudher that time, sure enough," said Barny.

"Take care, Barny," cried Jemmy and Peter together. "Blur an agers man, we'll be kilt if you don't go to them."

"Well, and we'll be lost if we turn out iv our *Nor-Aist coorse*, and that's as broad as it's long. Let them hit iz if they like; sure it 'ud be a pleasanther death nor starvin' at say. I tell you agin I'll turn out o' my *Nor-Aist coorse* for no man."

A shotted gun was fired. The shot hopped on the water as it passed before the hooker.

"Phew! you missed it, like your mammy's blessin'," said Barny.

"Oh murther!" said Jemmy, "didn't you see the ball hop aff the wather forninst you. Oh murther, what 'ud we ha' done if we wor there at all at all?"

"Why, we'd have taken the ball at the hop," said Barny, laughing, "accordin' to the ould sayin'."

Another shot was ineffectually fired.

"I'm thinking that's a Connaughtman that's shootin'," said Barny, with a sneer[1]. The allusion was so relished by Jemmy and Peter, that it excited a smile in the midst of their fears from the cannonade.

Again the report of the gun was followed by no damage.

"Augh! never heed them!" said Barny, contemptuously. "It's a barkin' dog that never bites, as the owld sayin' says," and the hooker was soon out of reach of further annoyance.

"Now, what a pity it was, to be sure," said Barny, "that I wouldn't go aboord to plaze them. Now, who's right? Ah, lave me alone always, Jimmy; did you ivir know me wrong yet?"

"Oh, you may hillow now that you're out o' the wood," said Jemmy, "but, accordin' to my idays, it was runnin' a grate rishk to be contrary wid them at all, and they shootin' balls afther us."

"Well, what matther?" said Barny, "since they wor only blind gunners, *an' I knew it*; besides, as I said afore, I won't turn out o' my *Nor-Aist coorse* for no man."

"That's a new turn you tuk lately," said Peter. "What's the raison you're runnin a Nor-Aist coorse now, an' we never hear'd iv it afore at all, till afther you quitted the big ship?"

"Why, thin, are you sitch an ignoramus all out," said Barny, "as not for to know that in navigation you must lie an a great many different tacks before you can make the port you steer for?"

"Only I think," said Jemmy, "that it's back intirely we're goin' now, and I can't make out the rights o' that at all."

"Why," said Barny, who saw the necessity of mystifying his companions a little, "you see, the captain towld me that I kum a round, an' rekimminded me to go th'other way."

"Faix, it's the first I ever heard o' goin' a round by say," said Jemmy.

"Arrah, sure, that's part o' the saycrets o'navigation, and the varrious branches o' knowledge that is requizit for a navigathor; an' that's what the captain, God bless him, and myself was discoorsin' an aboord; and, like a rale gentleman as he is, Barny, says he; Sir, says I; you've come the round, says he. I know that, says I, bekase I like to keep a good bowld offin', says I, in contrairy places. Spoke like a good sayman, says he. That's my prenciples, says I. They're the right sort, says he. But, says he (no offince), I think you wor wrong, says he, to pass the short turn in the ladie-shoes[2], says he. I know, says I, you mane beside the three-spike headlan'. That's the spot, says he, I see you know it. As well as I know my father, says I."

"Why, Barny," said Jemmy, interrupting him, "we seen no headlan' at all."

"Whisht, whisht!" said Barny, "bad cess to you, don't thwart me. We passed it in the night, and you couldn't see it. Well, as I was saying, I knew it as well as I know my father, says I, but I gev the preferrince to go the round, says I. You're a good sayman for that same, says he, an' it would be right at any other time than this present, says he, but it's onpossible now, tee-totally, on account o' the war, says he. Tare alive, says I, what war? An' didn't you hear o' the war? says he. Divil a word, says I. Why, says he, the Naygurs has made war on the king o' Chaynee, says he, bekase he refused them any more tay; an' with that, what did they do, says he, but they put a lumbaago on all the vessels that sails the round, an' that's the rayson, says he, I carry guns, as you may see; and I'd rekimmind you, says he, to go back, for you're not able for thim, an' that's jist the way iv it. An' now, wasn't it looky that I kem acrass him at all, or maybe we might be cotch by the Naygurs, and ate up alive."

"O, thin, indeed, and that's thrue," said Jemmy and Peter, "and when will we come to the short turn?"

"Oh never mind," said Barny, "you'll see it when you get there; but wait till I tell you more about the captain and the big ship. He said, you know, that he carried guns afeard o' the Naygurs, and in throth it's the hoight o'care he takes o'them same guns; and small blame to him, sure they might be the salvation of him. 'Pon my conscience, they're taken betther care of than any poor man's child. I heer'd him cautionin' the sailors about them, and given them ordhers about their clothes."

"Their clothes!" said his two companions at once in much surprise; "is it clothes upon cannons?"

"It's truth I'm tellin' you," said Barny. "Bad luck to the lie in it, he was talkin' about their aprons and their breeches."

"Oh, think o' that!" said Jemmy and Peter in surprise.

"An' 'twas all iv a piece," said Barny, "that an' the rest o' the ship all out. She was as nate as a new pin. Throth I was a'most ashamed to put my fut an the deck, it was so clane, and she painted every colour in the rainbow; and all sorts o' curosities about her; and instead iv a tiller to steer her, like this darlin' craythur iv ours, she goes wid a wheel, like a coach all as one; and there's the quarest thing you iver seen, to show the way, as the captain gev me to undherstan', a little round rowly-powly thing in a bowl, that goes waddlin' about as if it didn't know its own way, much more nor show any body their's. Throth myself thought that if that's the way they're obliged to go, that it's with a great deal of *fear and thrimblin'* they find it out."

Thus it was that Barny continued most marvellous accounts of the ship and the captain to his companions, and by keeping their attention so engaged, prevented their being too inquisitive as to their own immediate concerns, and for two days more Barny and the hooker held on their respective courses undeviatingly.

The third day, Barny's fears for the continuity of his *Nor-Aist coorse* were excited, as a large brig hove in sight, and the nearer she approached, the more directly she came athwart Barny's course.

"May the divil sweep you," said Barny, "and will nothin' else sarve you than comin' forninst me that away? Brig-a-hoy there!!" shouted Barny, giving the tiller to one of his messmates, and standing at the bow of his boat. "Brig-a-hoy there!—bad luck to you, go 'long out o' my *nor-aist coorse*." The brig, instead of obeying his mandate, hove to, and lay right ahead of the hooker. "Oh look at this!" shouted Barny, and he stamped on the deck with rage—"look at the blackguards where they're stayin', just a-purpose to ruin an unfort'nate man like me. My heavy hathred to you, *quit* this minit, or I'll run down an yes, and if we go to the bottom, we'll hant you for evermore—go 'long out o' that, I tell you. The curse o' Crummil an you, you stupid vagabones, that won't go out iv a man's nor-aist coorse!!"

From cursing Barny went to praying as he came closer. "For the tendher marcy o'heavin and lave my way. May the Lord reward you, and get out o' my nor-aist coorse! May angels make your bed in heavin and don't ruinate me this-a-way." The brig was immoveable, and Barny gave up in despair, having cursed and prayed himself hoarse, and finished with a duet volley of prayers and curses together, apostrophising the hard case of a man being "*done out of his nor-aist coorse*."

"A-hoy there!" shouted a voice from the brig, "put down your helm, or you'll be aboard of us. I say, let go your jib and foresheet—what are you about, you lubbers?"

'Twas true that the brig lay so fair in Barny's course, that he would have been aboard, but that instantly the manœuvre above alluded to was put in practice on board the hooker, as she swept to destruction towards the heavy hull of the brig, and she luffed up into the wind along side her. A very pale and somewhat emaciated face appeared at the side, and addressed Barny.—

"What brings you here?" was the question.

"Throth thin, and I think I might betther ax what brings *you* here, right in the way o' my *Nor-Aist coorse.*"

"Where do you come from?"

"From Kinsale; and you didn't come from betther place, I go bail."

"Where are you bound to?"

"To Fingall."

"Fingall—where's Fingall?"

"Why then ain't you ashaimed o' yourself an' not to know where Fingall is?"

"It is not in these seas."

"Oh, that's all you know about it," says Barny.

"You're a small craft to be so far at sea. I suppose you have provision on board?"

"To be sure we have; throth if we hadn't, this id be a bad place to go a beggin'."

"What have you eatable?"

"The finest o' scalpeens."

"What are scalpeeens?"

"Why you're mighty ignorant intirely," said Barny, "why scalpeens is pickled mackerel."

"Then you must give us some, for we have been out of every thing eatable these three days; and even pickled fish is better than nothing."

"It chanced that the brig was a West India trader, which unfavourable winds had delayed much beyond the expected period of time on her voyage, and though her water had not failed, every thing eatable had been consumed, and the crew reduced almost to helplessness. In such a strait the arrival of Barny O'Reirdon and his scalpeens was a most providential succour to them, and a lucky chance for Barny, for he got in exchange for his pickled fish a handsome return of rum and sugar, much more than equivalent to their value. Barny lamented much, however, that the brig was not bound for Ireland, that he might practise his own peculiar system of navigation; but as staying with the brig could do no good, be got himself put into his *Nor-Aist coorse* once more, and ploughed away towards home.

The disposal of his cargo was a great godsend to Barny in more ways than one. In the first place, he found the most profitable market he could have had; and, secondly, it enabled him to cover his retreat from the difficulty which still was before him of not getting to Fingal after all his dangers, and consequently being open to discovery and disgrace. All these beneficial results were not thrown away upon one of Barny's readiness to avail himself of every point in his favour; and, accordingly, when they left the brig, Barny said to his companions, "Why thin, boys, 'pon my conscience but I'm as proud as a horse wid a wooden leg this minit, that we met them poor unfort'nate craythers this blessed day, and was enabled to extind our charity to them. Sure an' it's lost they'd be only for our comin' acrass them, and we, through the blessin' o' God, enabled to do an act of marcy, that is, feedin' the hungry; and sure every good work we do here is before uz in heaven—and that's a comfort any how. To be sure, now that the scalpeens is sowld, there's no use in goin' to Fingal, and we may as well jist go home."

"Faix I'm sorry myself," said Jemmy, "for Terry O'Sullivan said it was an iligant place intirely, an' I wanted to see it."

"To the divil wid Terry O'Sullivan," said Barny, "how does he know what's an iligant place? What knowledge has he of iligance! I'll go bail he never was half as far a navigatin' as we—he wint the short cut I go bail, and never daar'd for to vinture the round, as I did."

"By dad we wor a great dale longer any how than he towld me he was."

"To be sure we wor," said Barny, "he wint skulkin' by the short cut, I tell you, and was afeard to keep a bowld offin' like me. But come, boys, let uz take a dhrop o' that bottle o' sper'ts we got out o' the brig. By gor it's well we got some bottles iv it; for I wouldn't much like to meddle wid that darlint little kag iv it antil we get home." The rum was put on its trial by Barny and his companions, and in their critical judgment was pronounced quite a good as the captain of the ship had bestowed upon them but that neither of those specimens of spirit was to be compared to whiskey. "By dad," says Barny, "they may rack their brains a long time before they'll make out a purtier invintion than *potteen*—that rum may do very well for thim that has the misforthin not to know betther; but the whiskey is a more nath'ral sper't accordin' to my idays." In this, as in most other of Barny's opinions, Peter and Jemmy coincided.

Nothing particular occurred for the two succeeding days, during which time Barny most religiously pursued his *Nor-Aist coorse*, but the third day produced a new and important event. A sail was discovered on the horizon, and in the direction Barny was steering, and a couple of hours made him tolerably certain that the vessel in sight was an American, for though it is needless to say that he was not very conversant in such matters, yet from the frequency of his seeing Americans trading to Ireland, his eye had become sufficiently accustomed to their lofty and tapering spars, and peculiar smartness of rig, to satisfy him that the ship before him was of transatlantic build: nor was he wrong in his conjecture.

Barny now determined on a manœuvre, classing him amongst the first tacticians at securing a good retreat.

Moreau's highest fame rests upon his celebrated retrograde movement through the Black-forest.

Xenophon's greatest glory is derived from the deliverance of his ten thousand Greeks from impending ruin by his renowned retreat.

Let the ancient and the modern hero "repose under the shadow of their laurels," as the French have it, while Barny O'Reirdon's historian, with a pardonable jealousy for the honour of his country, cuts down a goodly bough of the classic tree, beneath which our Hibernian hero may enjoy his "*otium cum dignitate*."

Barny calculated the American was bound for Ireland, and as she lay, *almost* as directly in the way of his "Nor-Aist coorse," as the West Indian brig, he bore up to and spoke her.

He was answered by a shrewd Yankee Captain.

"Faix an' it's glad I am to see your honor again," said Barny.

The Yankee had never been to Ireland, and told Barny so.

"Oh throth I couldn't forget a gintleman so aisy as that," said Barny.

"You're pretty considerably mistaken now, I guess," said the American.

"Divil a taste," said Barny, with inimitable composure and pertinacity.

"Well, if you know me so tarnation well, tell me what's my name." The Yankee flattered himself he had nailed Barny now.

"Your name, is it?" said Barny, gaining time by repeating the question, "Why what a fool you are not to know your own name."

The oddity of the answer posed the American, and Barny

took advantage of the diversion in his favor, and changed the conversation.

"By dad I've been waitin' here these four or five days, expectin' some of you would be wantin' me."

"Some of us!—How do you mean?"

"Sure an' arn't you from Amerikay?"

"Yes; and what then?"

"Well, I say I was waitin' for some ship or other from Amerikay, that ud be wantin' me. It's to Ireland you're goin' I dar' say."

"Yes."

"Well, I suppose you'll be wantin' a pilot," said Barny.

"Yes, when we get in shore, but not yet." "Oh, I don't want to hurry you," said Barny.

"What port are you a pilot of?"

"Why indeed, as for the matther o' that," said Barny, "they're all aiqual to me a'most."

"All?" said the American. "Why I calculate you couldn't pilot a ship into all the ports of Ireland."

"Not all at wanst (once), said Barny, with a laugh, in which the American could not help joining.

"Well, I say, what ports do you know best?"

"Why thin, indeed," said Barny, "it would be hard for me to tell; but wherever you want to go, I'm the man that'll do the job for you complate. Where is your honor goin'?"

"I won't tell you that—but do you tell me what ports you know best?"

"Why there's Watherford, and' there's Youghall, an' Fingal."

"Fingal! Where's that?"

"So you don't know where Fingal is. Oh, I see you're a sthranger, sir,—an' then there's Cork."

"You know Cove, then?"

"Is it the Cove o' Cork why?"

"Yes."

"I was bred an' born there, and pilots as many ships into Cove as any other two min *out* of it."

Barny thus sheltered his falsehood under the idiom of his language.

"But what brought you so far out to sea?" asked the captain.

"We wor lyin' out lookin' for ships that wanted pilots, and there kem an the terriblest gale o' wind off the land, an' blew us to say out intirely, an' that's the way iv it, your honor."

"I calculate we got a share of the same gale; 'twas from the nor-east."

"Oh, directly!" said Barny, "faith you're right enough, 'twas the *Nor-Aist coorse* we wor an sure enough; but no matther now that we've met wid you—sure we'll have a job home any how."

"Well, get aboard then," said the American.

"I will in a minit your honor, whin I jist spake a word to my comrades here."

"Why sure it's not goin' to turn pilot you are," said Jemmy, in his simplicity of heart.

"Whisht, you omadhaun!" said Barny, "or I'll cut the tongue out o' you. Now mind me, Pether. You don't undherstan' navigashin and the varrious branches o' knowledge, an' so all you have to do is to folly the ship when I get into her, an' I'll show you the way home."

Barny then got aboard the American vessel, and begged of the captain, that as he had been out at sea so long, and had gone through "a power o' hardship intirely," that he would be permitted to go below and turn in to take a sleep, "for in troth it's myself and sleep that is sthrayngers for some time," said Barny, "an' if your honor 'ill be plazed I'll be thankful if you won't let them disturb me antil I'm wanted, for sure till you see the land there's no use for me in life, an' throth I want a sleep sorely."

Barny's request was granted, and it will not be wondered at, that after so much fatigue of mind and body, he slept profoundly for four-and-twenty hours. He then was called, for land was in sight, and when he came on deck the captain rallied him upon the potency of his somniferous qualities and "calculated" he had never met any one who could sleep "four-and-twenty hours on a stretch, before."

"Oh, sir," said Barny, rubbing his eyes, which were still a little hazy, "whiniver *I* go to sleep *I pay attintion to it*."

The land was soon neared, and Barny put in charge of the ship, when he ascertained the first landmark he was acquainted with; but as soon as the Head of Kinsale hove in sight, Barny gave a "whoo," and cut a caper that astonished the Yankees, and was quite inexplicable to them, though, I flatter myself, it is not to those who do Barny the favor of reading his adventures.

"Oh! there you are, my darlint ould head! an' where's the head like you? throth its little I thought I'd ever set eyes an your good-looking faytures agin. But God's good!"

In such half muttered exclamations did Barny apostrophise each well-known point of his native shore, and when opposite the harbour of Kinsale, he spoke the hooker that was somewhat astern, and ordered Jemmy and Peter to put in there, and tell Molly immediately that he was come back, and would be with her as soon as he could, after piloting the ship into Cove. "But an your apperl don't tell Pether Kelly o' the big farm, nor indeed don't mintion to man nor mortial about the navigation we done antil I come home myself and make them sensible of it, bekase Jemmy and Pether, neither o' yiz is aqual to it, and doesn't undherstan' the branches o' knowledge requízit for discoorsin' o' navigation."

The hooker put into Kinsale, and Barny sailed the ship into Cove. It was the first ship he ever had acted the pilot for, and his old luck attended him; no accident befell his charge, and what was still more extraordinary, he made the American believe he was absolutely the most skilful pilot on the station. So Barny pocketed his pilot's fee, swore the Yankee was a gentleman, for which the republican did not thank him, wished him good bye, and then pushed his way home with what Barny swore was the easiest made money he ever had in his life. So Barny got himself paid for *piloting* the ship that *showed him the way home.*

All the fishermen in the world may throw their caps at this feat—none but an Irishman, I fearlessly assert, could have executed so splendid a *coup de finesse.*

And now, sweet readers (the ladies I mean), did you ever think Barny would get home? I would give a hundred of pens to hear all the guesses that have been made as to the probable termination of Barny's adventure. They would furnish good material, I doubt not, for another voyage. But Barny did make other voyages I can assure you; and, perhaps, he may appear in his character of navigator once more, if his daring exploits be not held valueless by an ungrateful world, as in the case of his great predecessor, Columbus.

As some *curious* persons (I *don't* mean the ladies), may wish to know what became of some of the characters who have figured in this tale, I beg to inform them that Molly continued a faithful wife and time-keeper, as already alluded to, for many years. That Peter Kelly was so leased with his share in the profits arising from the trip, in the ample return of rum and sugar, that he freighted a large brig with scalpeens to the West Indies, and went supercargo himself.

All he got in return was the yellow fever.

Barny profited better by his share; he was enabled to open a public-house, which had more custom than any ten within miles of it. Molly managed the bar very efficiently, and Barny "discoorsed" the customers most seductively; in short, Barny, at all times given to the *marvellous*, became a greater romancer than ever, and, for years, attracted even the gentlemen of the neighbourhood, who loved fun, to his house, for the sake of his magnanimous mendacity.

As for the hitherto triumphant Terry O'Sullivan, from the moment Barny's *Bingal* adventure became known, he was obligeds to fly the country, and was never heard of more, while the hero of the hooker became a greater man than before, and never was addressed by any other title afterwards than that of THE COMMODORE.

1. This is an allusion of Barny's to a prevalent saying in Ireland, addressed to a sportsman who returns home unsuccessful, "So you've killed what the Connaughtman shot at." Besides Barny, herein, indulges a provincial pique; for the people of Monster have a profound contempt for Connaught men.
2. Some offer Barny is making at latitudes.

# THE BURIAL OF THE TITHE

With the help of a surgeon he might yet recover.
SHAKSPEARE.

IT WAS A FINE MORNING in the autumn of 1832, and the sun had not yet robbed the grass of its dew, as a stout-built peasant was moving briskly along a small by-road in the county of Tipperary. The elasticity of his step bespoke the lightness of his heart, and the rapidity of his walk did not seem sufficient, even, for the exuberance of his glee, for every now and then the walk was exchanged for a sort of dancing shuffle, which terminated with a short capering kick that threw up the dust about him, and all the while he whistled one of those whimsical jig tunes with which Ireland abounds, and twirled his stick over his head in a triumphal flourish. Then off he started again in his original pace, and hummed a rolicking song, and occasionally broke out into soliloquy—"Why then, an isn't it the grate day intirely for Ireland, that is in it this blessed day? Whoo! your sowl to glory but we'll do the job complate—" and here he cut a caper.—"Divil a more they'll ever get, and it's only a pity they ever got any—but there's an ind o' them now—they're cut down from this out," and here he made an appropriate down stroke of his shillelah through a bunch of thistles that skirted the road. "Where will be their grand doin's now?—eh?—I'd like to know that. Where'll be their lazy livery sarvants?—ow! ow!!"—and he sprang lightly over a stile. "And what will they do for their coaches and four?" Here, a lark sprang up at his feet and darted into the air with its thrilling rush of exquisite melody.—"Faith, you've given me my answer sure enough, my purty lark—that's as much as to say, they may go whistle for them—oh, my poor fellows, how I pity yiz;"—and here he broke into a "too ra lal loo" and danced along the path:—then suddenly dropping into silence he resumed his walk, and applying his hand behind his head, cocked up his caubeen[1] and began to rub behind his ear, according to the most approved peasant practice of assisting the powers of reflection.—"Faix an it's mysef that's puzzled to know what'll the procthors, and the process sarvers,[1] and 'praisers[2] do at all. By gorra they must go rob *an the road*, since they won't be let to rob any more *in the fields*; robbin' is all that is left for them, for sure they couldn't turn to any honest thrade afther the coorses they have been used to. Oh what a power o' miscrayants will be out of bread for the want of their owld thrade of false swearin'. Why the vagabones will be lost, barrin' they're sent to *Bot*[3]—and indeed if a bridge could be built of false oaths, by my sowkins, they could sware themselves there without wettin' their feet."—Here he overtook another peasant, whom he accosted with the universal salutation of "God save you!"—"God save you kindly," was return for answer.—"And is it yourself that's there, Mikee Noonan?" said the one first introduced to the reader.

"Indeed it's mysef and nobody else," said Noonan; "an where is it you're goin' this fine mornin'?"

"An is it yourself that's axin' that same, Mikee?—why where is it I would be goin' but to the berrin?"

"I thought so in throth. Its yoursef that is always ripe and ready for fun."

"And small blame to me."

"Why then it was a mighty complate thing, whoever it was that thought of makin' a berrin out of it."

"And don't you know?"

"Not to my knowledge."

"Why then who 'ud you think now laid it all out."

"Faix I dunna—maybe 'twas Pether Conolly."

"No it wasn't, though Pether's a cute chap—guess again."

"Well, was it Phil Mulligan?"

"No it wasn't, though you made a good offer at it sure enough, for if it wasn't Phil, it was his sisther—"

"'Tare alive, is it Biddy, it was?"

"'Scure to the one else.—Oh she's the quarest craythur in life.—There's not a thrick out, that one's not up to, and more besides. By the powdhers o' war, she'd bate a field full o' lawyers at schkamin'—she's the Divil's Biddy."

"Why thin but it was a grate iday intirely."

"You may say that in throth—maybe it's we won't have the fun—but see who's before us there. Isn't it that owld Coogan?"

"Sure enough by dad."

"Why thin isn't he the rale fine ould cock to come so far to see the rights o' the thing."

"Faix he was always the right sort—sure in Nointy-eight, as I hear, he was malthrated a power, and his place rummaged, and himself a'most kilt, bekase he wouldn't inform an his neighbours."

"God's blessin' be an him an the likes av him that wouldn't prove thraitor to a friend in disthress."

Here they came up with the old man to whom they alluded—he was the remains of a stately figure, and his white hair hung at some length round the back of his head and his temples, while a black and well marked eyebrow overshadowed his keen gray eye—the contrast of the dark eyebrow to the white hair rendered the intelligent cast of his features more striking, and he was, altogether, a figure that one would not be likely to pass without notice. He was riding a small horse at an easy pace, and he answered the rather respectful salutation of the two foot passengers with kindness and freedom. They addressed him as "*Mr Coogan*," while to them he returned the familiar term "boys."

"And av coorse it goin' to the berrin you are, Mr Coogan, and long life to you."

"Aye, boys.—It's hard for an owld horse to leave off his thricks."

"Owld is it?—faix and it's yourself that has more heart in you this blessed mornin' than many a man that's not half your age."

"By dad I'm not a cowlt, boys, though I kick up my heels sometimes."

"Well, you'll never do it younger, sir,—but sure why wouldn't you be there when all the counthry is goin' I hear, and no wondher sure.—By the hole in my hat it's enough, so it is, to make a sick man lave his bed to see the fun that'll be in it, and sure it's right and proper, and shows the sperit that's in the counthry, when a man like yourself, Mr Coogan, joins the poor people in doin' it."

"I like to stand up for the right," answered the old man.

"And always was a good warrant to do that same," said Larry, in his most laudatory tone.

"Will you tell us who's that fornint us an the road there?" asked the old man, as he pointed to a person that seemed to make his way with some difficulty, for he laboured under an infirmity of limb that caused a grotesque jerking action in his walk, if walk it might be called.

"Why, thin, don't you know him, Mr Coogan? by dad I thought there wasn't a parish in the county that didn't know poor Hoppy Houligan."

It has been often observed before, the love of *soubriquet* that the Irish possess; but let it not be supposed that their nicknames are given in a spirit of unkindness—far from it. A sense of the ridiculous is so closely interwoven in an Irishman's nature, that he will even jest upon his *own* misfortunes; and while he indulges in a joke (one of the few indulgences he can command), the person that excites it may as frequently be the object of his openheartedness as his mirth.

"And is that Hoppy Houligan?" said old Coogan, "I often heerd of him, to be sure, but I never seen him before."

"Oh, then, you may see him before and behind now," said Larry; "and, indeed, if he had a match for that odd skirt of his coat, he wouldn't be the worse iv it; and in throth the cordheroys themselves aren't a bit too good, and there's the laste taste in life of his—"

"Whisht," said he old man, "he is looking back, and maybe he hears you."

"Not he in throth. Sure he's partly bothered."

"How can he play the fiddle then, and he bothered?" said Coogan.

"Faix an that's the very raison he *is* bothered; sure he moidhers the ears off of him intirely with the noise of his own fiddle. Oh he's a powerful fiddler."

"So I often heerd, indeed," said he old man.

"He bangs all the fiddlers in the counthry."

"And is in the greatest request," added Noonan.

"Yet he looks tatthered enough," said old Coogan.

"Sure you never seen a well dhrest fiddler yet," said Larry.

"Indeed, and now you remind me, I believe not," said the old man. "I suppose they all get more kicks than ha'pence, as the saying is."

"Divil a many kicks Hooligan gets; he's a great favorite intirely."

"Why is he in such distress then?" asked Coogan.

"Faith he's not in disthress at all; he's welkim every where he goes, and has the best of atin' and dhrinkin' the place affords, wherever he is, and picks up the coppers fast at the fairs, and is no way *necessiated* in life; though indeed it can't be denied, as he limps along there, that he has a great many *ups* and *downs* in the world."

This person, of whom the preceding dialogue treats, was a celebrated fiddler in "these parts," and his familiar name of Hoppy Houligan was acquired, as the reader may already have perceived, from his limping gait. This limp was the consequence of a broken leg, which was one of the consequences of an affray, which is the certain consequence of a fair in Tipperary. Houligan was a highly characteristic specimen of an Irish fiddler. As Larry Lanigan said, "You never seen a well drest fiddler yet;" but Houligan was a particularly ill fledged bird of the musical tribe. His corduroys have already been hinted at by Larry, as well as his coat, which had lost half the skirt, thereby partially revealing the aforesaid corduroys; or if one might be permitted to indulge in an image, the half skirt that remained served to produce a partial eclipse of the disc of corduroy. This was what we painters call *picturesque*. By the way, the vulgar are always amazed that some tattered remains of any thing is more prized by the painter than the freshest production in all its gloss of novelty. The fiddler's stockings, too, in the neglected falling of their folds round his leg, and the whisp of straw that fringed the opening of his gaping brogues, were valuable additions to the picture; and his hat—But stop,—let me not presume;—his hat it would be a vain attempt to describe. There are two things not to be described, which, to know what they are, you must see.

Those two things are Taglioni's dancing and an Irish fiddler's hat. The one is a wonder in *action*;—the other, an enigma in *form*.

Houligan's fiddle was as great a curiosity as himself, and like it master, somewhat the worse for wear. It had been broken some score of times, and yet, by dint of glue, was continued in what an antiquary would call "a fine state of preservation;" that is to say, there was rather more of glue than wood in the article. The stringing of the instrument was as great a piece of patchwork as itself; and exhibited great ingenuity on the part of its owner. Many was the knot above the finger-board and below the bridge; that is, when the fiddle was in its *best* order; for in case of fractures on the field of action, that is to say, at wake, patron, or fair, where the fiddler, unlike the girl he was playing for, had not two strings to his bow; in such case, I say, the old string should be knotted, wherever it might require to be, and I have heard it insinuated that the music was not a bit the worse of it. Indeed, the only economy that poor Houligan ever practised was in the strings of his fiddle, and those were an admirable exemplification of the proverb of "making both ends meet." Houligan's waistcoat, too, was a curiosity, or rather, a cabinet of curiosities; for he appropriated its pockets to various purposes;—snuff, resin, tobacco, a clasp-knife with half a blade, a piece of flint, a *doodeen*[4] and some bits of twine and ends of fiddle-strings were all huddled together promiscuously. Houligan himself called his waistcoat Noah's ark; for, as he said himself, there was a little of every thing in it, barring[5] money, and that would never stay in his company. His fiddle, partly enfolded in a scanty bit of old baize, was tucked under his left arm, and his right was employed in helping him to hobble along by means of a black-thorn stick, when he was overtaken by the three travellers already named, and saluted by all, with the addition of a query as to where he was going.

"An where would I be goin' but to the berrin'?" said Houligan.

"Throth it's the same answer I expected," said Lanigan. "It would be nothing at all without you."

"I've played at many a weddin'," said Houligan, "but I'm thinkin' there will be more fun at this berrin' than any ten weddin's."

"Indeed you may say that, Hoppy, aghra," said Noonan.

"Why thin, Hoppy jewel," said Lanigan, "what did the skirt o' your coat do to you that you left it behind you, and wouldn't let it see the fun?"

"'Deed then I'll tell you, Larry, my boy. I was goin' last night by the by-road that runs up at the back o' the owld house, nigh hand the Widdy Casey's, and I heerd that people was livin' in it since I thravelled the road last, and so I opened the owld iron gate that was as stiff in the hinge as a miser's fist, and the road ladin' up to the house lookin' as lonely as a churchyard, and the grass growin' out through it, and says I to myself, I'm thinkin' it's few darkens your doors, says I; God be with the time the owld squire was here, that staid at home and didn't go abroad out of his own counthry, lettin' the fine stately owld place go to rack and ruin; and faix I was turnin' back, and I wish I did; whin I seen a man comin' down the road, and so I waited till he kem near to me, and I axed if any one was up at the house; Yis, says he; and with that I heerd terrible barkin' intirely, and a great big lump of a dog turned the corner of the house and stud growlin' at me; I'm afeard there's dogs in it, says I to the man; Yis, says he, but they're quite (quiet); so, with that I wint my way, and he wint his way; but my jew'l, the minit I got into the yard, nine great vagabones of dogs fell an me, and I thought they'd ate me alive; and so they would I b'lieve, only I had a cowld bones o' mate and some praties that Mrs Magrane, God bless her, made me put in my pocket when I was goin' the road as I was lavin' her house that mornin' afther the christenin' that was in it, and sure enough lashings and lavings was there; O that's the woman has a heart as big as a king's, and her husband too, in throth; he's a dacent man and keeps mighty fine dhrink in his house. Well, as I was sayin', the cowld mate and praties was in my pocket, and by gor the thievin' morodin' villians o' dogs made a dart at the pocket and dragged it clane aff; and thin, my dear, with fightin' among themselves, sthrivin' to come at the mate, the skirt o' my coat was in smidhereens in one minit—divil a lie in it—not a tatther iv it was left together; and it's only a wondher I came off with my life."

"Faith I think so," said Lanigan; "and wasn't it mighty providintial they didn't get at the fiddle; sure what would the counthry do then?"

"Sure enough you may say that," said Houligan; "and then my *bread* would be gone as well as my *mate*. But think o' the unnatharal vagabone that towld me the dogs was quite; sure he came back while I was there, and I ups and towld him what a shame it was to tell me the dogs was quite. So they are quite, says he; sure there's nine o' them, and *only seven o' them bites*. Thank you, says I."

There was something irresistibly comic in the quiet manner that Houligan said, "Thank you, says I;" and the account of his canine adventure altogether excited much mirth amongst his auditors. As they pursued their journey many a joke was passed and repartee returned, and the laugh rang loudly and often from the merry little group as they trudged along. In the course of the next mile's march their numbers were increased by some half dozen, that, one by one, suddenly appeared, by leaping over the hedge on the road, or crossing a stile from some neighbouring path. All these new comers pursued the same route, and each gave the same answer when asked where he was going. It was universally this—

"Why, then, where would I be goin' but to the berrin'?"

At a neighbouring confluence of roads straggling parties of from four to five were seen in advance, and approaching in the rear, and the highway soon began to wear the appearance it is wont to do on the occasion of a patron, a fair, or a market day. Larry Lanigan was in evident enjoyment at this increase of numbers; and as the crowd thickened his exultation increased, and he often repeated his ejaculation, already noticed in Larry's opening soliloquy, "Why, then, an' isn't it a grate day intirely for Ireland!!!"

And now, horsemen were more frequently appearing, and their numbers soon amounted to almost a cavalcade;

and sometimes a car, that is to say, the car common to the country for agricultural purposes, might be seen, bearing a cargo of women; videlicet, "the good woman" herself, and her rosy-cheeked daughters, and maybe a cousin or two, with an *aid du camp* aunt to assist in looking after the young ladies. The roughness of the motion of this primitive vehicle was rendered as accommodating as possible to the gentler sex, by a plentiful shake down of clean straw on the car, over which a feather bed was laid, and the best quilt in the house over that, to make all smart, possibly a piece of hexagon patchwork of "the misthriss" herself, in which the tawdriest calico patterns served to display the taste of the rural sempstress, and stimulated the rising generation to feats of needlework. The car was always provided with a driver, who took such care upon himself "for a rayson he had:" he was almost universally what is called in Ireland "a clane boy," that is to say, a well made, good-looking young fellow, whose eyes were not put into his head for nothing; and these same eyes might be seen wandering backwards occasionally from his immediate charge, the dumb baste, to "take a squint" at some, or maybe *one*, of his passengers. This explains "the rayson he had" for becoming driver. Sometimes he sat on the crupper of the horse, resting his feet on the shafts of the car, and bending down his head to say something *tindher* to the *colleen* that sat next him, totally negligent of his duty as guide. Sometimes when the girl he wanted to be sweet on was seated at the back of the car, this relieved the horse from the additional burthen of his driver, and the clane boy would leave the horse's head and fall in the rear to *deludher* the craythur, depending on an occasional "hup" or "wo" for the guidance of the *baste*, when a too near proximity to the dyke by the road side warned him of the necessity of his interference. Sometimes he was called to his duty by the open remonstrance of either the mother or the aunt, or maybe a mischievous cousin, as thus: "Why then, Dinny, what are you about at all at all? God betune me and harm, if you warn't within an inch o' puttin' uz all in the gripe o' the ditch;—arrah, lave off your gostherin' there, and mind the horse, will you; a purty thing it 'ud be if my bones was bruk; what are you doin' there at all at the back o' the car, when it's at the baste's head you ought to be?"

"Arrah sure, the baste knows the way herself."

"Faix, I b'lieve so, for it's little behowlden to you she is for showin' her. Augh!!—murther!!—there we are in the gripe a'most."

"Lave off your screeching, can't you, and be quite. Sure the poor craythur only just wint over to get a mouthful o' the grass by the side o' the ditch."

"What business has she to be atin' now?"

"Bekase she's hungry, I suppose;—and why isn't she fed betther?"

"Bekase rogues stales her oats, Dinny. I seen you in the stable by the same token yistherday."

"Sure enough, ma'am, for I wint there to look for my cowlt that was missin'."

"I thought it was the *filly* you wor afther, Dinny," said a cousin with a wink; and Dinny grinned, and his sweetheart blushed, while the rest of the girls tittered, the mother pretending not to hear the joke, and bidding Dinny go mind his business by attending to the horse.

But lest I should tire my reader by keeping him so long on the road, I will let him find the rest of his way as well as he can to a certain romantic little valley, where a comfortable farm-house was situated beside a small mountain stream that tumbled along noisily over its rocky bed, and in which some ducks, noisier than the stream, were enjoying their morning bath. The geese were indulging in dignified rest and silence upon the bank; a cock was crowing and strutting with his usual swagger amongst his hens; a pig was endeavouring to save his ears, not from this rural tumult, but from the teeth of a half-terrier dog, who was chasing him away from an iron pot full of potatoes which the pig had dared to attempt some impertinent liberties with; and a girl was bearing into the house a pail of milk which she had just taken from the cow that stood placidly looking on, an admirable contrast to the general bustle of the scene.

Every thing about he cottage gave evidence of comfort on the part of its owner, and, to judge from the numbers without and within the house, you would say he did not want for friends; for all, as they arrived at its door, greeted Phelim O'Hara kindly, and Phelim welcomed each new-comer with a heartiness that did honor to his gray hairs. Frequently passing to and fro, busily engaged in arranging an ample breakfast in the barn, appeared his daughter, a pretty round-faced girl, with black hair and the long and silky-lashed dark gray eyes of her country, where merriment loves to dwell, and a rosy mouth whose smiles served at once to display her good temper and her fine teeth; her colour gets fresher for a moment, and a look of affectionate recognition brightens her eye, as a lithe young fellow springs briskly over the stepping stones that lead across the stream, and trips lightly up to the girl, who offers her hand in welcome. Who is the happy dog that is so well received by Honor O'Hara, the prettiest girl in that parish or the next, and the daughter of a "snug man" into the bargain?—It is the reader's old acquaintance, Larry Lanigan;—and maybe Larry did not give a squeeze extraordinary to the hand that was presented to him. The father received him well also; indeed, for that matter, the difficulty would have been to find a house in the whole district that Larry would *not* have been welcome in.

"So here you are at last, Larry," said old O'Hara; "I was wondering you were not here long ago."

"An' so I would, I thank you kindly," said Larry, "only I overtook owld Hoppy here, on the road, and sure I thought I might as well take my time, and wait for poor Hoppy, and bring my welkim along with me;" and here he shoved the fiddler into the house before him.

"The girls will be glad to see the pair o' yiz," said the old man, following.

The interior of the house was crowded with guests, and the usual laughing and courting so often described, as common to such assemblages, were going forward amongst the young people. At the farther end of the largest room in the cottage, a knot of the older men of the party was engaged in the discussion of some subject that seemed to carry deep interest along with it, and at the opposite extremity of the same room, a coffin of very rude construction lay on a small table; and around this coffin stood all the junior part of the company, male and female, and the wildness of their mirth, and the fertility of their jests, over this tenement of mortality and its contents, might have well startled a stranger for a moment, until he saw the nature of the deposit the coffin contained.

Enshrouded in a sheaf of wheat lay a pig, between whose open jaws a large potato was placed, and the coffin was otherwise grotesquely decorated.

The reader will wonder no doubt, at such an exhibition, for certainly never was coffin so applied before; and it is therefore necessary to explain the meaning of all this, and I believe Ireland is the only country in the world where the facts I am about to relate could have occurred.

It may be remembered that some time previously to the date at which my story commences, his majesty's ministers declared that there should be a "total extinction of tithes."

This declaration was received in Ireland by the great mass of the people with the utmost delight, as they fancied they should never have tithes to pay again. The peasantry in the neighbourhood of Templemore formed the very original idea of BURYING THE TITHE. It is only amongst an imaginative people that such a notion could have originated; and indeed there is something highly poetical in the conception. The tithe—that which the poor felt the keenest; that which they considered a tax on their industry; that which they, looked upon as an hereditary oppression; that hateful thing, they were told, was to be extinct, and, in joyous anticipation of the blessing, they determined to enact an emblematic interment of this terrible enemy.—I think it is not too much to call this idea a fine one; and yet, in the execution of it, they invested it with the broadest marking of the grotesque. Such is the strange compound of an Irish peasant, whose anger is often vented in a jest, and whose mirth is sometimes terrible.

I must here pause for a moment, and request it to be distinctly understood, that, in relating this story, in giving the facts connected with it, and in stating what the Irish peasant's feelings are respecting tithe, I have not the most distant notion of putting forward any opinions of my own on the subject. In the pursuit of my own quiet art, I am happily far removed from the fierce encounter of politics, and I do not wish to offend against the feelings or opinions of any one in my little volume; and I trust, therefore, that I may be permitted to give a sketch of a characteristic incident, as it came to my knowledge, without being mistaken for a partisan.

"I tell the tale as 'twas told to me."

I have said a group of seniors was collected at one end of the room, and, as it is meet to give precedence to age, I will endeavour to give some idea of what was going forward amongst them.

There was one old man of the party whose furrowed forehead, compressed eyebrows, piqued nose, and mouth depressed at the corners, at once indicated to a physiognomist a querulous temper. He was one of your doubters upon all occasions, one of the unfailing elements of an argument;—as he said himself, he was "dubersome" about every thing, and he had hence earned the name of Daddy Dubersome amongst his neighbours. Well, Daddy, began to doubt the probability that any such boon as the extinction of tithes was to take place, and said, he was "sartin sure 'twas too good news to be thrue."

"Tare anounty," said another, who was the very antithesis of Daddy in his credulous nature, "sure, didn't I see it myself in *prent*."

"I was towld often that things was in prent," returned Daddy, drily, "that come out lies afther, to my own knowledge."

"But sure," added a third, "sure, didn't the Prime Ear himself lay it all out before the Parleymint?"

"What Prime Ear are you talking about, man dear?" said Daddy, rather testily.

"Why, the Prime Ear of his Majesty, and no less. Is that satisfaction for you, eh?"

"Well, and who is the Prime Ear?"

"Why, the Prime Ear of his Majesty, I towld you before. You see, he is the one that hears of every thing that is to be done for the whole impire in partic'lar; and bekase he *hears* of every thing, that's the rayson he is called the Prime *Ear*—and a good rayson it is."

"Well, but what has that to do with the tithes? I ask you again," said Daddy with his usual pertinacity.

Here he was about to be answered by the former speaker, whose definition of "The Premier" had won him golden opinions amongst the by-standers,—when he was prevented by a fourth orator, who rushed into the debate with this very elegant opening—

"Arrah! tare-an-ouns, yiz are settin' me mad, so yiz are. Why, I wondher any one 'id be sitch a fool as to go arguefy with that crooked owld diciple there."

"Meanin' me?" said Daddy.

"I'd be sorry to contheradict you, sir;" said the other with an admirable mockery of politeness.

"Thank you, sir," said Daddy, with a dignity more comical than the other's buffoonery.

"You're kindly welkim, Daddy," returned the aggressor. "Sure, you never b'lieved any thing yit; and I wondher any one would throw away their time sthriviu' to rightify you."

"Come, boys," saidl O'Hara, interrupting the discourse, with a view to prevent further bickering, "there's no use talking about the thing now, for whatever way it is, sure we are met to bury the Tithe, and it's proud I am to see you all here to make merry upon the stringth of it, and I think I heerd Honor say this minit that every thing is ready in the barn without, so you'll have no difference of opinion about tackling to the breakfast, or I'm mistaken. Come, my hearties, the mate and the praties is crying, 'Who'll ate me?'—away wid you, that's your sort;"—and he enforced his summons to the feast by pushing his guests before him towards the scene of action.

This was an ample barn, where tables of all sorts and

sizes were spread, loaded with viands of the most substantial character: wooden forms, three-legged stools, broken-backed chairs, &c. &c. were in requisition for the accommodation of the female portion of the company, and the men attended first to their wants with a politeness which, though deficient in the external graces of polished life, did credit to their natures. The eating part of the business was accompanied with all the clatter that might be expected to attend such an affair; and when the eatables had been tolerably well demolished, O'Hara stood up in the midst of his guests and said he should propose to them a toast, which he knew all the boys would fill their glasses for, and that was, to drink the health of the King, and long life to him, for seeing into the rights of the thing, and doing "such a power" for them, and "more power to his elbow."—This toast was prefaced by a speech to his friends and neighbours upon the hardships of tithe in particular, spiced with the *laste taste in life* of politics in general; wherein the Repeal of the Union and Daniel O'Connell cut no inconsiderable figure; yet in the midst of the rambling address, certain glimpses of good sense and shrewd observation might be caught; and the many powerful objections he advanced against the impost that was to be "extinct" so soon, were put forward with a force and distinctness that were worthy of a better speaker, and might have been found difficult to reply to by a more accustomed hand. He protested that he thought he had lived long enough when he had witnessed in his own life-time two such national benefits as the Catholic Emancipation Bill and the Abolition of Tithes. O'Hara further declared, he was the happiest man alive that day only in the regard "of one thing, and that was, that his reverence, Father Hely (the priest) was not there amongst them;" and, certainly, the absence of the pastor on an occasion of festivity in the house of a snug farmer, is of rare occurrence in Ireland. "But you see," said O'Hara, "whin his rivirince heerd what it was we wor goin' to do, he thought it would be *purtier* on his part for to have nothin' whatsomivir to do with it, in hand, act, or part; and, indeed, boys, that shews a great deal of good breedin' in Father Hely."

This was quite agreed to by the company; and, after many cheers for O'Hara's speech, and some other toasts pertinent to the occasion, the health of O'Hara, as founder of the feast, with the usual addenda of long life, prosperity, &c. to him and his, was drunk, and then preparations were entered into for proceeding with the ceremony of the funeral.

"I believe we have nothing to wait for now," said O'Hara, "since you won't have any more to drink, boys; so let us set about it at once, and make a *clane* day's work of it."

"Oh, we're not quite ready yit," said Larry Lanigan, who seemed to be a sort of master of the ceremonies on the occasion.

"What's the delay?" asked O'Hara.

"Why, the chief *murners* is not arrived yit."

"What murners are you talkin' about, man?" said the other.

"Why, you know, at a *grand* berrin they have always chief murners, and there's a pair that I ordhered to be brought here for that same."

"Myself doesn't know any thing about murners," said O'Hara, "for I never seen any thing finer than the *keeners*[6] at a berrin; but Larry's up to the ways of the quolity, as well as of his own sort."

"But you wouldn't have keeners for the Tithe, would you? Sure, the keeners is to say all the good they can of the departed, and more if they can invint it; but, sure, the divil a good thing at all they could say of the Tithe, barrin' it was lies they wor tellin', and so it would only be throwin' away throuble."

"Thrue for you, Lanigan."

"Besides, it is like a grand berrin belongin' to the quol'ty to have chief murners, and you know the Tithe was aiqual to a lord or a king a'most for power."

In a short time the "murners," as Larry called them, arrived in custody of half a dozen of Larry's chosen companions, to whom he had entrusted the execution of the mission. These chief mourners were two tithe proctors who had been taken forcibly from their homes by the Lanigan party, and threatened with death unless they attended the summons of Larry to be present at "The Berrin."

Their presence was hailed with a great shout, and the poor devils looked excessively frightened; but they were assured by O'Hara they had nothing to fear.

"I depend an you, Mr O'Hara, for seeing us safe out of their hands," said one of them, for the other was dumb from terror.

"So you may," was the answer O'Hara returned. "Hurt nor harm shell not be put an you; I give you my word o' that."

"Divil a harm," said Larry. "We'll only put you into a shoot o' clothes that is ready for you, and you may look as melancholy as you plaze, for it is murners you are to be. Well, Honor," said he, addressing O'Hara's daughter, "have you got the mithres and vestments ready, as I towld you?"

"Yes," said Honor; "here comes Biddy Mulligan with them from the house, for Biddy herself helped me to make them."

"And who had a betther right?" said Larry, "when it was herself that laid it all out complate, the whole thing from the beginnin', and sure enough but it was a bright thought of her. Faix, he'll be the *looky* man that gets Biddy, yet."

"You had betther have her yourself, I think," said Honor, with an arch look at Larry, full of meaning.

"An it's that same I've been thinking of for some time," said Larry, laughing, and returning Honor's look with one that repaid it with interest. "But where is she at all? Oh, here she comes with the duds, and Mike Noonan afther her; throth, he's following her about all this mornin' like a sucking calf. I'm afeard Mikee is going to *sarcumvint* me wid Biddy; but he'd betther mind what he's at."

Here the conversation was interrupted by the advance of Biddy Mulligan, "and Mikee Noonan afther her," bearing some grotesque imitation of clerical vestments made of coarse sacking, and two enormous head-dress made of straw, in the fashion of mitres; these were decorated with black rags hung fantastically about them, while the vestments were smeared over with black stripes in no very regular order.

"Come here," said Larry to the tithe proctors; "come here, antil we put you into your *regimentals*."

"What are you goin' to do with us, *Mr* Lanigan?" said the frightened poor wretch, while his knees knocked together with terror.

"We are just going to make a pair o' bishops of you," said Lanigan; "and sure that's promotion for you."

"Oh, Mr O'Hara," said the proctor, "sure you won't let them tie us up in them sacks."

"Do you hear what he calls the iligant vestments we made a' purpose for him? They are sackcloth, to be sure, and why not—seeing as how that you are to be the chief murners? and sackcloth and ashes is what you must be dhressed in, accordin' to rayson. Here, my buck," said the rolicking Larry, "I'll be your vally de sham myself," and he proceeded to put the dress on the terrified tithe proctor.

"Oh, Mr Lanigan dear!" said he, " don't murther me, *if you plaze*."

"Murther you!—arrah, who's going to murther you? Do you think I'd dirty my hands wid killin' a snakin' tithe procthor?"

"Indeed, that's thrue, Mr Lanigan; it would not be worth your while."

"Here now," said Larry, "howld your head till I put the mithre an you, and make you a bishop complate. But wait a bit; throth, I was nigh forgettin' the ashes, and that would have been a great loss to both o' you, bekase you wouldn't be right murners at all without them, and the people would think you wor only *purtendin'*." This last bit of Larry's waggery produced great merriment amongst the bystanders, for the unfortunate tithe proctors were looking at that moment most doleful examples of wretchedness. A large shovelful of turf ashes was now shaken over their heads, and then they were decorated with their mitres. "Tut, man," said Larry to one of them, "don't thrimble like a dog in a wet sack. Oh, thin, look at him how pale he's turned, the dirty coward that he is. I tell you, we're not goin' to do you any hurt, so you needn't be lookin' in sitch mortial dhread. By gor, you're as white as a pen'orth o' curds in a sweep's fist."

With many such jokes at the expense of the tithe proctors, they were attired in their caricature robes and mitres, and presented with a pair of pitchforks, by way of crosiers, and were recommended at the same time to make hay while the sun shone, "bekase the fine weather would be lavin' them soon;" with many other bitter sarcasms, conveyed in the language of ridicule.

The procession was now soon arranged, and, as they

had their chief mourners, it was thought a good point of contrast to have their chief rejoicers as well. To this end, in a large cart they put a sow and her litter of pigs, decorated with ribands, a sheaf of wheat standing proudly erect, a bowl of large potatoes, which, at Honor O'Hara's suggestion, were *boiled*, that they might be *laughing* on the occasion, and over these was hung a rude banner, on which was written, "We may stay at home now."

In this cart, Hoppy Houligan, the fiddler, with a piper as a coadjutor, rasped and squeaked their best to the tune of "Go to the devil and shake yourself," which was meant to convey a delicate hint to the tithes for the future.

The whole assemblage of people, and it was immense, then proceeded to the spot where it was decided the tithe was to be interred, as the most fitting place to receive such a deposit, and this place was called by what they considered the very appropriate name of "The Devil's Bit[7]."

In a range of hills, in the neighbourhood where this singular occurrence took place, there is a sudden gap occurs in the outline of the ridge, which is stated to have been formed by his sable majesty taking a bite out of the mountain; whether it was spite or hunger that had made him do so, is not ascertained, but he evidently did not consider it a very savoury morsel; for it is said, he spat it out again, and the rejected *morceau* forms the rock of Cashel. Such is the wild legend of this wild spot, and here was the interment of the tithe to be achieved, as an appropriate addition to the "Devil's Bit."

The procession now moved onward, and, as it proceeded its numbers were considerably augmented. Its approach was looked for by a scout on every successive hill it came within sight of, and a wild halloo, or the winding of a cow's horn immediately succeeded, which called forth scores of fresh attendants upon "the berrin." Thus, their numbers were increased every quarter of a mile they went, until, on their arriving at the foot of the hill which they were to ascend, to reach their final destination, the multitude assembled presented a most imposing appearance. In the course of their march, the great point of attraction for the young men and women was the cart that bore the piper and fiddler, and the road was rather danced than walked over in this quarter. The other distinguished portion of the train was where the two tithe proctors played their parts of chief mourners. They were the delight of all the little ragged urchins in the country; the half-naked young vagabonds hung on their flanks, plucked at their vestments, made wry faces at them, called them by many ridiculous names, and an occasional lump of clay was slily flung at their mitres, which were too tempting a "cock shot" to be resisted. The multitude now wound up the hill, and the mingling of laughter, of singing, and shouting, produced a wild compound of sound, that rang far and wide. As they doubled an angle in the road, which opened the Devil's Bit full upon their view, they saw another crowd assembled there, which consisted of persons from the other side of the hills, who could not be present at the breakfast, nor join the procession, but who attended upon the spot where the interment was to take place. As soon as the approach of the funeral train was perceived from the top of the hill, the mass of people there sent forth a shout of welcome, which was returned by those from below.

Short space now served to bring both parties together, and the digging of a grave did not take long with such a plenty of able hands for the purpose. "Come, boys," said Larry Lanigan to two or three of his companions, "while they are digging the grave here, we'll go cut some sods to put over it when the thievin' tithe is buried; not for any respect I have for it in partic'lar, but that we may have the place smooth and clane to dance over aftherwards; and may I never shuffle the brogue again, if myself and Honor O'Hara won't be the first pair that 'll set you a patthern."

All was soon ready for the interment; the tithe coffin was lowered into the pit, and the shouting that rent the air was terrific.

As they were about to fill up the grave with earth, their wild hurra, that had rung out so loudly, was answered by a fierce shout at some distance, and all eyes were turned towards the quarter whence it arose, to see from whom it proceeded, for it was, evidently, a solitary voice that had thus arrested their attention.

Toiling up the hill, supporting himself with a staff, and bearing a heavy load in a wallet slung over his shoulders, appeared an elderly man whose dress proclaimed him at once to be a person who depended on eleemosynary contributions for his subsistence: and many, when they caught the first glimpse of him, proclaimed, at once, that it was "Tatther the Road" was coming.

"Tatther the Road" was the very descriptive name that had been applied to this poor creature, for he was always travelling about the highways; he never rested even at nights in any of the houses of the peasants, who would have afforded him shelter, but seemed to be possessed by a restless spirit, that urged him to constant motion. Of course the poor creature sometimes slept, but it must have been under such shelter as a hedge, or cave, or gravel pit might afford, for in the habitation of man he was never seen to sleep; and, indeed, I never knew any one who had seen this strange being in the act of sleep. This fact attached a sort of mysterious character to the wanderer, and many would tell you that "he wasn't right," and firmly believed that he never slept at all. His mind was unsettled, and though he never became offensive in any degree from his mental aberration, yet the nature of his distemper often induced him to do very extraordinary things, and whenever the gift of speech was upon him (for he was habitually taciturn), he would make an outpouring of some rhapsody, in which occasional bursts of very powerful language and striking imagery would occur. Indeed the peasants said that "sometimes 'twould make your hair stand an end to hear Tatther the Road make a *noration*."

This poor man's history, as far as I could learn, was a very melancholy one. In the rebellion of 98 his cabin had been burned over his head by the yeomanry, after every violation that could disgrace his hearth had been committed. He and his son, then little more than a boy, had attempted to defend their hut, and they were both left for dead. His wife and his daughter, a girl of sixteen, were also murdered. The wretched father, unfortunately, recovered his life, but his reason was gone for ever. Even in the midst of his poverty and madness, there was a sort of respect attached to this singular man. Though depending on charity for his meat and drink, he could not well be called a beggar, for he never asked for any thing—even on the road, when some passenger, ignorant of his wild history, saw the poor wanderer, a piece of money was often bestowed to the silent appeal of his rags, his haggard features, and his grizly hair and beard.

Thus eternally up and down the country was he moving about, and hence his name of "Tatther the Road."

It was not long until the old man gained the summit of the hill, but while he was approaching, many were the "wonders" what in the name of fortune could have brought Tatther the Road there.—"And by dad," said one, "he's pullin' fut[8] at a great rate, and its wondherful how an owld cock like him can clamber up the hill so fast."

"Aye," said another, "and with the woight he's carrying too."

"Sure enough," said a third. "Faix he's got a fine lob in his wallet to-day."

"Whisht!" said O'Hara.—"Here he comes, and his ears are as sharp as needles."

"And his eyes too," said a woman. "Lord be good to me, did you ever see poor Tatther's eyes look so terrible bright afore?"

And indeed this remark was not uncalled for, for the eyes of the old man almost gleamed from under the shaggy brows that were darkly bent over them, as, with long strides, he approached the crowd which opened before him, and he stalked up to the side of the grave and threw down the ponderous wallet, which fell to the ground with a heavy crash.

"You were going to close the grave too soon," were the first words he uttered.

"Sure, when the tithe is wanst buried, what more have we to do?" said one of the by-standers.

"Aye, you have put the tithe in the grave—but will it stay there?"

"Why indeed," said Larry Lanigan, "I think he'd be a bowld resurrection man that would come to rise it."

"I have brought you something here to lie heavy on it, and 'twill never rise more," said the maniac, striking forth his arm fiercely, and clenching his hand firmly.

"And what have you brought us, Agrah?" said O'Hara kindly to him.

"Look here," said the other, unfolding his wallet and displaying five or six large stones.

Some were tempted to laugh, but a mysterious dread of the wild being before them, prevented any outbreak of mirth.

"God help the craythur!" said a woman, so loud as to be heard. "He has brought a bag full o' stones to throw a top o' the tithes to keep them down—O wisha! wisha! poor craythur!"

"Aye—stones!"—said the maniac;"but do you know what stones these are? Look woman—" and his manner became intensely impressive from the excitement even of madness, under which he was acting.—"Look, I say—there's not a stone there that's not a curse—aye a curse so heavy that nothing can ever rise that falls under it."

"Oh I don't want to say aginst it, dear," said the woman.

The maniac did not seem to notice her submissive answer, but pursuing his train of madness, continued his address in his native tongue, whose figurative and poetical construction was heightened in its effect, by a manner and action almost theatrically descriptive.

"You all remember the Widow Dempsy. The first choice of her bosom was long gone, but the son she loved was left to her, and her heart was not quite lonely. And at the widow's hearth there was still a welcome for the stranger—and the son of her heart made his choice, like the father before him, and the joy of the widow's house was increased, for the son of her heart was happy.—And in due time the widow welcomed the fair-haired child of her son to the world, and a dream of her youth came over her, as she saw the joy of her son and her daughter, when they kissed the fair-haired child.—But the hand of God was heavy in the land, and the fever fell hard upon the poor—and the widow was again bereft,—for the son of her heart was taken, and the wife of his bosom also—and the fair-haired child was left an orphan. And the widow would have laid down her bones and died, but for the fair-haired child that had none to look to but her. And the widow blessed God's name and bent her head to the blow—and the orphan that was left to her was the pulse of her heart, and often she looked on his pale face with a fearful eye, for health was not on the cheek of the boy—but she cherished him tenderly.

"But the ways of the world grew crooked to the lone woman, when the son, that was the staff of her age, was gone, and one trouble, followed another, but still the widow was not quite destitute.—And what was it brought the heavy stroke of distress and disgrace to the widow's door?—The tithe! The widow's cow was driven and sold to pay a few shillings; the drop of milk was no longer in the widow's house, and the tender child that needed the nourishment, wasted away before the widow's eyes, like snow from the ditch, and died: and fast the widow followed the son of her heart and his fair-haired boy.

"And now, the home of an honest race is a heap of rubbish; and the bleak wind whistles over the hearth where the warm welcome was ever found; and the cold frog crouches under the ruins.

"These stones are from that desolate place, and the curse of God that follows oppression is on them.—And let them be cast into the grave, and they will lie with the weight of a mountain on the monster that is buried for ever."

So saying, he lifted stone after stone, and flung them fiercely into the pit; then, after a moment's pause upon its verge, he suddenly strode away with the same noiseless step in which he had approached, and left the scene in silence.

1. The *cabhein* was an ancient head-dress of gorgeous material, and the name is applied in derision to a shabby hat.
2. The crop being often valued in a *green state* in Ireland, the appraiser becomes a very obnoxious person.
3. Botany Bay.
4. The stump of a pipe.
5. Excepting.
6. Keeners are persons who sing the Ulican, or death wail, round the coffin of the deceased, and repeat the good deeds of the departed.
7. I think Ware mentions an ancient crown being dug up at "The Devil's Bit."
8. *Pull fut* is a figurative expression to express making haste.

# THE WHITE HORSE OF THE PEPPERS.

## A LEGEND OF THE BOYNE

### CHAP. I.

A horse! a horse! my kingdom for a horse!

IT WAS THE NIGHT OF the 2nd of July, in the year 1690, that a small remnant of a discomfited army was forming its position, in no very good order, on the slope of a wild hill on the borders of the county of Dublin. In front of a small square tower, a sentinel was pacing up and down, darkly brooding over the disastrous fight of the preceding day, and his measured tread was sometimes broken by the fierce stamp of his foot upon the earth, as some bitter thought and muttered curse arose, when the feelings of the man overcame the habit of the soldier. The hum of the arrival of a small squadron of horse came from the vale below, borne up the hill on the faint breeze that sometimes freshens a summer's night, but neither the laugh, nor the song, which so often enlivens a military post, mingled with the sound. The very trumpet seemed to have lost the inspiring tingle of its tone, and its blast sounded heavily on the ear of the sentinel.

"There come more of our retreating comrades;" thought he, as he stalked before the low portal it was his duty to guard.—"Retreating—curse the word!—shall we never do any thing but fall back and back before this d—d Dutchman and his followers? And yesterday too, with so fine an opportunity of cutting the rascals to pieces,—and all thrown away, and so much hard fighting to go for nothing. Oh, if Sarsefield had led us! we'd have another tale to tell." And here he struck the heavy heel of his war boot into the ground, and hurried up and down. But he was roused from his angry musing by the sound of a horse's tramp which indicated a rapid approach to the tower, and he soon perceived, through the gloom, a horseman approaching at a gallop. The sentinel challenged the cavalier, who returned the countersign, and was then permitted to ride up to the door of the tower. He was mounted on a superb charger, whose silky coat of milk-white was much travel-stained, and the heaviness of whose breathing told of recent hard riding. The horseman alighted: his dress was of a mixed character, implying that war was not his profession, though the troubled nature of the times had engaged him in it. His head had no defensive covering, he wore the slouched hat of a civilian common to the time, but his body was defended by the cuirass of a trooper, and a heavy sword, suspended by a broad cross belt, was at his side—these alone bespoke the soldier, for the large and massively mounted pistols that protruded from the holsters at his saddle-bow, were no more than any gentleman, at the time, might have been provided with.

"Will you hold the rein of my horse," said he to the sentry, "while I remain in the castle?"

"I am a sentinel, sir," answered the soldier, "and cannot."

"I will not remain more than a few minutes."

"I dare not, sir, while I'm on duty—but I suppose you will find some one in the castle who will take charge of your horse."

The stranger now knocked at the door of the tower, and after some questions and answers in token of amity had passed between him and those inside, it was opened.

"Let some one take charge of my horse," said he, "I do not want him to be stabled, as I shall not remain here long, but I have ridden him hard, and he is warm, so let him be walked up and down until I am ready to get into the saddle again." He then entered the tower, and was ushered into a small and rude apartment, where a man of between fifty and sixty years of age, seated on a broken chair, though habited in a rich *robe de chambre*, was engaged in conversation with a general officer, a man of fewer years, whose finger was indicating certain points upon a map, which, with many other papers, lay on a rude table before them. Extreme dejection was the prevailing expression that overspread the countenance of the elder, while there mingled with the sadness that marked the noble features of the other, a tinge of subdued anger, as certain suggestions he offered, when he laid his finger, from time to time, on the map, were received with coldness; if not with refusal.

"Here at least we can make a bold stand," said the general, and his eye flashed, and his brow knit as he spoke.

"I fear not, Sarsefield," said the king, for it was the unfortunate James the Second who spoke.

Sarsefield withdrew his hand suddenly from the map, and folding his arms, became silent.

"May it please you, my liege," said the horseman, whose entry had not been noticed by either Sarsefield or his sovereign. "I hope I have not intruded on your majesty."

"Who speaks?" said the king, as he shaded his eyes from the light that burned on the table, and looked into the gloom where the other was standing.

"Your enemies, my liege," said Sarsefield, with some bitterness, "would not be so slow to discover a tried friend of your majesty—'tis the White Horseman;" and Sarsefield, as he spoke, gave a look full of welcome and joyous recognition towards him.

The horseman felt, with the pride of a gallant spirit, all that the general's look and manner conveyed, and he bowed his head, respectfully, to the leader, whose boldness and judgment he so often had admired.

"Ha! my faithful White Horseman," said the king.

"Your majesty's poor and faithful subject, Gerald Pepper," was the answer.

"You have won the name of the White Horseman," said Sarsefield, "and you deserve to wear it."

The Horseman bowed.

"The general is right," said the king. "I shall never choose to remember you by any other name. You and your white horse have done good service."

"Would that they could have done more, my liege," was the laconic and modest reply.

"Would that every one," laying some stress on the word, "had been as true to the cause *yesterday*!" said Sarsefield.

"And what has brought you here?" said the king, anxious perhaps to escape from the thought which his general's last words had suggested.

"I came, my liege, to ask permission to bid your majesty farewell, and beg the privilege to kiss your royal hand."

"Farewell?" echoed the king, startled at the word. "Are *you*, too, going?—every one deserts me!" There was intense anguish in the tone of his voice, for, as he spoke, his eye fell upon a ring he wore, which encircled the portrait of his favourite daughter, Anne, and the remembrance that she, his own child, had excited the same remark from the lips of her father—that bitter remembrance came across his soul and smote him to the heart. He was suddenly silent—his brow contracted—he closed his eyes in anguish, and one hitter tear sprang from under either lid at the thought. He passed his hand across his face, and wiped away the womanish evidence of his weakness.

"Do not say I desert you, my liege," said Gerald Pepper. "I leave you, 'tis true, for the present, but I do not leave you until I see no way in which I can be longer useful. While in my own immediate district, there were many ways in which my poor services might be made available; my knowledge of the county, of its people and its resources, its passes and its weak points, were of service. But here, or farther southward, where your majesty is going, I can no longer do any thing which might win the distinction that your majesty and General Sarsefield are pleased to honour me with."

"You have still a stout heart, a clear head, a hold arm, and a noble horse," said Sarsefield.

"I have also, a weak woman and helpless children, general," said Gerald Pepper.

The appeal was irresistible—Sarsefield was silent.

"But though I cannot longer aid with my arm—my wishes and my prayers shall follow your majesty—and whenever I may be thought an agent to be made useful, my king has but to command the willing services of his subject."

"Faithfully promised," said the king.

"The promise shall be as faithfully kept," said his follower; "but before I leave, may I beg the favour of a moment's private conversation with your majesty?"

"Speak any thing you have to communicate before Sarsefield," said the king.

Gerald Pepper hesitated for a moment; he was struggling between his sovereign's command and his own delicacy of feeling; but overcoming the latter, in deference to the former, he said:

"Your majesty's difficulties with respect to money supplies,—"

"I know, I know," said the king, somewhat impatiently, "I owe you five hundred pieces."

"Oh! my liege," said the devoted subject, dropping on his knee before him, "deem me not so unworthy as to seek to remind your majesty of the trifle you did me honour to allow me to lay at your disposal; I only regret I had not the means of contributing more. It is not that; but I have brought here another hundred pieces, it is all I can raise at present, and if your majesty will further honor me by the acceptance of so poor a pittance, when the immediate necessities of your army may render every trifle a matter of importance, I shall leave you with a more contented spirit, conscious that I have done all within my power for my king." And, as he spoke, he laid on the table a purse containing the gold.

"I cannot deny that we are sorely straitened," said the king, "but I do not like,—"

"Pray do not refuse it, my liege," said Gerald, still kneeling—"do not refuse the last poor service your subject may ever have it in his power to do in your cause."

"Well," said the king, "I accept it—but I would not do so if I were not sure of having, one day, the means of rewarding your loyalty and generosity." And thus allowing himself to be the dupe of his own fallacious hopes, he took from poor Gerald Pepper the last hundred guineas he had in his possession, with that happy facility kings have always exhibited, in accepting sacrifices from enthusiastic and self-devoted followers.

"My mission here is ended now," said Gerald. "May I be permitted to kiss my sovereign's hand?"

"Would that all my subjects were as faithful," said James, as he held out his hand to Gerald Pepper, who kissed it respectfully, and then arose.

"What do you purpose doing when you leave me?" said the king.

"To return to my home as soon as I may, my liege."

"If it be my fate to be driven from my kingdom by my unnatural son-in-law, I hope he may be merciful to my people, and none may suffer from their adherence to the cause of their rightful sovereign."

"I wish, my liege," said Gerald, "that he may have half the consideration for his *Irish* subjects which your majesty had for your *English* ones;" and he shook his head doubtfully as he spoke, and his countenance suddenly fell[1].

A hard-drawn sigh escaped from Sarsefield, and then, biting his lip, and with knitted brow, he exchanged a look of bitter meaning with Gerald Pepper.

"Adieu then," said the king, "since you will go. See our

good friend to his saddle, Sarsefield. Once more, good night; King James will not forget the White Horseman." So saying, he waved his hand in adieu. Gerald Pepper bowed low to his sovereign, and Sarsefield followed him from the chamber. They were both silent till they arrived at the portal of the tower, and when the door was opened, Sarsefield crossed the threshold with the visitor, and stepped into the fresh air, which he inhaled audibly three or four times, as if it were a relief to him.

"Good night, General Sarsefield," said Gerald.

"Good night, my gallant friend," said Sarsefield, in a voice that expressed much vexation of spirit.

"Be not so much cast down, general," said Gerald, "better days may come, and fairer fields be fought."

"Never, never!", said Sarsefield. "Never was a fairer field than that of yesterday, never was a surer game if it had been rightly played. But there is a fate, my friend, hangs over our cause, and I fear that destiny throws against us."

"Speak not thus, general,—think not thus."

"Would that I could think otherwise—but I fear I speak prophetically."

"Do you then give up the cause?" said Gerald in surprise.

"No;" said Sarsefield, firmly, almost fiercely. "Never—I *may* die in the cause, but I will never desert it, as long as I have a troop to follow me—but I must not loiter here. Farewell! Where is your horse?"

"I left him in the care of one of the attendants."

"I hope you are well mounted."

"Yes; here comes my charger."

"What!" said Sarsefield, "the white horse!"

"Yes, surely," said Gerald; "you never saw me back any other."

"But after the tremendous fatigue of yesterday," said Sarsefield in surprise, "is it possible he is still fresh?"

"Fresh enough to serve my turn for to-night," said Gerald, as he mounted into the saddle. The white horse gave a low neigh of seeming satisfaction as his master resumed his seat.

"Noble brute!" said Sarsefield, as he patted the horse on the neck, which was arched into the proud bend of a bold steed who knows a bold rider is on his back.

"And now farewell, general," said Gerald, extending his hand.

"Farewell, my friend. Fate is unkind to deny the charm of a victorious cause to so gallant a spirit."

"There is more gallantry in remaining unshaken under defeat; and you, general, are a bright, example of the fact."

"Good night, good night," said Sarsefield, anxious to escape from hearing his own praise, and wringing the hand that was presented to him with much warmth: he turned towards the portal of the tower, but before he entered, Gerald again addressed him.

"Pray tell me, general, is your regiment here? Before I go, I would wish to take leave of the officers of that gallant corps, in whose ranks I have had the honour to draw a sword."

"They are not yet arrived. They are on the road, perhaps, by this time; but I ordered they should be the last to leave Dublin, for as, yesterday, they suffered the disgrace of being led the first out of the battle[2], I took care they should have the honor of being the last in the rear to-night, to cover our retreat."

"Then remember me to them," said Gerald.

"They can never forget the White Horseman," said Sarsefield; "and they shall hear you left the kind word of remembrance for them. Once more, good night."

"Good night, general; God's blessing be upon you!"

"Amen!" said Sarsefield; "and with you."

They then wrung each other's hand in silence. Sarsefield re-entered the tower, and Gerald Pepper giving the rein to his steed, the white horse left the spot as rapidly as he had approached it.

For some days, Gerald Pepper remained in Dublin, where he had ridden the night after his interview with the king. The house of a friend afforded him shelter, for he did not deem it prudent to be seen in public as his person was too well known, and his, services to King James too notorious, not to render such a course dangerous. He, therefore, was obliged to submit to being cooped up in an attic in his friend's house, while he stayed in the city. His sojourn in Dublin originated in his anxiety to hear what was going forward at head-quarters; for there was but too much reason to fear, from all former examples in Ireland, that forfeitures to a great extent would take place, and to ascertain whether his name should he amongst the proscribed was the object that detained him from his home. His patience, however, became exhausted, and one morning, when his friend came to speak with him previously to going forth into the city to see and hear what was stirring, Gerald said he could bear the restraint of his situation and the separation from his family no longer. "My poor Magdalene," said he, "can but ill endure the suspense attendant upon my protracted absence, and I fear her gentle nature will sink under so severe a trial; therefore, my excellent, my kind friend, to-morrow morning I will leave you."

"Perhaps a day or two more may set your mind at rest; or, at least, will end your suspense respecting the course about to be pursued with the adherents of the king."

"I wait no longer than to-day," said Gerald, "I am resolved."

His friend sallied forth, with this parting assurance from his guest, and had not been absent more than an hour or two, when he returned; a low tap at the door of Gerald's apartment announced his presence; the bolt was drawn, and he entered.

"Gerald!" said his friend, grasping his hand, and remaining silent.

"I understand," said Gerald; "I am a ruined man."

How deeply expressive of meaning mere voice and action become under the influence of feeling! Here the uttering of a name, and the grasping of a hand, were more potent than language; for words could not so soon have expressed the fatal truth, as the electric sympathy that conveyed to Gerald's mind the meaning of his friend. How mysterious the influence between thought and action! I do not mean the action that is the result of mere habit, but the action which we cannot avoid, being a law of nature, and which every one indulges in, under the influence of strong affections of the mind. Grief and joy, hope and despair, fear and courage, have each an action to distinguish them, as strongly marked as the distinctions which separate different species.

His friend made no other answer to Gerald's ejaculation, than a suppressed groan, and then another fierce grasp of the hand and a melancholy look into each other's eyes passed between them. They then parted palms, and each took a seat, and sat opposite to each other, for some minutes, in perfect silence. In that interval the minds of both were busily engaged. Gerald's thoughts flew back, at once, to his home, his dear home; he thought of his sweet Magdalene and his darling children. He saw Magdalene deprived of the comforts of life, without a roof to shelter her, and heard his babes cry for food, as they shivered in the cold; the thought overcame him, and he hid his face in his hands. The mind of his friend had been engaged, at the moment, as to what was the best course Gerald could pursue under existing circumstances, and his case, though hard, seemed not hopeless. Therefore, when he saw Gerald sink as he had done, unconscious of the bitter thought that overcame him, he rose from his seat, and laying his hand kindly on the shoulder of his friend, he said:

"Cheer up, cheer up, man! matters are not so desperate as to reduce you to despair at once. You are not the man I take you for, if such a blow as this, heavy though it be, overcome you."

Gerald looked up; his eye was bright and his countenance serene, as he met the compassionating look that was cast upon him; he had recovered all his self possession. The voice of his friend had dispelled the terrible vision that fancy had presented him with, and recalled his ideas from home, where his affectionate nature first prompted them to fly.

"I do not despair," he said. "But there was a dreadful thought arose, which quite unmanned me for the moment, but you see I am calm again."

"Yes, you look like, yourself now."

"And will not relapse, I promise you. When once I know the worst I am equal to meet my destiny, whatever it may be: and having said so much, tell me what that fate is. Ruined, I know I am; but tell me in what degree. Is my person denounced, as well as my patrimony plundered from me?"

"No. Your life and freedom are not menaced, but your property is forfeited, and, in all probability, many days will not elapse until you may be dispossessed by some new master."

"Days!" said Gerald, "hours you mean; these gentry make quick work of such matters. I must hasten home directly."

"Will not to-morrow answer?" asked his friend; "to-day may be profitably spent here, in consulting as to your best mode of proceeding, regarding the future."

"The lapse of one day might produce a loss of some consequence to a man who is robbed of every acre he has in the world."

"How?" asked his friend.

"I would like to be beforehand with the plunderers, that I might secure any small articles of value, such as jewels or plate, from their clutches."

"Surely, *these* are not included in the forfeiture of a man's lands."

"The troopers of the Prince of Orange will not be very nice in making such legal distinctions; therefore I will hasten home, and save all I can from the wreck."

"Before you go, one word more," said his friend. "If your property happen to fall to the lot of a trooper, as you say; one of these fellows would rather have a round sum of hard cash, than he encumbered with lands; and if you manage matters well, a few hundred pieces may buy off the invader. I have heard of thousands of broad acres being so saved, in Cromwell's time."

"That hope of rescue is debarred me," said Gerald; "all the disposable cash I had, I gave to the king."

"What! not a rouleau left?"

"The last hundred I could command, I gave him."

"That's unfortunate," said his friend; "the more so, as it is beyond my power to supply the want."

"I know it—I know it," said Gerald, impatiently, "don't name it. If Heaven be pleased to spare me life and health, I shall be able to weather the storm. I have as much plate and other valuables as, when converted into cash, will enable me to carry my family to France, and still leave some thing in my purse. At the French court, I hope I can reckon on a good reception, and I have my sword to offer to the service of the French king, and I doubt not, from the interest I think I can command, that I should find employment in the ranks of the gallant Louis."

"You have decided soon on your course of proceeding, Gerald," said his friend, somewhat surprised at the coolness and consideration he exhibited.

"Yes; and you wonder at it," said Gerald, "because you saw me cast down for a moment; but the bitter thought that overcame me is past. I see distinctly the path before me which will save my wife and children from want, and that once secured, I repine not, nor shall cast one regret after the property I have lost in a noble cause. Farewell, my friend! Thanks and blessings be your's, from me and mine, for all your care for me. Before I leave Ireland you shall see me again, but for the present, farewell!"

In ten minutes more, Gerald Pepper was in his saddle, and his trusty steed was bearing him to the home which cost him so much anxiety.

As he pushed his way rapidly along the road, his thoughts were so wholly engrossed by his present calamitous circumstances, that he heeded no outward object, nor even uttered one cheering word, or sound of encouragement, to his favourite horse; and it was not until the noble round tower of Swords rose upon his view, that he became conscious of how far he had progressed homewards, and of the speed with which he had been going; he drew the bridle when he arrived at the summit of the hill that commands the extensive plain which lies at the foot of the mountain range that skirts the counties of Dublin and Kildare, and stretches onward into Meath and Lowth, and the more northern counties. The mountains of Carlingford and Mourne spired upwards in their beautiful forms, where the extreme distance melted into blue haze, and the sea could scarcely be distinguished from the horizon: but nearer, on his right, its level line of blue was distinctly defined, as glimpses of it appeared over the woods of Feltrum and Malahide, occasionally broken by the promontory of Howth, the grotesque pinnacles of Ireland's Eye, and the bold island of Lambay.

As he was leisurely descending the hill into the village beneath him, a figure suddenly appeared on a bank that overhung the road, and leaped into the highway; he ran over towards Gerald, and clasping his knee with both hands, said, with fervour—

"God save you, Masther Gerald, dear! oh then is that yourself safe and sound again?"

"What!" said Gerald, in surprise, "Rory Oge!—by what chance are you here?"

"You may say chance, sure enough—wait a minit, and I'll tell you, for it's out o' breath I am with the race I made across the fields, without, when I seen you powdherin' down the road at the rate of a hunt, and afear'd I was you would be gone past and out o' call before I could get to the ditch."

"Is my family well?" said Gerald, "can you tell me?"

"They're all hearty."

"Thanks be to God," said Gerald, devoutly.

"Amen," responded Rory.

"My poor wife, I suppose, has been fretting?"

"Throth to be suree, an' no wondher; the poor misthiss; but she keeps up wondherful, and I was goin' to Dublin myself to look for you."

"You, Rory!"

"Yis, me, and why not? and very nigh missin' you I was, and would, only for Tareaway here," putting his hand on the neck of the horse; "for you wor so far off when I first got a sight o' you, that I think I wouldn't have minded you, but I knew the proud toss of Tareaway's head, more betoken the white coat of him makes him so noticeable."

"But who sent you to Dublin, to look for me?"

"Myself, and nobody else—it was my own notion; for I seen the misthiss was onaisy, and I had a misgivin' somehow that I'd come upon you, and sure enough I did, for here you are."

"But not in Dublin, Rory," said Gerald, who could not forbear a smile even in his sadness.

"Well, it's all one, sure," said Rory, "for here you are, and I found you, as I said before; and now, Masther Gerald dear, that I see you're safe yourself, will you tell me how matthers goes on wid the king and his cause?"

"Badly enough, I fear, Rory, and worse with his friends," said Gerald, with a heavy sigh.

Rory caught at his meaning with native intelligence, and looking up into his face with the most touching expression of affection and anxiety, said, "God keep uz from harm, Masther Gerald dear, and sure it's not yourself that is come to throuble, I hope."

"Yes, Rory," said Gerald, "I am a ruined man."

"Oh Masther Gerald dear, don't say that," said Rory, with much emotion. "Who dar' ruinate you?" said he, indignantly; and then, his voice dropping into a tone of tenderness, he added; "Who'd have the heart to ruinate you?"

"Those who have nothing to fear nor love me for, Rory," answered Gerald.

"Is it them vagabone Williamites—them thraitors to their king and their God and their counthry—them outlandish villians! The Peppers o' Ballygarth ruinated! Oh what will the counthry come to at all at all!! But how is it they *can* ruinate you, Masther Gerald?"

"By leaving me without house or land."

"You don't want to make me believe they'll dhrive you out o' Ballygarth?"

"Ballygarth is no longer mine, Rory. I shall not have an acre left me."

"Why, who *dar* for to take it from you?"

"Those who have power to do so now, Rory; the conquerors at the Boyne."

"Why, bad cess to them, sure they won the day there, and more's the pity," said Rory, "and what do they want more? Sure, when they won the day, that's enough;—we don't deny it; and sorry I am to say that same;—but sure that should contint any raisonable faction, without robbin' the people afther. Why, suppose a chap was impidint to me, and that I gev him a wallopin' for it, sure that 'ud be no raison why I should take the clothes aff his back, or rob him iv any thrifle he might have about him; and isn't it *all one*? Sure, instid of havin' a crow over him for bein' the best man, I'd only be a common robber, knockin' a man down for what I could get. And what differ is there betune the cases?"

"That you are only an humble man, Rory, and that the other person is a king."

"Well, and sure if he is a king, shouldn't he behave as *sitch*, and give a good example instead of doin' a dirty turn like that? Why should a king do what a poor man, like me, would be ashamed of?"

Here, Rory broke out into a mingled strain of indignation against the oppressor, and lament for the oppressed, and wound up by this very argumentative and convincing peroration—

"And so that furrin moroder, they call a king, is goin' to rob and plundher and murdher you intirely,—and for what, I'd like to know? Is it bekase you stud up for the rale king, your own king, and your counthry, it is? Bad fortune to him, sure, if he had any honor at all, he'd only like you the betther iv it; and, instead iv pursuin' you with his blackguard *four-futted* laws[3], it's plazed he ought to be that you didn't come acrass him yourself when your swoord was in your hand, and the white horse undher you. Oh, the yellow-faced thief! he has no gratitude!!"

A great deal more of equally good *reasoning* and abuse was indulged in by Rory, as he walked beside the white horse and his rider. Gerald remained silent until they arrived at the foot of the hill, and were about to enter the village, when he asked his companion what he intended doing, now he had found the object of his search.

"Why, I'll go back to be sure," said Rory, "and be of any use I can to you; but you had betther make no delay in life, Masther Gerald, but make off to the misthriss as fast as you can, for it's the heart of her will leap for joy when she claps her two good looking eyes on you."

"I intend doing so, Rory; and I will expect to see you to-morrow."

"It may be a thrifle later nor that, Masther Gerald, for I intind stoppin' in Swoords to-night; but you'll see me afore long, any how."

"Then, good bye, Rory, for the present," said Gerald, as he put spurs to his horse, and sweeping at a rapid pace round one of the angles of the picturesque castle that formerly commanded the entrance to the village, he was soon lost to the sight of Rory Oge, who sent many an affectionate look and blessing after him.

The appearance of Rory Oge was too sudden to permit

any explanation to be given to the reader of who he was, when first introduced into the story; but now that the horseman's absence gives a little breathing time, a word, or two, on the subject may not be inapposite.

Rory Oge was foster-brother to Gerald Pepper, and hence the affection and familiarity of address which existed and was permitted between them. In Ireland, as in Scotland, the ties thus originating between two persons who have been nurtured at the same breast, are held very dear, and were even more so, formerly, than now. Rory Oge might thus, as foster-brother to Gerald, have had many advantages, in the way of worldly comfort, which he not only did not seek for, but had even shunned. Making use of such advantages must have involved, at the same time, a certain degree of dependence, and this, the tone of his character would have rendered unpleasing to him. There was a restlessness in his nature, with which a monotonous state of being would have been incompatible; an independence of mind also, and a touch of romance, which prompted him to be a free agent. To all these influences was added a passionate love of music; and it will not, therefore, be wondered at, that Rory Oge had determined on becoming an erratic musician. The harp and the bagpipes he had contrived, even in his boyhood, to become tolerably familiar with; and when he had taken up the resolution of becoming a professed musician, his proficiency upon both instruments increased rapidly, until, at length, he arrived at a degree of excellence, as a performer, seldom exceeded. Ultimately, however, the pipes was the instrument he principally practised upon: his intuitive love of sweet sounds would have prompted him to the use of the harp, but the wandering life he led rendered the former instrument so much more convenient, from its portability, that it became his favourite, from fitness, rather than choice.

In the cool of the evening, Rory Oge was seated at the back of a cottage on the skirts of a village, and a group of people of both sexes were dancing on the green sod, in the rear of it, to the inspiring music of his pipes. More than an hour had been thus employed, and the twilight was advancing, when a fresh couple stood up to dance, and Rory, after inflating his bag and giving forth the deep hum of his drone, let forth his chaunter into one of his best jigs, and was lilting away in his merriest style; but the couple, instead of commencing the dance, joined a group of the bystanders, who seemed to have got their heads together upon some subject of importance, and listened to the conversation, instead of making good use of their own time, the day's declining light, and Rory's incomparable music.

At length they turned from the knot of talkers, and were going to dance, when the girl told her partner she would rather have another jig than the one Rory was playing. The youth begged of Rory to stop.

"For what?" said Rory.

"Aggy would rather have another jig," said her beau, "for she doesn't like the one you're playin'."

"Throth, it's time for her to think iv it," said Rory, "and I playin' away here all this time for nothin', and obleeged now to *put back the tune*. Bad cess to me, but it's too provokin', so it is;— and why couldn't you tell me so at wanst?"

"Now don't be angry, Rory," said Aggy, coming forward herself to appease his anger;—"I ax your pardon, but I was just listenin' to the news that they wor tellin'."

"What news?" said the piper. "I suppose they havn't fought another battle?"

"No; but one would think you wor a witch, Rory; for, if it's not a battle, there's a sojer in it."

"What sojer?" said Rory, with earnestness.

"Why, a sojer a' horseback rode into the town awhile agon, jist come down from Dublin, and is stoppin' down below at the Public."

A thought at once flashed across Rory's mind that the visit of a soldier at such a time might have some connexion with the events he had become acquainted with in the morning, and, suddenly rising from his seat, he said, "Faix, and I don't see why I shouldn't see the sojer as well as every body else, and so I'll go down to the Public myself."

"Sure, you won' go, Rory, until you give us the tune, and we finish our dance?"

"Finish, indeed," Rory; "why, you didn't begin it yet."

"No, but we will, Rory."

"By my sowl, you won't," said Rory very sturdily, unyoking his pipes at the same time.

"Oh, Rory," said Aggy, in great dismay,—"Rory—if you plaze."

"Well, I don't plaze; and there's an end iv it. I was bellowsing away there for betther nor ten minutes, and the divil a toe you'd dance, but talking all the time, and then you come and want me to put back the tune. Now, the next time you won't let good music be wasted; throth, it's not so plenty."

"Not such as your's, in throth, Rory," said Aggy, in her own little coaxing way.—"Ah, now, Rory!"

"'Twon't do, Aggy; you think to come over me now with the blarney; but you're late, says Boyce[4]:" and so saying, off he trudged, leaving the dancers in dudgeon.

He went directly to the Public, where he found an English officer of King William's cavalry had not only arrived, but intended remaining, and, to that end, was superintending the grooming of his horse, before he was put up for the night in a shabby little shed, which the landlady of the

Public chose to call stable. Here Rory Oge proceeded, and entered into conversation with the hostler, as a preliminary to doing the same with the soldier: this he contrived with the address so peculiar to his country and his class, and finding that the stranger intended going northward in the morning, the suspicion which had induced him to leave the dance and visit the Public, ripened into uneasiness as to the object of the stranger, and, desirous to arrive closer to the truth, he thought he might test the intentions of the trooper in a way which would not betray his own anxiety on the subject, at the same time that it would sufficiently satisfy him as to the other's proceedings. To this end, in the course of the desultory conversation which may be supposed to take place between three such persons as I have named, Rory ingeniously contrived to introduce the name of "Ballygarth," watching the Englishman closely at the moment, whose attention became at once awakened at the name, and, turning quickly to Rory, he said—

"Ballygarth, did you say?"

"Yis, your honour," said Rory, with the most perfect composure and seeming indifference, though, at the same time, the success of his experiment convinced him, that the man who stood before him was he who was selected to expel his beloved foster-brother from his home.

"How far is the place you name from this village?" asked the soldier.

"Indeed, it's not to say very convaynient," answered Rory.

"How many miles do you reckon it?"

"Indeed, an' that same would be hard to say."

"I think," said the hostler, "it would be about"—

"Twenty-four or twenty-five," interrupted Rory, giving the hostler a telegraphic kick on the shin, at the same time, by way of a hint not to contradict him.

"Aye, something thereaway," said the other, assenting and rubbing the intelligent spot.

"Why, Drokhe-da is not more than that from Dublin," said the trooper, in some surprise.

"It's Drogheda you mane, I suppose, sir," said Rory, noticing the English false pronunciation, rather than his remark of the *intentional* mistake as to the distance named.

"Aye, Droketty, or whatever you call it."

"Oh, that's no rule in life, your honour; for Ballygarth, you see, does not lie convaynient, and you have to go by so many cruked roads and little boreens to come at it, that it is farther off, when you get there, than a body would think. Faix, I know, I wish I was at the ind o' my journey there to-morrow, for it's a *long step* to go."

"Are you going there, to-morrow?" said the trooper.

"Nigh hand it, sir," said Rory, with great composure; and, turning to the hostler, he said, "That's a fine baste you're clainin', Pether."

"My reason for asking," said the soldier, "is that I am going in the same direction myself, and, as you say the road is intricate, perhaps you will show me the way."

"To be sure I will, your honor," said Rory, endeavouring to conceal his delight at the stranger's falling into his designs so readily. "At all events, as far as I go your road, you're heartily welkim to any sarvice I can do your honor, only I'm afeard I'll delay you an your journey, for indeed the haste I have is not the fastest."

"Shank's mare[5], I suppose," said Peter, with a wink.

"No; Teddy Ryan's horse," said Rory. "An' I suppose your honour will be for startin' in the mornin'?"

"Yes," said the soldier; and he thereupon arranged with

his intended guide as to the hour of their commencing their journey on the morrow; after which, the piper wished him good night, and retired.

The conjecture of Rory Oge was right as to the identity of the English soldier. He was one of those English adherents of King William, for whose gratification and emolument, an immediate commission had been issued for the enriching a greedy army, inflamed as well by religious animosity as cupidity, at the expense of the community at large. So indecent was the haste displayed to secure this almost indiscriminate plunder, that "no courts of judicature were opened for proceeding regularly and legally[6]." But a commission was issued, under which extensive forfeitures were made, and there was no delay in making what seizures they could: but this rapacious spirit defeated its own ends in some instances, for the unsettled state of the country rendered it difficult, if not impossible, to secure the ill-gotten good, from the headlong haste it was necessary to proceed with[7].

It was in the gray of the succeeding morning that Rory Oge stole softly from the back-door of the house of entertainment where he, as well as the English soldier, slept, and proceeded cautiously across the enclosure, in the rear of the house, to the shed where the horse of the stranger was stabled. Noiselessly he unhasped the door of rough boards, that swung on one leather hinge, and, entering the shed, he shook from his hat some corn into the beast's manger; and while the animal was engaged in dispatching his breakfast, Rory lifted his fore foot in a very workmanlike manner into his lap, and commenced, with a rasp, which he had *finessed* from a smith's forge the evening before for the purpose, to loosen the nails of the shoe. As soon as he had accomplished this to his satisfaction, he retired to his sleeping place, and remained there until summoned to arise when the soldier was ready to take the road.

At the skirts of the village, some delay occurred while Rory stopped at the house of one of his friends, who had promised him the loan of a horse for his journey, which arrangement he had contrived to make over night. It was not long, however, before Rory appeared, leading from behind the low hut of the peasant, by whom he was followed, a very sorry piece of horseflesh; after mounting, he held out his hand, first having passed it across his mouth and uttered a sharp sound, something resembling "thp[8]." The offered palm was met by that of his friend, after a similar observance on his part, and they shook hands heartily, while exchanging some words in their native tongue. Rory then signified to the Englishman that he was ready to conduct him.

The soldier cast a very discontented eye at the animal on which his guide was mounted, and Rory interpreted the look at once—

"Oh, indeed, he's not the best, sure enough. I towld your honor, last night, I was afeard I might delay you a little for that same; but don't be onaisy, he's like a singed cat, better nor he looks, and, if we can't go in a hand gallop, sure there's the owld sayin' to comfort us, that 'fair and aisy goes far in a day.'"

"We have a long ride before us, though," said the soldier, "and your horse, I'm afraid, will founder before he goes half way."

"Oh, don't be afeard av him in the laste," said Rory; "he's owld, to be sure, but an owld frind is preferrable to a new inimy."

Thus, every objection on the part of the Englishman was met by Rory with some old saying, or piece of ingenuity of his own, in answer; and after some few minutes of conversation, they dropped into silence and jogged along.

In some time, the notice of the stranger was attracted by the singular and picturesque tower of Lusk that arose on their sight, and he questioned Rory as to its history and use.

"It's a church it is," said his guide.

"It looks more like a place of defence," said the soldier; "it is a square tower with circular flankers."

"To be sure, it is a place of difince," said Rory. "Isn't it a place of difince agin the devil, (God bless us) and all his works; and mighty great people is proud to be berrid in it for that same. There is the Barnewells, (the lords of Kingsland I mane), and they are berrid in it time beyant tellin', and has an iligant monument in it, the lord himself and his lady beside him, an the broad o' their backs, lyin' *dead*, done to the life[9]."

There was scarcely any tower or house which came within view of the road they pursued, that did not present Rory with an occasion for giving some account of it, or recounting some tale connected with it, and thus many a mile was passed over. It must be confessed, to be sure, that Rory had most of the conversation to himself, as the soldier helped him very little; but as Rory's object was to keep his attention engaged and while away the time, and delay him on the road as long as he could, he did not relax in his efforts to entertain, however little reciprocity there was on that score, between him and his companion. At last, he led him from the high road into ever small by-way that could facilitate his purpose of delaying, as well as of tiring the trooper, and his horse too, to say nothing of his plan of having a shoe lost by the charger in a remote spot. Many a wistful glance was thrown on the fore shoe, and, at last, he had the pleasure to see it cast, unnoticed by the rider. This, Rory said nothing about, until they had advanced a mile or two, and then, looking down for some time as if in anxious observation, he exclaimed, "By dad, I'm afeard your horse's fore shoe is gone."

The dragoon pulled up immediately and looked down; "I believe it is the off foot," said he.

"It's the *off* shoe, any how," said Rory; "and that's worse."

The dragoon alighted and examined the foot thus deprived of its defence, and exhibited a good deal of silent vexation;—"It is but a few days since I had him shod," said he.

"Throth, then, it was a shame for whoever *done* it, not to make a betther job iv it," said Rory.

The Englishman then inspected the remaining shoes of his horse, and finding them fast, he noticed the singularity of the loss of one shoe under such circumstances.

"Oh, that's no rule in life," said Rory, "for you may remark that a horse never throws two shoes at a time, but only one, by way of a warnin' as a body may say, to jog your memory that he wants a new set; and, indeed, that same is very *cute* of a dumb baste;—and I could tell your honor a mighty quare story of a horse I knew wanst, and as reg'lar as the day o' the month kem round——"

"I don't want to hear any of your stories," said the Englishman, rather sullenly; "but can you tell me how I may have this loss speedily repaired?"

"Faix, an' I could tell your honor *two* stories easier nor *that*, for not a forge I know nigher hand to this than one that in Duleek."

"And how far is Duleek?"

"'Deed, an' it's a good step."

"What do you call a good step?"

"Why it 'ill take a piece of a day to go there."

"Curse you," said the dragoon, at last, provoked beyond his constitutional phlegm at such evasive replies; "can't you say how many miles?"

"I ax your honor's pardon," replied his guide, who now saw that trifling would not answer: "To the best o' my knowledge, we are aff o' Duleek about five miles, or thereaway."

"Confound it!" said the soldier—"Five miles, and this barbarous road, and your long miles into the bargain."

"Sure, I don't deny the road is not the best," said Rory; "but if it's not good, sure we give you good measure at all events."

It was in vain that the Englishman grumbled; Rory had so ready and so queer an answer to every objection raised by the soldier, that, at last, he remounted, and was fain to content himself with proceeding at a very slow pace along the vile by-road they travelled, lest he might injure the hoof of his charger.

And now, Rory having effected the first part of his object, set all his wits to work how he could make the rest of the road as little tiresome as possible to the stranger; and he not only succeeded in effecting this, but he managed, in the course of the day, to possess himself of the soldier's secret, touching the object of his present journey.

In the doing this, the scene would have been an amusing one to a third person: it was an encounter between phlegm and wit—a trial between English reserve and Irish ingenuity.

By the way, it is not unworthy of observation, that a common spring of action influences the higher and the lower animals, under the circumstances of oppression and pursuit. The oppressed and the pursued have only stratagem to encounter force, or escape destruction. The fox and other animals of the chase are proverbial for their cunning, and every conquered people have been reduced to the expedient of finesse, as their last resource.

The slave-driver tells you that every negro is a liar. It is the violation of charity on the one hand that induces the violation of truth on the other; and weakness, in all cases, is thus driven to deceit, as its last defence against power.

The soldier, in the course of his conversation with his guide, thought himself very knowing when he said, in a careless way, that he believed there was some one of the name of Pepper lived at Ballygarth.

"Some one, is it?" said Rory, looking astonished; "Oh! is that all you know about it? *Some one*, indeed! By my conscience an' it's plenty of them there is. The counthry is overrun with them."

"But I speak of Pepper of Ballygarth," said the other.

"The *Peppers* o' Ballygarth you mane; for they are livin' all over it as thick as rabbits in the back of an owld ditch."

"I mean he who is called Gerald Pepper?"

"Why then, indeed, I never heerd him calle that-a-way before, and I dunna which o' them at all you mane; for you see there is so many o' them, as I said before, that we are obleeged to make a differ betune them by invintin' names for them; and so we call smooth skinned chap that is among them, White Pepper, and a dark fellow (another o' the family) Black Pepper; and there's a great long sthreel that is christened Long Pepper; and there is another o' them that is tindher an one of his feet, and we call him Pepper-*corn*; and there is a fine dashin' well grown blade, the full of a door he is, long life to him, and he is known by the name of Whole Pepper; and it's quare enough, that he is married to a poor little starved bound of a wife, that has the bittherest tongue ever was in a woman's head, and so they call her Ginger; and I think that is a *highly saisoned* family for you. Now, which o' them is it you mane? is it White Pepper, or Black Pepper, or Long Pepper, or Whole Pepper, or Pepper-corn?"

"I don't know any of them," said the soldier; "Gerald Pepper is the man I want."

"Oh, you *do* want him then," said Rory, with a very peculiar intonation of voice. "Well, av coorse, if you want him, you'll find him; but look forenint you there; there you may see the owld abbey of Duleek;"—and he pointed to the object as he spoke.

This was yet a mile, or so, distant, and the day was pretty well advanced by the time the travellers entered the village. Rory asked the soldier where it was his honor's pleasure to stop, while he got his horse shod, and recommended him to go to the abbey, where, of course, the monks would be proud to give "any accommodation in life" to a gentleman like him. But this proposal the soldier did not much relish; for though stout of heart, as most of his countrymen, he was loath to be tempted into any situation where he would have considered himself, to a certain degree, at the mercy of a parcel of Popish monks;—and poisoned viands and drugged wine were amongst some of the objections which his Protestant imagination started at the proposal. He inquired if there was not any Public in the village, and being answered in the affirmative, his resolution was taken at once, of sheltering and getting some refreshment there while his horse should be under the hands of the blacksmith.

Here again, Rory's roguery came into practice; the blacksmith of the village was his relative, and after depositing the fatigued and annoyed soldier at the little *auberge*, Rory went for the avowed purpose of getting the smith to "do the job," but, in reality, to send him out of the way; and this was easily done, when the motive for doing so was communicated. On his return to the Public, there was a great deal of well-affected disappointment on Rory's part at the absence of his near relation, the smith, as he told the betrayed trooper how "provoking it was that he wasn't in the forge at that present,—but was expected at every hand's turn, and that the very first instant minute he kem home, Ally (that was his wife) would run up and tell his honor, and the horse should be shod in *no* time."

"In no time?" said the soldier, with a disappointed look; "You know I want to have him shod *in* time."

"Well, sure, that's what I mane," said Rory; "that is, it will be jist *no time at all* antil he *is* shod."

"Indeed, an' you may believe him, your honor," said mine host of the Public, coming to the rescue, "for there's no one he would do a sthroke o' work sooner for, than Rory Oge here, seem' that he is of his own flesh and blood, his own cousin wance removed."

"Faith he is farther *removed* than that," replied Rory, unable to contain a joke; "he is a more *distant* relation than you think; but he'll do the work with a heart and a half, for all that, as soon as he comes back; and, indeed, I think your honor might as well make yourself comfortable here antil that same time, and the sorra betther enthertainmint you'll meet betune this and the world's end, than the same man will give you; Lanty Lalor I mane, and there he is stan'in' forninst you; and it's not to his face I'd say it, but behind his back too, and often did, and will agin, I hope."

"Thank you kindly, Rory," said Lanty, with a how and scrape.

Some refreshment was accordingly prepared for the soldier, who, after his fatigue, was nothing loath to comfort the inward man; the more particularly, as it was not merely the best, but the only thing he could do, under existing circumstances; and after gorging profusely on the solids, the fluids were next put under contribution, and, acting on the adage that "good eating requires good drinking," he entered into the feeling of the axiom with an earnestness that Sancho Panza himself could not have outdone, either in the spirit or the letter.

Rory was in attendance all the time, and still played his game of engaging the stranger's attention as much as possible, with a view to divert him from his prime object, and make him forget the delays which were accumulated upon him. It was in this spirit that he asked him if he ever "heerd tell of the remarkable place that Duleek was."

"*We* made the place remarkable enough the other day," said the soldier, with the insolence which the habit of domination produces in little minds, "when we drove your flying troops through the pass of Duleek, and your runaway king at the head of them. I was one of the fifty who did it[10]."

Rory, influenced by the dear object he had in view, smothered the indignation he felt rising to his throat; and as he might not exhibit anger, he had recourse to sarcasm, and said,

"In throth, your honor, I don't wondher at all at the brave things you done, in the regard that it was at Duleek; and sure Duleek was always remarkable for havin' the bowldest things done there, and about, ever since the days of the 'Little Waiver.'"

"What Little Weaver?" said the soldier.

"Why then, an' did you never hear of the Little Waiver of Duleek Gate?"

"Never."

"Well, that's wondherful!!" said Rory.

"I don't see how it's wonderful," said the trooper, "for how could I hear of the Weaver of Duleek when I have been living in England all my life?"

"Oh murther!" said Rory, in seeming amazement, "an' don't they know about The Little Waiver o' Duleek Gate, in England?"

"No," said the trooper; "how should they?"

"Oh then what a terrible ignorant place England must be, not for to know about that!!!"

"Is it so *very* wonderful then?" asked the man whose country was thus aspersed.

"Wondherful!" said Rory "By my sowl, it is *that*, that is wondherful."

"Well, tell it to me then," said the soldier.

"Now, suppose I was for to tell you, you see, the divil a one taste you'd believe a word iv it; and it's callin' me a fool you'd be; and you'd be tired into the bargain before I was half done, for it's a long story, and if you stopped me I'd be lost."

"I won't stop you."

"But you won't b'lieve it; and that's worse."

"Perhaps I may," said the other, whose curiosity began to waken.

"Well, that same is a promise any how, and so here goes;" and Rory then related, with appropriate voice and gesture, the following Legend.

1. At the battle of the Boyne, when the Irish were driving the enemy with great slaughter before them, James was heard often to exclaim, "Oh spare my English subjects."

2. Sarsefield's regiment, after having repeatedly repulsed the enemy, was obliged to leave the field in order to protect the person of the king, who chose to fly unnecessarily soon.
3. Some mystification of Rory's about "*forfeited.*"
4. When the Lord Thomas Fitzgerald discovered that treason was within his castle of Maynooth, the traitor (Parese, I believe) was ordered for immediate execution in the Bass Court of the fortress; there he endeavoured to save his life by committing a double treason, and offered to betray the secrets of the English besiegers, but a looker-on exclaimed, "You're late!" His name was Boyce; and hence the saying which exists to this day."
5. One's own legs.
6. *Leland's Ireland*, book vi. chap. 7.
7. The sweeping forfeitures made at this period were such, that many were driven by the severity, rather than inclination, to take part with the adherents of King James, their very existence depending on the overthrow of William's power. This protracted the contest so much, that it was lamented even by many of *King William's own party*. In a letter from the Secretary of the Lords Justices to Ginckle, there occurs this passage: "But I see our civil officers regard more adding fifty pounds a year to the English interest in this kingdom, than saving England the expense of fifty thousand. I promise myself it is for the king's, the allies', and England's interest, to *remit most or all of the forfeitures*, so that we could immediately bring the kingdom under their majesties' obedience."—*Leland's Ireland*, book vi. chap. 7.
8. This practice is continued to this day, and is supposed to propitiate good fortune.
9. This very fine monument of the Barnewalls (of the period of Elizabeth, I believe) has been lamentably abused, by having some iron bars inserted into the recumbent effigies upon it,

for the purpose of supporting a pulpit. It is a pity that piety and propriety are sometimes at variance.

10. It was at Schomberg's suggestion that this pass was looked to; William had not attended to it, and, much to Schomberg's disappointment, sent only fifty dragoons to observe it. Leland remarks, that had not the king (James) been so scandalously intent on flight, the English dragoons must have been slaughtered to a man, and the pass made good.

# CHAP. II.—THE LEGEND OF THE LITTLE WEAVER OF DULEEK GATE. A TALE OF CHIVALRY

YOU SEE, THERE WAS A Waiver lived, wanst upon a time, in Duleek here, hard by the gate, and a very honest industherous man he was, by all accounts. He had a wife, and av coorse they had childhre, and small blame to them, and plenty of them, so that the poor little Waiver was obleeged to work his fingers to the bone a'most, to get them the bit and the sup; but he didn't begridge that, for he was an industherous cravther, as I said before, and it was up airly and down late wid him, and the loom never standin' still. Well, it was one mornin' that his wife called to him, and he sitting very busy throwin' the shuttle, and says she, "Come here," says she, "jewel, and ate your brekquest, now that it's ready." But he never minded her, but wint an workin'. So in a minit or two more, says she, callin' out to him agin, "Arrah! lave off slavin' yourself, my darlin', and ate your bit o' brekquest while it is hot."

"Lave me alone," says he, and he dhruv the shuttle fasther nor before.

Well, in a little time more, she goes over to him where he sot, and, says she, coaxin' him like, "Thady dear," says she, "the stirabout[1] will be stone cowld if you don't give over that weary work and come and ate it at wanst."

"I'm busy with a patthern here that is brakin' my heart," says the Waiver, "and antil I complate it and masther it intirely, I won't quit."

"Oh, think o' the iligant stirabout, that 'ill be spylte intirely."

"To the divil with the stirabout," says he.

"God forgive you," says she, "for cursin' your good brekquest."

"Aye, and you too," says he.

"Throth you're as cross as two sticks this blessed morning, Thady," says the poor wife, "and it's a heavy handful I have of you when you are cruked in your temper; but stay there if you like, and let your stirabout grow cowld, and not a one o' me 'ill ax you agin;" and with that off she wint, and the Waiver, sure enough, was mighty crabbed, and the more the wife spoke to him the worse he got, which, you know, is only nath'ral. Well, he left the loom at last, and wint over to the stirabout, and what would you think but whin he looked at it, it was as black as a crow; for you see, it was in the hoighth o' the summer, and the flies 'lit upon it to that degree, that the stirabout was fairly covered with them.

"Why then bad luck to your impidince," says the Waiver,

"would no place sarve you but that? and is it spyling my brequest yiz are, you dirty bastes?" And with that, bein' altogether cruked tempered at the time, he lifted his hand, and he made one great slam at the dish o' stirabout, and killed no less than three score and tin flies at the one blow. It was three score and tin exactly, for he counted the carcases one by one, and laid them out an a clane plate, for to view them.

Well, he felt a powerful sperit risin' in him, when he seen the slaughther he done, at one blow, and with that, he got as consaited as the very dickens, and not a sthroke more work he'd do that day, but out he wint, and was fractious and impidint to every one he met, and was squarein' up into their faces and sayin', "Look at that fist! that's the fist that killed three score and tin at one blow—Whoo!"

With that all the neighbours thought he was crack'd[2], and faith the poor wife herself thought the same whin he kem home in the evenin', afther spendin' every rap he had in dhrink, and swaggerin' about the place, and lookin' at his hand every minit.

"Indeed an' your hand is very dirty, sure enough, Thady jewel," says the poor wife, and thrue for her, for he rowled into a ditch comin' home. "You'd betther wash it, darlin'."

"How dar' you say dirty to the greatest hand in Ireland?" says he, going to bate her.

"Well, it's nat dirty," says she.

"It is throwin' away my time I have been all my life," says he, "livin' with you at all, and stuck at a loom' nothin' but a poor Waiver, when it is Saint George or the Dhraggin I ought to be, which is two of the siven champions o' Christendom."

"Well, suppose they christened him twice as much," says the wife, "sure what's that to uz?"

"Don't put in your prate," says he, "you ignorant sthrap,"

says he. "You're vulgar, woman—you're vulgar—mighty vulgar; hut I'll have nothin' more to say to any dirty snakin' thrade again—divil a more waivin' I'll do."

"Oh, Thady dear, and what'll the children do then?"

"Let them go play marvels," says he.

"That would be but poor feedin' for them, Thady."

"They shan't want for feedin'," says he, "for it's a rich man I'll be soon, and a great man too."

"Usha, but I'm glad to hear it, darlin',—though I dunna how it's to be, but I think you had betther go to bed, Thady."

"Don't talk to me of any bed, but the bed o' glory, woman," says he,—lookin' mortial grand.

"Oh! God send we'll all be in glory yet," says the wife, crassin' herself; "but go to sleep, Thady, for this present."

"I'll sleep with the brave yit," says he.

"Indeed an' a brave sleep will do you a power o' good, my darlin'," says she.

"And it's I that will be the knight!!" says he.

"All night, if you plaze, Thady," says she.

"None o' your coaxin," says he. "I'm detarmined on it, and I'll set off immediantly, and be a knight arriant."

"A what!!!" says she.

"A knight arriant, woman."

"Lord be good to me, what's that?" says she.

"A knight arriant is a rale gintleman," says he, "going round the world for sport, with a swoord by his side, takin' whatever he plazes,—for himself; and that's a knight arriant," says he.

"Just a'most like yourself, sir," said Rory, with a sly sarcastic look at the trooper, who sat listening to him with a sort of half stupid, half drunken wonder.

Well, sure enough, he wint about among his neighbours the next day, and he got an owld kittle from one, and a saucepan from another, and he took them to the tailor, and he sewed him up a shuit o' tin clothes like any knight arriant, and he borrowed a pot lid, and *that*, he was very partic'lar about, bekase it was his shield, and he wint to a friend o' his, a painther and glazier, and made him paint an his shield, in big letthers—

"I'M THE MAN OF ALL MIN,
THAT KILL'D THREE SCORE AND TIN,
AT A BLOW."

"When the people sees *that*," says the Waiver to himself, "the sorra one will dar' for to come near me."

And with that, he towld the wife to scour out the small iron pot for him, "for," says he, "it will make an iligant helmet;"—and when it was done, he put it an his head, and the wife said, "Oh, murther, Thady jewel, is it puttin' a great heavy iron pot an your head you are, by way iv a hat?"

"Sartinly," says he, "for a knight arriant should always have *a woight an his brain*."

"But, Thady dear," says the wife, "there's hole in it, and it can't keep out the weather."

"It will be the cooler," says he, puttin' it an him;—"besides, if I don't like it, it is aisy to stop it with a wisp o' sthraw, or the like o' that?'

"The three legs of it looks mighty quare, stickin' up,"—says she.

"Every helmet has a spike stickin' out o' the top of it," says the weaver, "and if mine has three, it's only the grandher it is."

"Well," says the wife, getting bitther at last, "all I can say is, it isn't the first sheep's head was dhress'd in it."

"*Your sarvant, ma'am,*" says he; and off he set.

Well, he was in want of a horse, and so he wint to a field hard by, where the miller's horse was grazin', that used to carry the ground corn round the counthry. "This is the idintical horse for me," says the waiver; "he is used to carryin' flour and male; and what am I but the *flower* o' shovelry in a coat o' *mail*; so that the horse won't be put out iv his way in the laste."

But as he was ridin' him out o' the field, who, should see him but the miller. "Is it stalin' my horse you are, honest man?" says the miller.

"No," says the waiver, "I'm only goin' to *ax*ercise him," says he, "in the cool o' the evenin'; it will be good for his health."

"Thank you kindly," says the miller, "but lave him where he is, and you'll obleege me."

"I can't afford it," says the waiver, runnin' the horse at the ditch.

"Bad luck to your impidince," says the miller, "you've as much tin about you as a thravellin' tinker, but you've more brass. Come back here, you vagabone," says he.

But he was late;—away galloped the waiver, and took the road to Dublin, for he thought the best thing he could do was to go to the King o' Dublin—(for Dublin was a grate place thin, and had a king iv its own)—and he thought, may be, the King o' Dublin would give him work. Well, he was four days goin' to Dublin, for the baste was not the best, and the roads worse, not all as one was now; but there was no turnpikes then, glory be to God[3]!! Whin he got to Dublin, he wint sthrait to the palace, and whin he got into the coort yard he let his horse go and graze about the place, for the grass was growin' out betune the stones; every, thing was flourishin' thin, in Dublin, you see. Well, the king was lookin' out of his dhrawin' room windy, for divarshin, whin the waiver kem in; but the waiver pretended not to see him, and he wint over to a stone sate, undher the windy—for you see, there was stone sates all round about the place for the accommodation o' the people—for the king was a dacent, obleegin' man:—well, as I said, the waiver wint over and lay down an one o' the sates, just undher the king's windy, and purtended to go asleep; but he took care to turn out the front of his shield that hd the letthers an it—well, my dear, with that the king calls out to one of the lords of his coort that was standin' behind him, howldin' up the skirt of his coat, accordin' to rayson, and says he, "Look here," says he, "what do you think of a vagabone like that, comin' undher my very nose to go sleep? It is thrue I'm a good king," says he, "and I 'commodate people by havin' sates for them to sit down and enjoy the raycreation and contimplation of seem' me here, lookin' out a' my drawin' room windy, for divarshin; but that is no rayson they are to *make* a hotel o' the place, and come and sleep here.—Who is it at all?" says the king.

"Not a one o' me knows, plaze your majesty."

"I think he must be a furriner[4]," says the king, "bekase his dhress is outlandish."

"And doesn't know manners, more betoken," says the lord.

"I'll go down and *circumspect* him myself," says the king:—"folly me," says he to the lord, wavin' his hand at the same time in the most dignacious manner.

Down he wint accordianly, followed by the lord; and when he wint over to where the waiver was lying, sure the first thing he seen was his shield with the big letthers an it, and with that, says he to the lord, "By dad," says he, "this is the very man I want."

"For what, plaze your majesty?" says the lord.

"To kill that vagabone dhraggin, to be sure," says the king.

"Sure, do you think he could kill him," says the lord, "when all the stoutest knights in the land wasn't aiquil to it, but never kem back, and was ate up alive by the cruel desaiver."

"Sure, don't you see there," says the king, pointin' at the shield, "that he killed three score and tin at one blow; and the man that done *that*, I think, is a match or any thing."

So, with that, he wint over to the waiver and shuck him by the shouldher for to wake him, and the waiver rubbed his eyes as if just wakened, and the king says to him, "God save you," says he.

"God save you kindly," says the waiver, *purtendin'* he was quite onknowst who he was spakin' to.

"Do you know who I am," says the king, "that you make so free, good man?"

"No indeed," says the waiver, "you have the advantage o' me."

"To be sure I have," says the king, *moighty high*; "sure, ain't I the king o' Dublin?" says he.

The waiver dhropped down an his two knees forninst the king, and says he, "I beg God's pardon and your's for the liberty I tuk; plaze your holiness, I hope you'll excuse it."

"No offince," says the king; "get up, good man.—And what brings you here?" says he.

"I'm in want o' work, plaze your riverince," says the waiver.

"Well, suppose I give you work?" says the king.

"I'll be proud to sarve you, my lord," says the waiver.

"Very well," says the king. "You kill'd three score and tin at one blow, I undherstan'," says the king.

"Yis," says the waiver; "that was the last thrifle o' work I done, and I'm afeard my hand 'ill go out o' practice if I don't get some job to do, at wanst."

"You shall have a job immediantly," says the king. "It is not three score and tin or any fine thing like that; it is only a blaguard dhraggin, that is disturbin' the counthry and ruinatin' my tinanthry wid aitin' their powlthry, and I'm lost for want of eggs," says the king.

"Throth thin, plaze your worship," says the waiver, "you look as yollow as if you swallowed twelve yolks, this minit."

"Well, I want this dhraggin to be killed," says the king. "It will be no throuble in life to you; and I am only sorry that it isn't betther worth your while, for he isn't worth fearin' at all; only I must tell you, that he lives in the county Galway, in the middle of a bog, and he has an advantage in that."

"Oh, I don't value it in the laste," says the waiver; "for the last three score and tin I killed was in a *soft place*."

"When will you undhertake the job then?" says the king.

"Let me at him at wanst," says the waiver.

"That's what I like," says the king; "you're the very man for my money," says he.

"Talkin' of money," says the waiver, "by the same token, I'll want a thrifle o' change from you for my thravellin' charges."

"As much as you plaze," says the king; and with the word, he brought him into his closet, where there was an owld stockin' in an oak chest, burstin' wid goolden guineas.

"Take as many as you plaze," says the king: and sure enough, my dear, the little waiver stuffed his tin clothes as full as they could howld with them.

"Now, I'm ready for the road," says the waiver.

"Very well," says the king; "but you must have a fresh horse," says he.

"With all my heart," says the waiver, who thought he might as well exchange the miller's owld garron for a betther.

And maybe it's wondherin' you are, that the waiver would think of goin' to fight the dhraggin afther what he heerd about him, when he was purtendin' to be asleep: but he had no sitch notion: all he intended was,—to fob the goold, and ride back again to Duleek with his gains and a good horse. But you see, cute as the waiver was, the king was cuter still; for these high quolity, you see, is great desaivers; and so the horse the waiver was put an, was larned an purpose; and sure, the minit he was mounted, away powdhered the horse, and the divil a toe he'd go but right down to Galway. Well, for four days he was goin' evermore, antil at last the waiver seen a crowd o' people runnin' as if owld Nick was at their heels, and they shoutin' a thousand murdhers and cryin', "The dhraggin, the dhraggin!" and he couldn't stop the horse nor make him turn back, but away he pelted right forninst the terrible baste that was comin' up to him, and there was the most *nefaarious* smell o' sulphur, savin' your presence, enough to knock you down; and faith the waiver seen he had no time to lose, and so he threwn himself off the horse and made to a three that was growin' nigh hand, and away he clambered up into it as nimble as a cat; and not a minit had he to spare, for the dhraggin kem up in a powerful rage, and he devoured the horse, body and bones, in less than no time; and then he began to sniffle and scent about for the waiver, and at last he clapt his eye an him, where he was, up in the three, and says he, "In throth, you might as well come down out o' that," says he, "for I'll have you as sure as eggs is mate."

"Divil a fut I'll go down," says the waiver.

"Sorra care, I care," says the dhraggin, "for you're as good as ready money in my pocket this minit; for I'll lie undher this three," says he, "and, sooner or later you must fall to my share;" and sure enough he sot down, and began to pick his teeth with his tail, afther the heavy brekquest he made that mornin' (for he ate a whole village, let alone the horse), and he got dhrowsy at last, and fell asleep; but before he wint to sleep, he wound himself all round about the three, all as one as a lady windin' ribbon round her finger, so that the waiver could not escape.

Well, as soon as the waiver knew he was dead asleep, by the snorin' of him—and every snore he let out of him was like a clap o' thundher—

Here the trooper began to exhibit some symptoms of following the dragon's example,—and perhaps the critics will say, no wonder,—but Rory, notwithstanding, pursued the recital of the legend.

That minit, the waiver began to creep down the three, as cautious as a fox; and he was very nigh hand the bottom, when, bad cess to it, a thievin' branch he was dipindin' an, bruk, and down he fell right a top o' the dhraggin: but if he did, good luck was an his side, for where should he fall but with his two legs right acrass the dhraggin's neck, and, my jew'l, he laid howlt o' the baste's ears, and there he kept his grip, for the dhraggin wakened and endayvoured for to bite him; but, you see, by raison the waiver was behind his ears, he could not come at him, and, with that, he endayvoured for to shake him off; but the divil a stir could he stir the waiver; and though he shuk all the scales an his body, he could not turn the scale agin the waiver.

"By the hokey, this is too bad intirely," says the dhraggin; "but if you won't let go," says he, "by the powers o' wildfire, I'll give you a ride that 'ill astonish your siven small sinses, my boy;" and, with that, away he flew like mad; and where do you think did he fly? by dad, he flew sthraight for Dublin—divil a less. But the waiver bein' an his neck was a great disthress to him, and he would rather have had him an *inside passenger*; but, any way, he flew and he flew till he kem *slap* up agin the palace o' the king; for, bein' blind with the rage, he never seen it, and he knocked his brains out; that is, the small thrifle he had, and down he fell spacheless. An' you see, good luck would have it, that the king o' Dublin was lookin' out iv his dhrawin-room windy, for divarshin, that day also, and whin he seen the waiver ridin' an the fiery dhraggin (for he was blazin' like a tar-barrel), he called out to his coortyers to come and see the show. "By the powdhers o' war, here comes the knight arriant," says the king, "ridin' the dhraggin that's all afire, and if he gets *into the palace*, yiz must be ready wid the *fire ingines*[5]," says he, "for to *put him out*." But when they seen the dhraggin fall outside, they all run down stairs and scampered into the palace-yard for to circumspect the *curosity*; and by the time they got down, the waiver had got off o' the dhraggin's neck, and runnin' up to the king, says he, "Plaze your holiness," says he, "I did not think myself worthy of killin' this facetious baste, so I brought him to yourself for to do him the honor of decripitation by your own royal five fingers. But I tamed him first, afore I allowed him the liberty for to *dar'* to appear in your royal prisince, and you'll oblige me if you'll just make your mark with your own hand upon the onruly baste's neck." And with that, the king, sure enough, dhrew out his swoord and took the head aff the *dirty* brute, as *clane* as a new pin. Well, there was great rejoicin' in the coort that the dhraggin was killed; and says the king to the little waiver, says he, "You are a knight arriant as it is, and so it would be no use for to knight you over agin; but I will make you a lord," says he.

"Oh Lord!" says the waiver, thundersthruck, like, at his own good luck.

"I will," says the king; "and as you are the first man I ever heer'd tell of that rode a dhraggin, you shall be called Lord *Mount* Dhraggin," says he.

"And where's my estates, plaze your holiness?" says the waiver, who always had a sharp look-out afther the main chance.

"Oh, I didn't forget that," says the king. "It is my royal pleasure to provide well for you, and for that rayson I make you a present of all the dhraggins in the world, and give you power over them from this out," says he[6].

"Is that all?" says the waiver.

"All?" says the king. "Why you ongrateful little vagabone, was the like ever given to any man before?"

"I b'lieve not, indeed," says the waiver; "many thanks to your majesty."

"But that is not all I'll do for you," says the king; "I'll give you my daughther too, in marriage," says he. Now, you see, that was nothin' more than what he promised the waiver in

his first promise; for, by all accounts, the king's daughther was the greatest dhraggin ever was seen, and had the divil's own tongue, and a beard a yard long, which she *purtended* was put an her, by way of a penance, by Father Mulcahy, her confissor; but it was well known was in the family for ages, and no wondher it was so long, by rayson of that same.

Rory paused.—He thought that not only the closed eyes but the heavy breathing of the soldier, gave sure evidence of sleep; and in another minute, an audible snore gave notice that he might spare himself any further trouble; and, forthwith, the chronicler of THE LITTLE WEAVER stole softly out of the room.

1. Porridge.
2. Deranged.
3. I must crave pardon for this little anachronism of Rory's; for I believe there were not any turnpike laws enacted in Ireland until early in Anne's reign.
4. Foreigner.
5. Showing the great antiquity of these machines.
6. Not any of this curious property remains, save what is left in the memory of the chronicler; and I regret to say, a great many Irish estates are in the same sorry condition.

   One interesting relic, however, has escaped the otherwise universal decay that has fallen on the noble house of Mount Dragon. It is the genealogy and armorial bearings of the family, which will; no doubt, afford matter of speculation to the antiquary. Perhaps the ingenious Sir William Betham, Ulster King, could give some further information on the subject.

"Thady or Thaddeus, Patriarch of this familye, was of Phœnician descente. There is a tradytione in y^e^ familye that y^e^ arte of waivynge was firste introduced into Irelonde by themme from Tyre, theye being thence called Tyros, since y^e^ whiche tyme alle beginners so-everre, are so-called. Hence alsoe is it inferred that y^e^ Redde Kertle, which prevails amongste y^e^ Irishers is of y^e^ true Tyrian Dye; which hath soe moche disturbed y^e^ repose of y^e^ curious, heretofore.

"Thisse noble familye beareth for theire achievemente and hathe for theire SHIELDE, a potte lidde propperre, quarterlye of three: Argente, Azure, and Gules: Ande overre all a younge chylde displayed, proper.[1] The same withinne a Horse collarr propperre, charged as an honnorrable distinction for valoure and prowesse with 'Drag-onnet.'[2]

"CRESTE. Onne a waiverrs shuttle Or. a potte, charged with Stirre-a-bowte and potter-sticke—all propperre.[3]

"SUPPORTERS. Dexterre a Dragonne Gules, winges elevated Or—Sinisterre a flie Azure.[4]

"MOTTOE. I flie."[5]

1. This allusion to the weaver's large family, by a child, *three quarterly*, is very happy.
2. A play on the word Dragon (a practice common in ancient heraldry), in allusion to the use of the horse collar and the conquered monster.
3. *Very* proper.
4. A blue bottle, evidently.
5. A triple allusion to the weaver's first heroic deed, his masterly retreat from the dragon, and his homeward victorious flight upon him.

# CHAP. III.—CONCLUSION OF THE WHITE HORSE OF THE PEPPERS

LET THE DIVISION I HAVE made in my chapters serve, in the mind of the reader, as an imaginary boundary between the past day and the ensuing morning. Let him, in his own fancy, also, settle how the soldier watched, slept, dreamt, or waked through this interval. Rory did not make his appearance, however; he had left the Public on the preceding evening, having made every necessary arrangement for carrying on the affair he had taken in hand; so that the Englishman, on inquiry, found Rory had departed, being "obliged to lave the place early on his own business, but sure his honor could have any accommodation in life he wanted, in the regard of a guide, or the like o' that."

Now, for this, Rory had provided also, having arranged with the keepers of the Public, to whom he confided every thing connected with the affair, that in case the trooper should ask for a guide, they should recommend him a certain young imp, the son of Rory's cousin, the blacksmith, and one of the most mischievous, knowing, and daring young vagabonds in the parish.

To such guidance therefore, did the Englishman commit himself on this, the third day of his search after the lands of the Peppers, which still remained a *Terra Incognita* to him; and the boy, being previously tutored upon the duties he was to perform in his new capacity, was not one likely to enlighten him upon the subject. The system of the preceding day was acted upon, except the casting of the horse's shoe; but by-roads and crooked lanes were put in requisition, and every avenue, but the one really leading to his object, the trooper was made to traverse.

The boy affected simplicity or ignorance, as best suited his purposes, to escape any inconvenient interrogatory or investigation on the part of the stranger, and, at last, the young guide turned up a small rugged lane, down whose gentle slope some water was slowly trickling amongst stones and mud. On arriving at its extremity, he proceeded to throw down some sods, and pull away some brambles, which seemed to be placed there as an artificial barrier to an extensive field that lay beyond the lane.

"What are you doing there?" said the soldier.

"Makin' a convenience for your honor to get through the gap," said the boy.

"There is no road there," said the other.

"Oh no, plaze your honor," said the young rascal, looking up in his face with an affectation of simplicity that might have deceived Machiavel himself.—"It's not a road, sir, but a short cut."

"Cut it as short then as you can, my boy," said the soldier (the only good thing he ever said in his life), "for your short cuts in this country are the longest I ever knew—I'd rather go a round."

"So we must go round, by the bottom o' this field, sir, and then, over the hill beyant there, we come out an the road."

"Then there is a road beyond the hill?"

"A fine road, sir," said the boy, who, having cleared a passage for the horseman, proceeded before him at a smart pace, and led him down the slope of the hill to a small valley, intersected by a sluggish stream which ran at its foot. When the boy arrived at this valley, he stepped briskly across it, though the water splashed up about his feet at every bound he gave, and dashing on through the stream, he arrived at the other side by the time the trooper had reached the nearer one. Here, the latter was obliged to pull up, for his horse, at the first step sank so deep, that the animal instinctively withdrew his foot from the treacherous morass.

The trooper called after his guide, who was proceeding up the opposite acclivity, and the boy turned round.

"I can't pass this, boy," said the soldier.

The boy faced the hill again, without any reply, and recommenced his ascent at a rapid pace.

"Come back, you young scoundrel, or I'll shoot you," said the soldier, drawing his pistol from his holster. The boy still continued his flight, and the trooper fired—but ineffectually—upon which the boy stopped, and after making a contemptuous action at the Englishman, rushed up the acclivity and was soon beyond the reach of small arms, and shortly after out of sight, having passed the summit of the hill.

The Englishman's vexation was excessive, at finding himself thus left in such a helpless situation. For a long time he endeavoured to find a spot in the marsh he might make his crossing good upon, but in vain,—and after nearly an hour spent in this useless endeavour, he was forced to turn back and strive to unravel the maze of twisting and twining through which he had been led, for the purpose of getting on some highway, where a chance passenger might direct him in finding his road.

This he failed to accomplish, and darkness at length overtook him, in a wild country to which he was an utter stranger. He still continued, however, cautiously to progress along, the road on which he was benighted, and at length the twinkling of a distant light raised some hope of succour in his heart.

Keeping this beacon in view, the benighted traveller made his way, as well as he might, until, by favor of the glimmer he so opportunely discovered, he, at last, found himself in front of the house whence the light proceeded. He knocked at the door, which, after two or three loud summonses, was opened to him, and then, briefly stating the distressing circumstances in which he was placed, he requested shelter for the night.

The domestic who opened the door retired to deliver the stranger's message to the owner of the house, who immediately afterwards made his appearance, and, with a reserved courtesy, invited the stranger to enter.

"Allow me first to see my horse stabled," said the soldier.

"He shall be cared for," said the other.

"Excuse me, sir," returned the blunt Englishman, "if I wish to see him in his stall. It has been a hard day for the poor brute, and I fear one of his hoofs is much injured, how far, I am anxious to see."

"As you please, sir," said the gentleman, who ordered a menial to conduct the stranger to the stable.

There, by the light of a lantern, the soldier examined the extent of injury his charger had sustained, and had good reason to fear that the next day would find him totally unserviceable. After venting many a hear curse on Irish roads and Irish guides, he was retiring from the stable, when his attention was attracted by a superb white horse, and much as he was engrossed by his present annoyance, the noble proportions of the animal were too striking to be overlooked; after admiring all his points, he said to the attendant, "What a beautiful creature this is—"

"Throth, you may say that," was the answer.

"What a charger he would make!"

"Sure enough."

"He must be very fleet?"

"As the win'."

"An leaps?"

"Whoo!—over the moon, if you axed him."

"That horse must trot at least ten miles the hour."

"Tin!—faix it wouldn't be convaynient to him to throt undher fourteen,"—and with this assurance on the part of the groom, they left the stable.

On being led into the dwelling house, the stranger found the table spread for supper, and the owner of the mansion, pointing to a chair, invited him to partake of the evening meal.

The reader need scarcely be told that the invitation came from Gerald Pepper, for, I suppose, the white horse in the stable has already explained whose house chance had directed the trooper to, though all his endeavours to find it had proved unavailing.

Gerald still maintained the bearing which characterized his first meeting with the Englishman on his threshold—it was that of reserved courtesy. Magdalene, his gentle wife, was seated near the table, with an infant child sleeping upon her lap; her sweet features were strikingly expressive of sadness; and as the stranger entered the apartment, her eye was raised in one timorous glance upon the man whose terrible mission she was too well aware of, and the long lashes sank downwards again upon the pale cheek, which recent sorrow had robbed of its bloom.

"Come, sir," said Gerald, "after such a day of fatigue as your's has been, some refreshment will be welcome;" and the Englishman presently, by deeds, not words, commenced giving ample evidence of the truth of the observation. As the meal proceeded, he recounted some of the mishaps that had befallen him, all of which Gerald knew before, through

Rory Oge, who was in the house at that very moment, for obvious reasons, he did not make his appearance, and at last, the stranger put the question to his host, if he knew any one in the neighbourhood called Gerald Pepper.

Magdalene felt her blood run cold, but Gerald quietly replied, there was a person of that name thereabouts.

"Is his property a good one?" said the trooper.

"Very much reduced of late," replied Gerald.

"Ballygarth they call it," said the soldier; "is that far from here?"

"It would puzzle me to tell you how to go to it from this place," was the answer.

"It is very provoking," said the trooper; "I have been looking for it these three days, and cannot find it, and nobody seems to know where it is."

Magdalene, at these words, felt a momentary relief, yet still she scarcely dared to breathe.

"The truth is," continued the soldier, "that I am entitled under the king's last commission to the property, for all Pepper's possessions have been forfeited."

The baby, as it slept in its mother's lap, smiled as its legalised despoiler uttered these last words, and poor Magdalene, smote to the heart by the incident, melted into tears; but by a powerful effort, she repressed any audible evidence of grief, and, shading her eyes with her hand, her tears dropped in silence over her sleeping child.

Gerald observed her emotion, and found it difficult to master his own feelings.

"Now it is rather hard," continued the soldier, "that I have been hunting up and down the country for this confounded place, and can't find it. I thought it a fine thing, but I suppose it's nothing to talk of, or somebody would know of it; and more provoking still, we soldiers have yet our hands so full of work, that I only got four days' leave, and to-morrow night I am bound to return to Dublin, or I shall be guilty of a breach of duty; and how I am to return, with my horse in the disabled state in which this detestable country has left him, I cannot conceive."

"You will be hard run to accomplish it," said Gerald.

"Now will you make a bargain with me?" said the soldier.

"Of what nature?" said Gerald.

"There"—said the soldier, throwing down on the table a piece of folded parchment,—"there is the debenture entitling the holder thereof to the property I have named. Now, I must give up looking for it, for the present, and I am tired of hunting after it, into the bargain; besides, God knows when I may be able to come here again. You are on the spot, and may make use of this instrument, which empowers you to take full possession of the property whatever it may be; to you it *may* be valuable. At a word then, if I give you this debenture, will you give me the white horse that is standing in your stable?"

Next to his wife and children, Gerald Pepper loved his white horse; and the favourite animal so suddenly and unexpectedly named startled him, and, strange as it may appear, he paused for a moment; but Magdalene, unseen by the soldier, behind whom she, was seated, clasped her outstretched hands in the action of supplication to her husband, and met his eye with an imploring look that, at once, produced his answer.

"Agreed!" said Gerald.

"'Tis a bargain," said the soldier; and he tossed the debenture across the table as the property of the man whom it was intended to leave destitute.

Having thus put his host into possession of his own property, the soldier commenced spending the night pleasantly, and it need not be added that Gerald Pepper was in excellent humour to help him.

As for poor Magdalene, when the bargain was completed, her heart was too full to permit her to remain longer, and hurrying to the apartment where the elder children were sleeping, she kissed them passionately, and throwing herself on her knees between their little beds, wept profusely, as she offered the fervent outpourings of a grateful heart to Heaven, for the ruin so wonderfully averted from their innocent heads.

Stories must come to an end, like every thing else of this world, and so *my* story is ended, as all stories should be, when there is no further vitality left in them: for though some *post mortem* experiments are occasionally made by those who expect, by a sort of Galvanic influence, to persuade their readers that the subject is not quite dead yet, the practice is so generally unsuccessful, that I decline becoming an operator in that line;—therefore, let me hasten to my conclusion.

The next morning, the English soldier was in his saddle at an early hour, and he seemed to entertain all the satisfaction of an habitual horseman, in feeling the stately tread of the bold steed beneath him. The white horse champed his bit, and by his occasional curvettings, evinced a consciousness that his accustomed rider was not on his back; but the firm seat and masterly hand of the soldier shortly reduced such slight marks of rebellion into obedience, and he soon bade Gerald Pepper farewell.

The parting was rather brief and silent; for to have been other, would not have accorded with the habits of the one, nor suited the immediate humour of the other. In answer to the spur of the soldier, the white horse galloped down the avenue of his former master's domain, and left behind him the fields in which he had been bred. Gerald Pepper looked after his noble steed while he remained within sight, and thought no one was witness to the tear he dashed from his eye when he turned to re-enter his house. But there were two who saw and sympathised in the amiable weakness—his gentle Magdalene and the faithful Rory Oge. The latter, springing from behind an angle of the house where he had stood concealed, approached his foster-brother, and said—

"Thrue, for you, indeed, Masther Gerald, it is a pity so it is, and a murther intirely; but sure there's no help for it; and though the white horse is a loss, there is no denyin' it, yet, 'pon my conscience, I'm mighty proud this blessed minit *to see that fellow lavin' the place!*"

Gerald Pepper entertained, throughout his life, an affectionate remembrance of his gallant horse: even more,—the stall where he last stood, and the rack and manger, where he had last fed under the roof of his master, were held sacred, and were ordered to remain in the state the favourite had left them; and to perpetuate to his descendants the remembrance of the singular event which had preserved to him his estate, the white horse was introduced into his armorial bearings, and is at this day, one of the heraldic distinctions of the family.

As the reader may have some wish to know what became of the *historical* personages that figure in this story, I refer him to the History of England for King James; and for General Sarsefield I am enabled to account, by getting a sight of a rare old print of that distinguished officer, underneath which, the following curious lines record his fate:—

"Oh, Patrick Sarsefield! Ireland's wonder!
Who fought in the field like any thunder,
One of King James's great commanders,
Now lies the food of crows in Flanders.
Och! hone!—Och! hone!—Och! hone!"

# THE CURSE OF KISHOGUE

## INTRODUCTION

I DO NOT MEAN TO say that cursing is either moral or polite, but I certainly *do* think, that if a man curse at all, he has a right to curse after what fashion he chooses. Now, I am not going to curse, nor swear neither, but to write, concerning the very superior curse, as above named, and I have premised the foregoing conditions, seeing, that entertaining such an opinion on the subject, no moralist can find fault with me for the minor offence of introducing a curse to my own taste. Let not the polite world either startle at the word, "Introduction." I do not intend to force cursing into their notice or their company; I mean the word "introduction" purely in a literary sense; and lastly, therefore, to the literary I would say a few words on the matter.

There has beeen already known to the literary world, a celebrated curse, called "The Curse of Kehama," and I hope I may not be considered too presumptuous in the intention of putting forward a curse to their notice, as its "Companion."

Something of the sort I think, has been wanted, and should I win the distinction of being considered the person who has supplied the deficiency, I hope Doctor Southey will allow me the further happiness of dedicating the story to him. There are sufficient points of difference in the two curses to make a variety for the reader's entertainment, and yet one point of curious coincidence between them—the drinking of a cup.—Now, as regards the variety, Kehama's curse was, that he could not die; while poor Kishogue's was, that he did. As to the coincidence, Kehama and Kishogue have their interest materially involved in the drinking of a cup; yet, in the very coincidence, there is a charming want of similitude, for Kehama, in not having the cup to drink, and Kishogue in having it to drink, and refusing it, produce such different consequences, that it is like the same note being sounded by two voices, whose qualities are so unlike, that no one could believe the note to be the same. But, lest I should anticipate my story, I will close my observations on the rival merits of the two epics, and request the reader, in pursuance of my desire of being permitted to tell my story according to my own fancy, to step in with me for a few minutes into the next chapter, which is no genteeler place than a sheebeen house.

# THE SHEEBEEN HOUSE

A jug of punch, a jug of punch,
The tune he sung was a jug of punch.

OLD BALLAD.

I HAD BEEN WANDERING OVER a wild district, and thought myself fortunate, in default of better quarters, to alight upon a sheebeen house, the *auberge* of Ireland. It had been raining heavily,—I was wet, and there was a good turf fire to dry me. From many hours of exercise, I was hungry; and there was a good rasher of bacon and a fresh egg to satisfy the cravings of nature; and to secure me from cold, as a consequence of the soaking I had experienced, there was a glass of pure "mountain dew" at my service—so pure, that its rustic simplicity had never been contaminated by such a worldly knowledge as the king's duty. What more then might a reasonable man want, than a sheebeen house, under such circumstances?

Ah!—we who are used to the refinements of life, can never imagine how very little may suffice, upon occasion, to satisfy our *natural* wants, until we have been reduced by circumstances to the knowledge. The earthen floor of the sheebeen never for an instant suggested the want of a carpet; the absence of a steel grate did not render the genial heat of the blithely blazing fire less agreeable. There was no vagrant hankering after a haunch of venison as I despatched my rasher of bacon, which hunger rendered so palatable; and I believe "poteen," under the immediate circumstances in which I was placed, was more acceptable than the best flask of "*Chateau Margaux*."

When I arrived at the house, the appearance of a well dressed stranger seeking its hospitality created quite a "sensation:" the bare-legged girl, who acted in the capacity of waiter, was sent driving about in all directions; and I could overhear the orders issued to her by "the misthriss" from time to time, while I was drying myself before the fire.

"Judy—here,—come here, Judy, I tell you.—See!"—Then, in an under tone, "Get ready the quol'ty[1] room;—hurry it up soon." Then away trotted Judy; but before she had gone many steps there was another call.

"And, Judy!"

"Well, ma'am."

"Put a candle in the tin sconce."

"Sure Terry Regan has the sconce within there." Pointing to an adjoining apartment where some peasants were very busy in making merry.

"Well, no matther for that; scoop out a pratee[2] and that I'll do well enough for Terry—sure he knows no betther—and take the sconce for the gintleman."

I interrupted her here, to beg she would not put herself to any inconvenience on my account, for I was very comfortable where I was, before her good fire.

"Oh, as for the fire your honor, Judy shall put some 'live[3] turf an the hearth, and you'll be as snug as you plaze."

"Yes, but I should be very lonesome, sitting there all night by myself, and I would much rather stay where I am; this fire is so pleasant, you'll hardly make another as good to-night, and I like to see people about me."

"Indeed, an no wonher, sir, and that's thrue; but I'm afeard you'll find *them* men dhrinkin' within there, throublesome;

they're laughin' like mad."

"So much the better," said I; "I like to see people happy."

"Indeed and your honor's mighty agreeable; but that's always the way with a gintleman—it makes no differ in life to the *rale* quol'ty."

"Say no more about it," said I, "I beg of you; I can enjoy myself here by this good fire, and never mind the sconce, nor any thing else that might inconvenience you; but let me have the rasher as soon as you can, and some more of that good stuff you have just given me, to make some punch, and I will be as happy as a king."

"Throth then you're aisely satisfied, sir; but sure, as I said before, a rale gintleman takes every thing as it comes."

Accordingly, the rasher was dressed on the fire before which I sat, and it was not long before I did honour to the simple fare; and being supplied with the materials for making punch, I became my own brewer on the occasion.

In the mean time, the mirth grew louder in the adjoining compartment of the house; and Terry Regan, before alluded to, seemed to be a capital master of the revels; and while I enjoyed my own tipple beside the lively fire, I had all the advantage of overhearing the conversation of Terry and his party. This was of a very motley description: the forthcoming sporting events on a neighbouring race-course, the last execution at the county jail, and an approaching fair, were matters of discussion for some time; but these gave place, at last, to the politics of the day.

It was the period when the final downfall of Napoleon had created such a sensation, and it was a long time before the peasantry of Ireland could believe that the hero of France was so utterly discomfited. He had long been a sort of idol to them, and the brilliancy of his successes, for years, had led them into the belief that he was invincible. There is, perhaps, in the lower orders in general, a tendency to admire military heroes, but this is peculiarly the case amongst the Irish, and Alexander and Julius Cæsar are names more familiar to them than a stranger could well believe. But their love of Buonaparte, and their exultation in his triumphs, had a deeper motive than mere admiration of a warrior:—what that motive was, it would be foreign to my pages to touch upon, therefore, let me resume.

The conversation amongst these peasant politicians turned upon Buonaparte's imprisonment at St Helena, and some of the party, unwilling to believe it, doubted the affair altogether.

"By the powdhers o' war," said one, "I'll never b'lieve that he's a presoner. Tut—who could take him pres'ner? There's none o' them aiqual to it."

"Oh, I'm afeard it's too thrue it is," said another.

"An' you b'liev it then?" said a third.

"Faix I do. Sure Masther[4] Frank—the captain, I mane, said he seen him there himself."

"Tare-an-ouns, did he see him in airnest?"

"Sure enough faith, with his own two eyes."

"And was he in chains, like a *rale* pres'ner?"

"Oh, no, man alive! sure they wouldn't go for to put a chain an *him*, like any other housebraker, or the like o' that."

"Well, sure I heerd them makin' spaches about it at the meetin' was beyant in the town last summer; and a gintleman out o' Dublin, that *kem down an purpose*, had the *hoith* o' fine language all about it; and I remember well he said these very words:—'They will never *blot* the *stain* from their *annuals*; and when he *dies* it will be a *livin'* disgrace to them: for what can he do but die, says he, *non compossed* as

# THE JUG OF PUNCH.

Moderato.
As I was sit ting in my room, One
pleasant evening in the month of June, I heard a thrush singing
in a bush, And the tune he sung was a jug o' punch,
Too ra loo! too ra loo! too ra loo!
too ra loo! a jug o' punch, a jug o' punch, The
tune he sung was a jug o' punch.

he is by the wide oceant, chained, undher a burnin' *climax* to that *salutary* rock? Oh! think o' that!!'—So you see he was chained, accordin' to his account."

"But, Masther Frank, I tell you, says he seen him; and there's no chain an him at all; but he says he is *there* for sartin."

"Oh, murther, murther!—Well, if he's there, sure he's a pres'ner, and that'll brake his heart."

"Oh, thrue for you—think o' Bonyparty bein' a pres'ner like any other man, and him that was able to go over the whole world wherever he plazed, being obleeged to live an a rock."

"Aye," said the repeater of the *spache*, "and the villains to have him undher that burnin' climax. I wondher what is it."

"I didn't hear Masther Frank say a word about that. Oh, what will my poor Bony do at all at all!!"

"By dad, it is hard for to say."

"By gor!" said Terry Regan, who had been hitherto a silent listener, "I dunna what the divil he'll do wid himself now, *barrin' he takes to dhrink*."

"Faix, an' there is great comfort in the sup, sure enough," said one of his companions.

"To be sure there is," said Terry.—"Musha, thin, Phil," said he to one of the party, "give us 'The Jug o' Punch,' the sorra betther song you have than that same, and sure it's just the very thing that will be *nate and opprobrious* at this present, as they say in the spaches at the char'ty dinners."

"Well, I'll do my endayvour, if it's plazin' to the company," said Phil.

"That's your sort," said Terry. "Rise it! your sowl!"

Phil then proceeded to sing, after some preliminary hums and hahs and coughing to clear his voice, the following old ballad; the burden of which I have chosen as the epigraph of this chapter.

What more divarshin might a man desire
Than to be sated by a nate turf fire,
And by his side a purty wench,
And on the table a jug o' punch?
    Toor a loo, &c.

The Muses twelve and Apollio famed,
In *Castilian* pride dhrinks *pernicious*[5] sthrames;
But I would not grudge them tin times as much,
As long as I had a jug o' punch.
    Toor a loo, &c.

Then the mortial gods dhrinks their necthar wine,
And they tell me claret is very fine;
But I'd give them all, just in a bunch,
For one jolly pull at a jug o' punch.
    Toor a loo, &c.

The docthor fails with all his art,
To cure an imprission an the heart;
But if life was gone—within an inch
What would bring it back like a jug o' punch?
    Toor a loo, &c.

But when I *am* dead and in my grave,
No costly tomb-stone will I crave;
But I'll dig a grave both wide and deep,
With a jug o' punch at my head and feet.

Toor a loo, toor a loo, toor a loo, fol lol dhe roll;
A jug o' punch! a jug o' punch!!
Oh! more power to your elbow, my jug o' punch!

Most uproarious applause followed this brilliant lyric, and the thumping of fists and pewter pots on the table testified the admiration the company entertained for their minstrel.

"My sowl, Phil!" said Terry Regan, "it's betther and betther you're growing every night I hear you; the real choice spent is in you that improves with age."

"Faith, an' there's no choicer spert than this same Mrs Muldoody has in her house," said one of the party, on whom the liquor had begun to operate, and who did not *take* Terry Regan's allusion.

"Well, fill your glass again with it," said Terry, doing the honors, and then, resuming the conversation and addressing Phil again, he said, "Why then Phil, you have a terrible fine voice."

"Troth an' you have, Phil," said another of the party, "it's a pity your mother hadn't more of yez,—oh that I may see the woman that desarves you, and that I may dance at your weddin'!"

"Faix, an' I'd rather sing at my own wake," said Phil.

"Och that you may be able!" said Terry Regan, but I'm afeard there'll be a man hanged the day you die."

"Pray for yourself, Terry, if you plaze," said Phil.

"Well, sing us another song then."

"Not a one more I remimber," said Phil.

"Remimber!" said Terry, "bad cess to me, but you know more songs than would make the fortune of a ballad singer."

"Throth I can't think of one."

"Ah, don't think at all man, but let the song out of you, sure it'll come of itself if you're willin'."

"Bad cess to me if I remimber one."

"Oh, I'll jog your mimory," said Terry, "sing us the song you deludhered owld Roony's daughther with."

"What's that?" said Phil.

"Oh, you purtind not to know, you desaiver."

"Throth an' I don't," said Phil.

"Why, bad fortune to you, you know it well—sure the poor girl was never the same since she heerd it, you kem over her so, with the tindherness."

"Well, what was it, can't you tell me?"

"It was, 'the Pig that was in Aughrim.'"

"Oh that's a beautiful song, sure enough, and it's too thrue it is. Oh *them* vagabone staymers that's goin' evermore to England, the divil a pig they'll lave in the counthry at all."

"Faix, I'm afeard so—but that's no rule why you should not sing the song. Out with it, Phil, my boy."

"Well, here goes," said Phil, and he commenced singing in a most doleful strain, the following ballad:

### THE PIG THAT WAS IN AUGHRIM

The pig that was in Aughrim was dhruv to foreign parts,
And when he was goin' an the road it bruk the owld sow's heart.
"Oh," says she, "my counthry's ruin'd and desarted now by all.
And the rise of pigs in England will insure the counthry's fall.
For the landlords and the pigs are all goin' hand in hand—"

"Oh stop, Phil, jewel," said the fellow who had been doing so much honor to Mrs Muldoody's liquor—"Stop, Phil, my darlin!"—and here he began to cry in a fit of drunken tenderness. "Oh! stop, Phil—that's too much for me—oh, I can't stand it at all. Murther, murther, but it's heart breakin', so it is."

After some trouble on the part of his companions, this tender-hearted youth was reconciled to hearing "the Pig that was in Aughrim" concluded, though I would not vouch for so much on the part of my readers, and therefore I will quote no more of it. But he was not the only person who began to be influenced by the potent beverage that had been circulating, and the party became louder in their mirth and more diffuse in their conversation, which, occasionally was conducted on the good old plan of a Dutch concert, where every man plays his own tune. At last, one of the revellers, who had just sufficient sense left to know it was time to go, yet not sufficient resolution to put his notion in practice, got up and said "Good night, boys."

"Who's that sayin' good night?" called out Terry Regan, in a tone of indignation.

"Oh it's only me, and it's time for me to go, you know yourself, Terry, said the deserter—"and the wife will be as mad as a hatter if I stay out longer."

"By the powers o' Moll Kelly, if you had three wives you mustn't go yet," said the president.

"By dad I must, Terry."

"Ah then, why?"

"Bekase I must."

"That's so good a raison, Barny, that I'll say no more—only, mark my words:—You'll be sorry."

"*Will* be sorry," said Barny.—"Faix, an' it's sorry enough *I am*—and small blame to me; for the company's pleasant and the dhrink's good."

"And why won't you stay then?"

"Bekase I must go, as I towld you before."

"Well, be off wid you at wanst, and don't be spylin' good company if you won't stay. Be off wid you, I tell you, and don't be standin' there with your hat in your hand like an ass betune two bundles o' hay, as you are, but go if you're goin'—and the Curse of Kishogue an you!"

"Well, good night, boys," said the departing reveller.

"Faix, you shall have no good night from uz. You're a bad fellow, Barny Corrigan—so the Curse o' Kishogue an you!"

"Oh, tare an ouns," said Barny, pausing at the door, "don't put the curse an a man that is goin' the road, and has to pass by the Rath[6], more betoken, and no knowin' where the fairies would be."

"Throth, then, and I will," said Terry Regan, increasing in energy, as he saw Barny was irresolute—"and may the Curse o' Kishogue light on you again and again!"

"Oh, do you hear this!!!" exclaimed Barny, in a most comical state of distress.

"Aye!" shouted the whole party, almost at a breath; "the Curse o' Kishogue an you—and *your health to wear it!*"

"Why, then, what the dickens do you mane by that curse?" said Barny. "I thought I knew all the curses out, but I never heerd of the Curse o' Kishogue before."

"Oh you poor ignorant craythur," said Terry, "where were you born and bred at all at all? Oh signs on it, you were always in a hurry to brake up good company, or it's not askin' you'd be for the maynin' of the Curse o'Kishogue."

"Why then, what *does* it mane?" said Barny, thoroughly posed.

"Pull off your caubeen and sit down forninst me there,

and tackle to the dhrink like a man, and it is I that will enlighten your benighted undherstandin', and a beautiful warnin' it will be to you all the days o' your life, and all snakin' chaps like you, that would be in a hurry to take to the road and lave a snug house like this, while there was the froth an the pot or the head an the naggin."

So Barny sat down again, amidst the shouts and laughter of his companions, and after the liquor had passed merrily round the table for some time, Terry, in accordance with his promise, commenced his explanation of the malediction that had brought Barny Corrigan back to his seat; but before he began, he filled a fresh glass, and, profiting by the example, I will open a fresh chapter.

1. Quality. The term applied to persons of the higher classes.
2. A potatoe, with a hole scooped out of it, is, often, a succedaneum for a candlestick amongst the peasantry.
3. Lighted turf.
4. The junior male branches of a family are always called "Master" by the peasantry, no matter what their age may be. I have seen *Masther* Toms and *Masther* Franks who had counted half a century.
5. How beautifully are Castaly and Parnassus treated here!
6. Fairies are supposed to haunt all old mounds of earth, such as Raths, Tumuli, &c. &c.

# THE CURSE OF KISHOGUE

"Ireland is the only country in the world where they would make a comedy out of such a d—n—ble tragedy."

REMARK OF A LATE JUDICIOUS AND JUDICIAL FRIEND.

YOU SEE THERE WAS WANST a mighty dacent boy, called Kishogue—and not a complater chap was in the siven parishes nor himself—and for dhrinkin' or coortin' (and by the same token he was a darlint among the girls, he was so bowld), or cudgellin', or runnin', or wrastlin', or the like o' that, none could come near him; and at patthern, or fair, or the dance, or the wake, Kishogue was the flower o'the flock.

Well, to be sure, the gintlemen iv the counthry did not belove him so well as his own sort—that is the *eldherly* gintlemen, for as to the young 'squires, by gor they loved him like one of themselves, and betther a'most, for they knew well, that Kishogue was the boy to put them up to all sorts and sizes of divilment and divarshin, and that was all they wanted—but the owld, studdy (steady) gintlemen—the responsible people like, didn't give into his ways at all—and, in throth, they used to be thinkin' that if Kishogue was out of the counthry, body and bones, that the counthry would not be the worse iv it, in the laste, and that the deer, and the hares, and the pattheridges wouldn't be scarcer in the laste, and that the throut and the salmon would lade an aisier life:—but they could get no howlt of him good or bad, for he was as cute as a fox, and there was no sitch thing as getting him at an amplush, at all, for he was like a weasel, a'most—*asleep wid his eyes open.*

Well; that's the way it was for many a long day, and Kishogue was as happy as the day was long, antil, as bad luck id have it, he made a mistake one night, as the story goes, and by dad how he could make the same mistake was never cleared up yet, barrin' that the night was dark, or that Kishogue had a dhrop o' dhrink in; but the mistake *was* made, and *this* was the mistake, you see; that he consaived he seen his own mare threspassin' an the man's field, by the road side, and so, with that, he cotched the mare—that is, the mare, to all appearance, but it was not his own mare, but the squire's horse, which he tuk for his own mare,—all in a mistake, and he thought that she had sthrayed away, and not likin' to see *his* baste threspassin' an another man's field, what does he do, but he dhrives home the horse *in a mistake*, you see, and how he could do the like is hard to say, excep'n that the night was dark, as I said before, or that he had a dhrop too much in; but, howsomever the mistake was made, and a sore mistake it was for poor Kishogue, for he never persaived it at all, antil three days afther, when the polisman kem to him and towld him he should go along with him.

"For what?" says Kishogue.

"Oh, you're mighty innocent," says the polisman.

"Thrue for you, sir," says Kishogue, as quite (quiet) as a child. "And where are you goin' to take me, may I make bowld to ax, sir?" says he.

"To jail," says the Peeler[1].

"For what?" says Kishogue.

"For staalin' the 'squire's horse," says the Peeler.

"It's the first I heerd of it," says Kishogue.

"Throth then, 'twon't be the last you'll hear of it," says the other.

"Why, tare an ouns, sure it's no housebrakin' for a man to dhrive home his own mare," says Kishogue.

"No," says the Peeler, "but it is *burglaarious* to sarcumvint another man's horse," says he.

"But supposin' 'twas a mistake," says Kishogue.

"By gor, it'll be the *dear* mistake to you," says the polisman.

"That's a *poor* Case," says Kishogue.

But there was no use in talkin'—he might as well have been whistlin' jigs to a milestone as sthrivin' to invaigle the polisman, and the ind of it was, that he was obleeged to march off to jail, and there he lay in lavendher, like Paddy Ward's pig, antil the 'sizes kem an, and Kishogue, you see, bein' of a high sperrit, did not like the iday at all of bein' undher a complimint to the King for his lodgin'. Besides, to a chap like him, that was used all his life to goin' round the world for sport, the thoughts o' confinement was altogether contagious, though indeed his friends endayvoured for to make it as agreeable as they could to him, for he was mightily beloved in the counthry, and they wor goin' to see him mornin', noon, and night—throth, they led the turnkey a busy life lettin' them in and out, for they wor comin', and goin' evermore, like Mulligan's blanket.

Well, at last the 'sizes kem an, and down kem the sheriffs, and the judge and the jury, and the witnesses, all book-sworn to tell nothin' but the born thruth: and with that, Kishogue was the first that was put an his thrial for not knowin' the differ betune his own mare and another man's horse, for they wished to give an example to the counthry, and he was bid to howld up his hand at the bar (and a fine big fist he had of his own, by the same token), and up he held it—no ways danted at all, but as bowld as a ram. Well, then, a chap in a black coat and a frizzled wig and spectacles gets up, and he reads and reads, that you'd think he'd never have done readin'; and it was all about Kishogue—as we heerd afther—but could not make out at the time—and no wondher: and in throth, Kishogue never done the half of what the dirty little ottomy was readin' about him—barrin' he knew lies iv him; and Kishogue himself, poor fellow, got frekened at last, when he heerd him goin' an at that rate about him, but afther a bit, he tuk heart and said:

"By this and by that, I never done the half o' that any how."

"Silence in the coort!!!" says the crier—puttin' him down that-a-way. Oh there's no justice for a poor boy at all!

"Oh murther," says Kishogue, "is a man's life to be swore away afther this manner, and mustn't spake a word?"

"Howl' your tongue!" says my lord the judge. And so afther some more jabberin' and gibberish, the little man in the spectacles threwn down the paper and asked Kishogue if he was guilty or not guilty.

"I never done it, my lord," says Kishogue.

"Answer as you are bid, sir," says the spectacle man.

"I'm innocent, my lord!" says Kishogue.

"Bad cess to you, can't you say what you're bid," says my lord the judge;—"*Guilty* or *not* guilty."

"Not guilty," says Kishogue.

"I don't believe you," says the judge.

"Small blame to you," says Kishogue; "you're ped for hangin' people, and you must do something for your wages."

"You've too much prate, sir," says my lord.

"Faix then, I'm thinkin' it's yourself and your friend the hangman will cure me o' that very soon," says Kishogue.

And thrue for him, faith, he wasn't far out in sayin' that same, for they murthered him intirely. They brought a terrible sight o' witnesses agin him, that swore away his life an the cross examination; and indeed suite enough, it *was* the crossest examination altogether I ever seen. Oh they wor the bowld witnesses, that would *sware a hole in an iron pot* any day in the year. Not but that Kishogue's friends done their duty by him. Oh they stud to him like men and swore a power for him, and sthrove to make out a *lullaby* for him; maynin', by that same, that he was asleep in another place, at the time;—but it wouldn't do, they could not make it *plazin'* to the judge and the jury; and my poor Kishogue was condimned for to die; and the judge put an his black cap, and indeed it is not becomin', and discoorsed the hoighth of fine language, and gev Kishogue a power o' good advice, that it was a mortyal pity Kishogue didn't get sooner; and the last words the judge said was, "The Lord have marcy an your sowl!"

"Thank'ee, my lord," says Kishogue; "though indeed it is few has luck or grace afther your prayers."

And sure enough faith; for the next Sathurday Kishogue was ordhere'd out to be hanged, and the sthreets through which he was to pass was mighty throng; for in them days, you see, the people used to be hanged outside o' the town, not all as one as now, when we're hanged genteelly out o' the front o' the jail; but in them days they did not attind to the comforts o' the people at all, but put them into a cart, all as one a conthrairy pig goin' to market, and stravaiged them through the town to the gallows, that was full half a mile beyant it; but to be sure, whin they kem to the corner of the crass streets, where the Widdy Houlaghan's public-house was then, afore them dirty swaddlers[2] knocked it down and built a meetin'-house there, bad cess to them, sure they're spylin' divarshin wherever they go,—when they kem there, as I was tellin' you, the purcesshin was always stopped, and they had a fiddler and mulled wine for the divarshin of the pres'ner, for to rise his heart for what he was to go through; for, by all accounts, it is not plazin' to be goin' to be hanged, supposin' you die in a good cause itself, as my uncle Jim towld me whin he suffer'd for killin' the gauger. Well, you see, they always stopped tin minutes at the public-house, not to hurry a man with his dhrink, and, besides, to give the pres'ner an opportunity for sayin' an odd word or so to a frind in the crowd, to say nothin' of its bein' mighty improvin' to the throng, to see the man lookin' pale at the thoughts o' death, and maybe an idification and a warnin' to thim that was inclined to sthray. But however it happened, and the like never happened afore nor sence; hut, as bad luck would have it, that day, the divil a fiddler was there whin Kishogue dhruv up in the cart, no ways danted at all; but the minit the cart stopped rowlin' he called out as stout as a ram, "Sind me out Tim Riley here;"—Tim Riley was the fiddler's name,—"sind me out Tim Riley here," says he, "that he may rise my heart wid The Rakes o' Mallow[3];" for he was a Mallow man, by all accounts, and mighty proud of his town. Well, av coorse the tune was not to be had, bekase Tim Rile was not there, but was lyin' dhrunk in a ditch at the same time comin' home from confission, and when poor Kishogue heerd that he could not have his favorite tune, it wint to his heart to that degree, that he'd hear of no comfort in life, and he bid them dhrive him an, and put him out o' pain at wanst.

"Oh take the dhrink any how, aroon," says the Widdy Houlaghan, who was mighty tindher-hearted, and always attinded the man that was goin' to be hanged with the dhrink herself, if he was ever so grate a sthranger; but if he was a find of her own, she'd go every fut to the gallows wid him and see him suffer: Oh she was a darlint! Well,—"Take the dhrink, Kishogue my jewel," says she, handin' him up a brave big mug o' mulled wine, fit for a lord,—but he wouldn't touch it;—"Take it out o' my sight," says he, "for my heart is low becase Tim Riley desaived me, whin I expected to die game, like one of the Rakes o' Mallow! Take it out o' my sight," says he, puttin' it away wid his hand, and sure 'twas the first time Kishogue was ever known to refuse the dhrop o' dhrink, and many remarked that it was *the change before death* was comin' over him.

Well, away they rowled to the gallows, where there was no delay in life for the pres'ner, and the sheriff asked him if he had any thing to say to him before he suffered; but Kishogue hadn't a word to throw to a dog, and av coorse he said nothin' to the sheriff, and wouldn't say a word that might be improvin' even to the crowd, by way of an idification; and indeed a sore disappointment it was to the throng, for they thought he would make an iligant dyin' speech; and the prenthers there, and the ballad-singers, all ready for to take it down complate, and thought it was a dirty turn of Kishogue to chate them out o' their honest penny, like; but they owed him no spite, for all that, for they considhered his heart was low an account of the disappointment, and he was lookin' mighty pale while they wor makin' matthers tidy for him; and indeed, the last words he said himself was, "Put me out o' pain at wanst, for my heart is low bekase Tim Riley desaived me, whin I thought he would rise it, that I might die like a rale Rake o' Mallow!" And so, to make a long story short, my jew'l, they done the business for him: it was soon over wid him; it was just one step wid him, aff o' the laddher into glory; and to do him justice, though he was lookin' pale, he died bowld, and put his best leg foremost.

Well, what would you think, but just as all was over wid him there was a shout outside o' the crowd, and a shilloo that you'd think would split the sky; and what should we see gallopin' up to the gallows, but a man covered with dust an a white horse, to all appearance, but it wasn't a white horse but a black horse, only white wid the foam he was dhruv to that degree, and the man hadn't a breath to dhraw, and couldn't spake, but dhrew a piece o' paper out of the breast of his coat and handed it up to the sheriff; and, my jew'l, the sheriff grewn as white as the paper itself, when he clapt his eyes an it; and, says he, "Cut him down—cut him down this minute!!" says he; and the dhragoons made a slash at the messenger, but he ducked his head and sarcumvinted them. And then the sheriff shouted out, "Stop, you villians, and bad luck to yiz, you murtherin' vagabones," says he to the sojers; "is it goin' to murther the man you wor?—It isn't him at all I mane, but the man that's hangin'. Cut *him* down, says he: and they cut him down; but it was no use. It was all over wid poor Kishogue; he was as dead as small-beer, and as stiff as a crutch.

"Oh, tare an ouns," says the sheriff, tarin' the hair aff his head at the same time, with the fair rage, "Isn't it a poor case that he's dead, and here is a reprieve that is come for him; but, bad cess to him," says he, "it's his own fault, he wouldn't take it aisy."

"Oh millia murther, millia murther!" cried out the Widdy Houlaghan, in the crowd. "Oh, Kishogue, my darlint, why did you refuse my mull'd wine? Oh, if you stopped wid me to take your dhrop o' dhrink, you'd be alive and merry now!"

So that is the maynin' of the Curse o' Kishogue; for you see, Kishogue was hanged *for lavin' his liquor behind him*.

1. So called from being established by Sir Robert Peel.
2. Methodists.
3. A favourite tune.

# THE FAIRY FINDER

He got a halfpenny—but it was a rap.

Riddle me, riddle me, riddle me right;
Tell me what I dreamt last night.

"FINDING A FORTUNE," IS A phrase often heard amongst the peasantry of Ireland. If any man from small beginnings arrives at wealth, in a reasonable course of time, the fact is scarcely ever considered as the result of perseverance, superior intelligence, or industry; it passes as a by-word through the country that "he found a fortin';" whether by digging up a "a crok o' goold" in the ruins of an old abbey, or by catching a Leprechaun and forcing him to "deliver or die," or discovering it behind an old wainscot, is quite immaterial: the *when* or the *where* is equally unimportant, and the thousand are satisfied with the rumour, "He found a fortin'." Besides, going into particulars destroys romance,—and the Irish are essentially romantic,—and their love of wonder is more gratified in considering the change from poverty to wealth as the result of superhuman aid, than in attributing it to the mere mortal causes of industry and prudence.

The crone of every village has plenty of stories to make her hearers wonder how fortunes have been arrived at by extraordinary short cuts; and as it has been laid down as an axiom, "That there never was a fool who had not a greater fool to admire him," so there never was any old woman who told such stories without plenty of listeners.

Now, Darby Kelleher was one of the latter class, and there was a certain collioch[1] who was an extensive dealer in the marvellous, and could supply "wholesale, retail, and for exportation," any customer such as Darby Kelleher, who not only was a devoted listener, but also made an occasional offering at the cave of the sibyl, in return for her oracular communication. This tribute generally was tobacco, as the collioch was partial to chewing the weed; and thus, Darby returned a *quid pro quo*, without having any idea that he was giving a practical instance of the foregoing well known pun.

Another constant attendant at the hut of the hag, was Oonah Lenehan, equally prone to the marvellous with Darby Kelleher, and quite his equal in idleness. A day never passed without Darby and Oonah paying the old woman a visit. She was sure to be "at home," for age and decrepitude rendered it impossible for her to be otherwise, the utmost limit of her ramble from her own chimney corner being the seat of sods outside the door of her hut, where, in the summer time, she was to be found, so soon as the sunbeams fell on the front of her abode, and made the seat habitable for one whose accustomed vicinity to the fire rendered heat indispensable to comfort. Here she would sit and rock herself to and fro in the hot noons of July and August, her own appearance and that of her wretched cabin being in admirable keeping. To a fanciful beholder the question might have suggested itself, whether the hag was made for the hovel, or it for her; or whether they had grown into a likeness of one another, as man and wife are said to do, for there were many points of resemblance between them. The tattered thatch of the hut was like the straggling hair of its mistress, and Time, that had grizzled the latter, had covered the former with gray lichens. To its mud walls, a strong likeness was to be found in the tint of the old woman's shrivelled skin; they were both seriously out of the perpendicular; and the rude mud and wicker chimney of the edifice having toppled over the gable, stuck out, something in the fashion of the doodeen or short pipe that projected from the old woman's upper story; and so they both were smoking away from morning till night; and to complete the similitude sadly, both were poor,—both lonely,—both fast falling to decay.

Here were Darby Kelleher and Oonah Lenehan sure to meet every day. Darby might make his appearance thus:—

"Good morrow kindly, granny."

"The same to you, avic," mumbled out the crone.

"Here's some 'baccy for you, granny."

"Many thanks to you, Darby. I didn't lay it out for seeing you so airly, the day."

"No, nor you wouldn't neither, only I was passin' this a way, runnin' an arrand for the squire, and I thought I might as well step in and ax you how you wor."

"Good boy, Darby."

"Throth an' it's a hot day that's in it, this blessed day. Phew! Faix it's out o' breath I am, and mighty hot intirely; for I was runnin' a'most half the way, bekase it's an arrand you see, and the squire towld me to make haste, and so I did, and wint acrass the fields by the short cut; and as I was passin' by the owld castle, I remimbered what you towld me a while agon, granny, about the crock o' goold that is there *for sartin*, if any one could come upon it."

"An' that's thrue indeed, Darby, avick—and never heerd any other the longest day I can remember."

"Well well! think o' that!! Oh then it's he that 'll be the lucky fellow that finds it."

"Thrue for you, Darby; but that won't be *antil it is laid out* for some one to rise it."

"Sure that's what I say to myself often; and why mightn't it be my chance to be the man that it was laid out for to find it."

"There's no knowin'," mumbled the crone, mysteriously, as she shook the ashes out of her tobacco pipe, and replenished the *doodeen* with some of the fresh stock Darby had presented.

"Faix, an' that's thrue, sure enough. Oh but you've a power o' knowledge, granny!! Sure enough indeed, there's no knowin'; but they say there's great virtue in dhrames."

"That's ondeniable, Darby," said the hag, "and by the same token maybe you'd step into the house and bring me out a bit o' 'live turf[2] to light my pipe."

"To be sure, granny," and away went Darby to execute the commission.

While he was raking from amongst the embers on the hearth, a piece of turf sufficiently "alive" for the purpose, Oonah made her appearance outside the hut, and gave the usual cordial salutation to the old woman; just as she had done her civility, out came Darby, holding the bit of turf between the two extremities of an osier twig, bent double for the purpose of forming a rustic tongs.

"Musha an' is that you Darby?" said Oonah.

"Who else would it be?" said Darby.

"Why you towld me over an hour agone, down there in the big field, that you wor in a hurry."

"And so I am in a hurry, and wouldn't be here, only I jist stepped in to say God save you to the mother here, and to light her pipe for her, the craythur."

"Well, don't be standin' there, lettin' the coal[3] go black out, Darby," said the old woman; "but let me light my pipe at wanst."

"To be sure, granny," said Darby, applying the morsel of lighted ember to the bowl of her pipe, until the process of ignition had been effected. "And now, Oonah, my darlint, if you're so sharp an other people, what the dickens brings you here, when it is mindin' the geese in the stubbles you ought to be, and not here? What would the misthriss say to that, I wondher?"

"Oh I left them safe enough, and they're able to take care of themselves for a bit, and I wanted to ax the granny about a dhrame I had."

"Sure so do I," said Darby; "and you know *first come first sarved* is a good owld sayin'. And so, granny, you own to it that there's a power o' vartue in dhrames?"

A long-drawn whiff of the pipe was all the hag vouchsafed in return.

"Oh then but that's the iligant tabaccy! musha but it's fine and one a'most, it's so good. Long life to you, Darby—paugh!!"

"You're kindlly welkim, granny. An' as I was sayin' about the dhrames— you say there's a power o' virtue in them"

"Who says agin it?" said the hag authoritatively, and looking with severity on Darby.

"Sure an' it's not me you'd suspect o' the like? I was only goin' to say that *myself* had a mighty sharp dhrame last night, and sure I kem to ax you about the maynin' av it."

"Well avic, tell us your dhrame," said the hag, sucking her pipe with increased energy.

"Well you see," said Darby, "I dhremt I was goin' along a road, and that all of a suddint I kem to *crass* roads, and you know there's grate vartue in crass roads."

"That's thrue, avourneen!—paugh!!—go an."

"Well, as I was sayin', I kem to the crass roads, and soon afther I seen four walls; now I think the four walls *manes* the owld castle."

"Likely enough, avic."

"Oh," said Oonah, who was listening with her mouth as wide open as if the faculty of hearing lay there, instead of in her ears, "sure you know the owld castle has only *three* walls, and how could that be it?"

"No matther for that," said the crone, "it *ought* to have four, and that's the same thing."

"Well, well! I never thought o' that," said Oonah, lifting her hands in wonder; "sure enough so it ought!"

"Go an Darby," said the hag.

"Well, I thought the gratest sight o' crows ever I seen flew out o' the castle, and I think *that* must mane the goold there is in it."

"Did you count how many there was?" said the hag, with great solemnity.

"Faith, I never thought o' that," said Darby, with an air of vexation.

"Could you tell me, itself, wor they odd or even, avic?"

"Faix, an' I could not say for *sartin*."

"Ah, that's it!!" said the crone, shaking her head in token of disappointment. "How can I tell the maynin' o' your dhrame, if you don't know how it kem out exactly?"

"Well granny, but don't you think the crows was *likely* for goold?"

"Yis—if they flew heavy."

"Throth then, an' now I remimber they did fly heavy, and I said to myself there would be rain soon, the crows was flyin' so heavy."

"I wish you didn't dhrame o' rain, Darby."

"Why granny? What harm is it?"

"Oh nothin', only it comes in a crass place there."

"But it doesn't spile the dhrame, I hope?"

"Oh no. Go an."

"Well, with that, I thought I was passin' by Doolins the miller's, and says he to me, Will you carry home this sack o' male for me? Now you know, male is money, every fool knows."

"Right avic."

"And so I tuk the sack o' male an my shouldher, and I thought the woight iv it was killin' me, just as if it *was* a sack o' goold."

"Go an Darby."

"And with that I thought I met with a cat, and that, you know, manes an ill-nathur'd woman."

"Right Darby."

"And says she to me, Darby Kelleher says she, you're mighty yollow, God bless you; is it the jandhers you have? says she. Now wasn't that mighty sharp? I think the jandhers manes goold?"

"Yis, iv it was the yollow jandhers you dhremt iv, but not the black jandhers."

"Well, it *was* the yollow jandhers."

"Very good avic; that's makin' a fair offer at it."

"I thought so myself," said Darby, "more by token when there was a dog in my dhrame next; and that's a frind, you know."

"Right avic."

"And he had a silver collar an him."

"Oh bad luck to that silver collar Darby; what made you dhrame o' silver at all?"

"Why what harm?"

"Oh I thought you knew betther nor to dhrame o' silver; why, cushla machree, sure silver is a disappointment all the world over."

"Oh murther!" said Darby, in horror, "and is my dhrame spylte (spoiled) by that blackguard collar?"

"Nigh hand indeed, but not all out. It would be spylte only for the dog, but the dog is a frind, and so it will be only a frindly disappointment, or maybe a fallin' out with an acquaintance."

"Oh what matther," said Darby, "so the dhrame is to the good still!!"

"The dhrame *is* to the good still; but tell me if you dhremt o' three sprigs o' *spare*mint at the ind iv it?"

"Why then, now I could not say for sartin, bekase I was nigh wakin' at the time, and the dhrame was not so clear to me."

"I wish you could be sartin o' that."

"Why, I have it an my mind that there *was* sparemint in it, bekase I thought there was a garden in part iv it, and the sparemint was *likely* to be there."

"Sure enough, and so you did dhrame o' the three sprigs o' sparemint."

"Indeed I could a'most make my book-oath that I dhremt iv it. I'm partly sartin, if not all out."

"Well, that's raysonable. It's a good dhrame, Darby."

"Do you tell me so!"

"'Deed an' it is, Darby. Now wait till the next quarther o' the new moon, and dhrame again then, and you'll see what'll come of it."

"By dad an' I will, granny. Oh but it's you *has* taken the maynin' out of it beyant every thing; and faix if I find the crock, it's yourself won't be the worse iv it; but I must be goin', granny, for the squire bid me to hurry, or else I would stay longer wid you. Good mornin' to you—good mornin' Oonah! I'll see you to-morrow sometime, granny." And off went Darby, leisurely enough.

The foregoing dialogue shows the ready credulity of poor Darby; but it was not in his belief of the "vartue of dhrames" that his weakness only lay. He likewise had a most extensive creed as regarded fairies of all sorts and sizes, and was always on the look-out for a Leprechaun. Now a Leprechaun is a fairy of peculiar tastes, properties, and powers, which it is necessary to acquaint the reader with. His taste as to occupation is very humble, for he employs himself in making shoes, and he loves retirement, being fond of shady nooks where he can sit alone, and pursue his avocation undisturbed. He is quite a hermit in this respect, for there is no instance on record of two Leprechauns being seen together. But he is quite a beau in his dress, notwithstanding, for he wears a red square cut coat, richly laced with gold, waistcoat and inexpressibles of the same, cocked hat, shoes, and buckles. He has the property of deceiving, in so great a degree, those who chance to discover him, that none have ever yet been known whom he has not overreached in the "keen encounter of the wits," which his meeting with mortals always produces. This is occasioned by his possessing the power of bestowing unbounded wealth on whoever can keep him within sight until he is weary of the *surveillance*, and gives the ransom demanded, and to this end, the object of the mortal who is so fortunate as to surprise one, is to seize him, and never withdraw his eye from him, until the threat of destruction forces the Leprechaun to produce the treasure; but the sprite is too many for us clumsy witted earthlings, and is sure, by some device, to make us avert our eyes, when he vanishes at once.

This Enchanted Cobbler of the meadows, Darby Kelleher was always on the look out for. But though so constantly on the watch for a Leprechaun, he never had got even within sight of one, and the name of the Fairy Finder was bestowed upon him in derision. Many a trick too was played on him; sometimes a twig stuck amongst long grass, with a red rag hanging upon it, has betrayed Darby into a cautious observance and approach, until a nearer inspection, and a laugh from behind some neighbouring hedge, have dispelled the illusion. But this, though often repeated, did not cure him, and no turkey-cock had a quicker eye for a bit of red, or flew at it with greater eagerness, than Darby Kelleher, and he entertained the belief that one day or other he would reap the reward of all his watching, by finding a Leprechaun in good earnest.

But that was all in the hands of Fate, and must be waited for: in the mean time there was the castle and the "crock o' goold" for a certainty, and, under the good omens of the "sharp dhrame" he had, he determined on taking that affair in hand at once. For his companion in the labour of digging, and pulling the ponderous walls of the castle to pieces, he selected Oonah, who was, in the parlance of her own class, "a brave two-handed long-sided jack," and as great a believer in dreams and omens as Darby himself; besides, she promised profound secrecy, and agreed to take a small share of the treasure for her reward in assisting to discover it.

For about two months Darby and Oonah laboured in vain; but at last, something came of their exertions. In the course of their work, when they occasionally got tired, they would sit down to rest themselves and talk over their past disappointments and future hopes. Now it was during one of these intervals of repose that Darby, as he was resting himself on one of the coign-stones of the ruin, suddenly discovered——that he was in love with Oonah.

Now Oonah happened to be thinking much in the same sort of way about Darby, at that very moment, and the end of the affair was, that Darby and Oonah were married the Sunday following.

The calculating Englishman will ask, did he find the treasure before he married the girl? The unsophisticated boys of the sod never calculate on these occasions; and the story goes that Oonah Lenehan was the only treasure Darby discovered in the old castle. Darby's acquaintances were in high glee on the occasion, and swore he got *a great lob*—for Oonah, be it remembered, was on the grenadier scale, or what in Ireland is called: "the full of a door," and the news spread over the country in some such fashion as this—

"Arrah, an' did you hear the news?"

"What news?"

"About Darby Kelleher."

"What of him?"

"Sure he found a fairy at last."

"Tare an ounty!"

"Thruth I'm tellin' you.—He's married to Oonah Lenehan."

"Ha! ha! ha! by the powers it's she that is the rale fairy! musha, more power to you Darby, but you've cotched it in airnest now!"

But the fairy he had caught did not satisfy Darby so far as to make him give up the pursuit for the future. He was still on the watch for a Leprechaun; and one morning as he was going to his work, he stopped suddenly on his path, which lay through a field of standing corn, and his eye became riveted on some object with the most eager expression. He crouched, and crawled, and was making his way with great caution towards the point of his attraction, when he was visited on the back of the head with a thump that considerably disturbed his visual powers, and the voice of his mother, a vigorous old beldame, saluted his ear at the same time with a hearty "Bad luck to you, you lazy thief, what are you slindging there for, when it's minding your work you ought to be?"

"Whisht! whisht! mother," said Darby, holding up his hand in token of silence.

"What do you mane, you omadhawn?"

"Mother, be quiet, I bid you! Whisht! I see it."

"What do you see?"

"Stoop down here. Straight forninst you, don't you see it as plain as a pikestaff?"

"See what?"

"That little red thing."

"Well, what of it?"

"See there, how it stirs. Oh murther! it's goin' to be off afore I can catch it. Oh murther! why did you come here at all, makin' a noise and frightenin' it away?"

"Frightenin' what, you big fool?"

"The Leprechaun there. Whisht! it is quiet agin!"

"May the d—l run a huntin' wid you for a big omadhaun; why, you born nath'ral, is it that red thing over there you mane?"

"Yis, to be sure it is; don't spake so loud, I tell you."

"Why, bad scran to you, you fool, it's a poppy it is, and nothin' else;" and the old woman went over to the spot where it grew, and plucking it up by the roots threw it at Darby, with a great deal of abuse into the bargain, and bade him go mind his work, instead of being a "slindging vagabone, as he was."

It was some time after this occurrence, that Darby Kelleher had a meeting with a certain Doctor Dionysius Mac Finn, whose name became much more famous than it had hitherto been, from the wonderful events that ensued in consequence.

Of the doctor himself it becomes necessary to say something: his father was one Paddy Finn, and had been so prosperous in the capacity of a cow doctor, that his son Denis, seeing the dignity of a professor in the healing art must increase in proportion to the nobleness of the animal he operates upon, determined to make the human, instead of the brute creation, the object of his care. To this end he was assisted by his father, who had scraped some money together in his humble calling, and having a spice of ambition in him, as well as his aspiring son, he set him up in the neighbouring village as an apothecary. Here Denny enjoyed the reputation of being an "iligant bone-setter," and cracked skulls, the result of *fair* fighting, and whisky fevers, were treated by him on the most approved principles. But Denny's father was gathered unto *his* fathers, and the son came into the enjoyment of all the old man's money: this, considering his condition, was considerable, and the possession of a few hundred pounds so inflated the apothecary, that he determined on becoming a "Doctor" at once. For this purpose he gave up his apothecary's shop, and set off—where do you think?—To Spain. Here he remained for some time, and returned to Ireland, declaring himself a full physician of one of the '

Spanish universities; his name of Denny Finn transformed into Doctor Dionysius Mac Finn, or, as his neighbours chose to call it, Mac Fun, and fun enough the doctor certainly gave birth to. The little money he once had was spent in his pursuit of professional honors, and he returned to his native place with a full title and an empty purse, and his practice did not tend to fill it. At the same time there was a struggle to keep up appearances. He kept a horse, or what he intended to be considered as such, but 'twas only a pony, and if he had but occasion to go to the end of the village on a visit, the pony was ordered on service. He was glad to accept an invitation to dinner whenever he had the luck to get one, and the offer of a bed even, was sure to be accepted, because that insured breakfast the next morning. Thus, poor Doctor Dionysius made out the cause. Often asked to dinner from mingled motives of kindness and fun, for while good dinner was a welcome novelty to the doctor, the absurdities of his pretension and manner rendered him a subject of unfailing diversion to his entertainers. Now he had gone the round of all the snug farmers and country gentlemen in the district, but at last, he had the honor to receive an invitation from *the* squire himself, and on the appointed day Doctor Dionysius bestrode his pony, attired in the full dress of a Spanish physician, which happens to be *red* from head to foot, and presented himself at "The Hall."

When a groom appeared to take his "horse" to the stable, the doctor requested that his steed might be turned loose into the lawn, declaring it to be more wholesome for the animal, than being cooped up in a house; the saddle and bridle were accordingly removed, and his desire complied with.

The doctor's appearance in the drawing-room, attired as he was, caused no small diversion, but attention was speedily called off from him by the announcement of dinner, that electric sound that stimulates a company at the same instant, and supersedes every other consideration whatsoever. Moreover, the squire's dinners were notoriously good, and the doctor profited largely by the same that day, and lost no opportunity of filling his glass with the choice wines that surrounded him. This he did to so much purpose, that the poor little man was very far gone when the guests were about to separate.

At the doctor's request the bell was rung, and his horse ordered, as the last remaining few of the company were about to separate, but every one of them had departed, and still there was no announcement of the steed being at the door. At length a servant made his appearance, and said it was impossible to catch the doctor's pony.

"What do you mean by 'catch'?" said the squire. "Is it not in the stable?"

"No, sir."

Here an explanation ensued, and the squire ordered a fresh attempt to be made to take the fugitive; but, though many fresh hands were employed in the attempt, the pony baffled all their efforts;—every manœuvre, usually resorted to on such occasions, was vainly put in practice. He was screwed up into corners, but no sooner was he there than, squeeling and flinging up his heels, he broke through the blockade;—again his flank was turned by nimble runners, but the pony was nimbler still; a sieve full of oats was presented as an inducement, but the pony was above such vulgar tricks, and defied all attempts at being captured.

This was the mode by which the doctor generally secured the offer of a bed, and he might have been successful in this instance, but for a knowing old coachman who was up to the trick, and out of pure fun chose to expose it; so, bringing out a huge blunderbuss, he said,—"Never mind—just let me at him, and I'll engage I'll make him stand."

"Oh, my good man," said the doctor, "pray don't take so much trouble;—just let me go with you;" and proceeding to the spot where the pony was still luxuriating on the rich grass of the squire's lawn, he gave a low whistle, and the little animal walked up to his owner with as much tractability as a dog. The saddling and bridling did not take much time, and the doctor was obliged to renounce his hopes of a bed and the morrow's breakfast, and ride home—or homewards, I should say, for it was as little his destiny as his wish to sleep at home that night, for he was so overpowered with his potations, that he could not guide the pony, and the pony's palate was so tickled by the fresh herbage, that he wished for more of it, and finding a gate, that led to a, meadow, open by the road side, he turned into the field, where he very soon turned the doctor into a ditch, so that they had bed and board between them to their heart's content.

The doctor and his horse slept and ate profoundly all night, and even the "rosy-fingered morn," as the poets have it, found them in the continuance of their enjoyment. Now it happened that Darby Kelleher was passing along the path that lay by the side of the ditch where the doctor was sleeping, and on perceiving him, Darby made as dead a set as ever pointer did at game.

The doctor, be it remembered, was dressed in red. Moreover he was a little man, and his gold-laced hat and ponderous shoe-buckles completed the resemblance to the being that Darby took him for. Darby was at last certain that he had discovered a Leprechaun, and amaze so riveted him to the spot, and anxiety made his pulse beat so fast, that he could not move nor breathe for some seconds. At last he recovered himself, and stealing stealthily to the spot where the doctor slept, every inch of his approach made him more certain of the reality of his prize; and when he found himself within reach of it, he made one furious spring, and flung himself on the unfortunate little man, fastenining his tremendous fist on his throat, at the same time exclaiming in triumph, "Hurra!—by the hoky, I have you at last!!"

The poor little doctor, thus rudely and suddenly aroused from his tipsy sleep, looked excessively bewildered when he opened his eyes, and met the glare of ferocious delight that Darby Kelleher cast upon him, and he gurled out, "What's the matter?" as well as the grip of Darby's hand upon his throat would permit him.

"Goold's the matther," shouted Darby—"Goold!—Goold!!—Goold!!!"

"What about Goold?" says the doctor.

"Goold!—yallow goold—that's the matther."

"Is it Paddy Goold that's taken ill again?" said the doctor, rubbing his eyes. "Don't choke me my good man; I'll go immediately," said he, endeavouring to rise.

"By my sowl, you won't," said Darby tightening his hold.

"For mercy's sake let me go!" said the doctor.

"Let you go indeed!—ow! ow!"

"For the tender mercy"—

"Goold! goold! you little vagabone!"

"Well I'm going, if you let me."

"Divil a step;"—and here he nearly choked him.

"Oh! murder!—for God's sake!"

"Whisht!!—you thief—how *dar* you say God, you divil's imp!!!"

The poor little man, between the suddenness of his waking, and the roughness of the treatment he was under, was in such a state of bewilderment, that for the first time he now perceived he was lying amongst grass and under bushes, and rolling his eyes about, he exclaimed—

"Where am I?—God bless me!"

"Whisht! you little cruked ottomy—by the holy farmer, if you say God agin, I'll cut your throat."

"What do you hold me so tight for?"

"Just for fear you'd vanish you see. Oh I know you well."

"Then my good man, if you know me so well, treat me with proper respect, if you please."

"Divil send you respect. Respect indeed! that's a good thing. Musha bad luck to your impidence, you thievin' owld rogue."

"Who taught you to call such names to your betters, fellow?—How dare you use a professional gentleman so rudely?"

"Oh, do you hear this!!—a profissionil gintleman!—Arrah, do you think I don't know you, you little owld cobbler?"

"Cobbler!—Zounds, what do you mean, you ruffian? Let me go sirrah!" and he struggled violently to rise.

"Not a taste, 'scure to the step you'll go out o' this till you give me what I want."

"What do you want then?"

"Goold—goold!"

"Ho! ho! so you're a robber, sir; you want to rob me, do you?"

"Oh! what robbery it is!!—throth that won't do, as cunnin' as you think yourself; you won't frighten me that way. Come, give it at wanst—you may as well. I'll never let go my grip o' you antil you hand me out the goold."

"'Pon the honour of a gentleman, gold nor silver is not in my company. I have fourpence halfpenny in my breeches pocket, which you are welcome to if you let go my throat."

"Four pence ha'pny!!!—Why, then, do you think me sitch a *gom*, all out, as to put me off wid four pence hap'ny; throth, for three sthraws, this minit I'd thrash you within an inch o' your life for your impidince. Come, no humbuggin'; out with the goold!"

"I have no gold. Don't choke me: if you murder me, remember there's law in the land. You'd better let me go."

"Not a fut. Gi' me the goold, I tell you, you little vagabone!!" said Darby, shaking him violently.

"Don't murder me, for Heaven's sake!"

"I will murdher you if you don give me a hatful o' goold this minit."

"A hatful of gold!—Why, who do you take me for?"

"Sure I know you're! a Leprechaun, you desaiver o' the world!"

"A Leprechaun!" said the doctor, in mingled indignation and amazement. "My good man, you mistake."

"Oh, how soft I am!—'Twon't do, I tell you. I have you, and I'll howld you;—long I've been lookin' for you, and I cotch you at last, and by the 'tarnal o' war I'll have your life or the goold."

"My good man, be merciful—you mistake—I'm no Leprechaun;—I'm Doctor Mac Finn."

"That won't do either! you think to desaive me, but 'twont do:—just as if I didn't know a docthor from a Leprechaun. Gi' me the goold, you owld chate!"

"I tell you I'm Doctor Dionysius Mac Finn. Take care what you're about!—there's law in the land;—and I think I begin to know you. Your name is Kelleher!"

"Oh, you cunnin' owld thief! oh, then but you are the complate owld rogue; only I'm too able for you. You want to freken me, do you?—Oh, you little scrap o' deception, but you are deep!"

"Your name is Kelleher—I remember. My good fellow, take care;—don't you know I'm Doctor Mac Finn—don't you see I am?"

"Why thin but you have the dirty yollow pinched look iv him, sure enough; but don't I know you've only put in an you to desaive me; besides, the doctor has dirty owld tatthers o' black clothes an him, and isn't as red as a sojer like you."

"That's an accident, my good man."

"Gi' me the goold this minit, and no more prate wid you."

"I tell you, Kelleher"——

"Howld your tongue, and gi' me the goold."

"By all that's"——

"Will you give it?"

"How can I?"

"Very well. You'll see what the ind of it 'ill be," said Darby, rising, but still keeping his iron grip of the doctor. "Now, for the last time, I ask you, will you gi' me the goold? or, by the powers o' wild fire, I'll put you where you'll never see daylight antil you make me a rich man."

"I have no gold, I tell you."

"Faix then I'll keep you till you find it," said Darby, who tucked the little man under his arm, and ran home with him as fast as he could.

He kicked at his cabin door for admittance when he reached home, exclaiming—

"Let me in! let me in!—Make haste; I have him."

"Who have you?" said Oonah, as she opened the door.

"Look at that!" said Darby in triumph; "I cotch him at last?"

"Weira then, is it a Leprechaun, it is?" said Oonah.

"Divil a less," said Darby, throwing down the doctor on the bed, and still holding him fast. "Open the big chest,

Oonah, and we'll lock him up in it, and keep him antil he gives us the goold."

"Murder! murder!" shouted the doctor. "Lock me up in a chest!!"

"Gi' me the goold, then, and I won't."

"My good man, you know I have not gold to give."

"Don't believe him, Darby jewel," said Oonah, "them Leprechauns is the biggest liars in the world."

"Sure I know that!" said Darby, "as well as you. Oh! all the throuble I've had wid him; throth only I'm aiqual to a counsellor for knowledge, he'd have namplushed me long ago;"

"Long life to you, Darby dear!"

"Mrs Kelleher," said the doctor.

"Oh Lord!" said Oonah, in surprise, "did you ever hear the like o' that?—how he knows my name!"

"To be sure he does," said Darby, "and why nat? sure he's a fairy, you know."

"I'm no fairy, Mrs Kelleher. I'm a doctor—Doctor Mac Finn."

"Don't b'lieve him, darlin'," said Darby. "Make haste and open the chest."

"Darby Kelleher," said the doctor, "let me go, and I'll cure you whenever you want my assistance."

"Well, I want your assistance now," said Darby, "for I'm very bad this minit wid poverty; and if you cure me o' that, I'll let you go."

"What will become of me?" said the doctor in despair, as Darby carried him towards the big chest which Oonah had opened.

"I'll tell you what'll become o' you," said Darby, seizing a hatchet that lay within his reach;—"by the seven blessed candles, if you don't consint before night to fill me that big chest full o' goold, I'll chop you as small as aribs (herbs) for the pot." And Darby crammed him into the box.

"Oh, Mrs Kelleher, be merciful to me," said the doctor, "and whenever you're sick I'll attend you."

"God forbid!" said Oonah; "it's not the likes o' you I want when I'm sick;—attind me, indeed! bad luck to you, you little imp, maybe you'd run away with my babby, or it's a *Banshee* you'd turn yourself into, and sing for my death. Shut him up Darby; it's not looky to be howldin' discoorse wid the likes iv him."

"Oh!" roared the doctor; as his cries were stifled by the lid of the chest being closed on him. The key was turned, and Oonah sprinkled some holy water she had in a little bottle that hung in one corner of the cabin over the lock; to prevent the fairy having any power upon it.

Darby and Oonah now sat down in consultation on their affairs, and began forming their plans on an extensive scale, as to what they were to do with their money, for have it they must, now that the Leprechaun was fairly in their power. Now and then Darby would rise and go over to the chest, very much as one goes to the door of a room where a naughty child has been locked up, to know "if it be good yet," and giving a thump on the lid would exclaim, "Well, you little vagabone, will you gi' me the goold yet?"

A groan and a faint answer of denial was all the reply he received.

"Very well, stay there; but, remember, if you don't consint before night I'll chop you to pieces." He then got his bill-hook, and began to sharpen it close by the chest, that the Leprechaun might hear him; and when the poor doctor heard this process going forward, he felt more dead than alive; the horrid scraping of the iron against the stone being interspersed with occasional interjectional passages from

Darby, such as, "Do you hear that you thief? I'm gettin' ready for you." Then away he'd rasp at the grind-stone again, and, as he paused to feel the edge of the weapon, exclaim, "By the powers I'll have it as sharp as a razhir."

In the meantime it was well for the prisoner that there were many large chinks in the chest, or suffocation from his confinement would have anticipated Darby's pious intentions upon him; and when he found matters likely to go so hard with him, the thought struck him at last, of affecting to be what Darby mistook him for, and regaining his freedom by stratagem.

To this end, when Darby had done sharpening his bill-hook, the doctor replied, in answer to one of Darby's summonses for gold, that he saw it was in vain longer to deny giving it, that Darby was too cunning for him, and that he was ready to make him the richest man in the country.

"I'll take no less than the full o' that chest," said Darby.

"You'll have ten times the full of it, Darby," said the doctor, "if you'll only do what I bid you."

"Sure I'll do anything."

"Well, you must first prepare the mystificand-herumbrandherum."

"Tare an ouns, how do I know what that is?"

"Silence, Darby Kelleher, and attend to me: that's a magical ointment, which I will show you how to make; and whenever you want gold, all you have to do is to rub a little of it on the point of a pick-axe or your spade, and dig wherever you please, and you will be sure to find treasure."

"Oh, think o' that! faix an I'll make plenty of it when you show me. How is it made?"

"You must go into the town, Darby, and get me three things, and fold them three times in three rags torn out of the left side of a petticoat that has not known water for a year."

"Faith, I can do that much any how," said Oonah, who began tearing the prescribed pieces out of her under garment—

"And what three things am I to get you?"

"First bring me a grain of salt from a house that stands at cross-roads."

"Crass roads!" said Darby, looking significantly at Oonah; "By my sowl, but it's my dhrame's comin' out!"

"Silence, Darby Kelleher," said the doctor with solemnity; "mark me, Darby Kelleher;"—and then he proceeded to repeat a parcel of gibberish to Darby, which he enjoined him to remember, and repeat again; but as Darby could not, the doctor said he should only write it down for him, and, tearing a leaf from his pocket-book, he wrote in pencil a few words, stating the condition he was in, and requesting assistance. This slip of paper he desired Darby to deliver to the apothecary in the town, who would give him a drug that would complete the making of the ointment.

Darby went to the apothecary's as he was desired, and it happened to be dinner time when he arrived. The apothecary had a few friends dining with him, and Darby was detained until they chose to leave the table, and go, in a body, to liberate the poor little doctor. He was pulled out of the chest amidst the laughter of his liberators and the fury of Darby and Oonah, who both made considerable fight against being robbed of their prize. At last the doctor's friends got him out of the house, and proceeded to the town to supper, where the whole party kept getting magnificently drunk, until sleep plunged them into dizzy dreams of Leprechauns and Fairy Finders.

The doctor for some days swore vengeance against Darby, and threatened a prosecution; but his friends recommended him to let the matter rest, as it would only tend to make the affair more public, and get him nothing but laughter for damages.

As for Darby Kelleher, nothing could ever persuade him that it was not a *real* Leprechaun he had caught, which by some villanous contrivance, on the Fairy's part, changed itself into the semblance of the doctor; and he often said the great mistake he made was "givin' the little vagabone so much time, for that if he done right he'd have set about cutting his throat at wanst."

As the superstitious reader may have been disappointed in not hearing of a real fairy in the foregoing tale, I will now give an account of a meeting between two superhuman beings; and as prose is too heavy a material wherewith to treat such a subject, I will attempt the story in rhyme.

1. Old woman.
2. In Ireland the tobacco in a pipe is very generally ignited by the application of a piece of burning turf—or, as it is figuratively called, 'live turf.
3. The peasantry often say "a coal o' turf."

# THE LEPRECHAUN AND THE GENIUS

Hibernia's Genius passed one day
Through one of her sweet mountain vallies,
Whose emerald Verdure is begot
Where Sun with Show'r so frequent dallies.

Turning around a granite rock,
She popp'd upon a shady nook,
Where, whisp'ring to some blushing flow'rs,
There lisp'd an amatory brook.

It was the very place for love;
For vows, that never should be broken,

And forty other silly things,
That never, never, should be spoken.

Fancy her wonder then, when in
This sweetest "place for lovers only,"
She saw a Cobbler——making love?
No;—making brogues—and all *alonée.*

*Alonée, proudée*, like a child,
None more conceited could you meet;
Though his pride was not for his own,
But for his neighbour's greater *feet.*

Like most conceited men too, he
Was little, and like little men
Was very active too; in short,
With him 'twas, " Cut and come again."

And on he cut, and on he stitch'd,
And seem'd to be in greatest gig,
For every stitch he gave his brogue,
He put another in his wig.[1]

Sips from a bottle oft were taken,
In which, from mountain side, a few
Bright dew-drops from the heath were shaken;
In fact his drink was, *mountain dew.*

The Genius,—(by the by 'tis odd
What lots of geniuses we boast here;)
First, as a lady always ought,
Look'd round about to see the coast clear.

For she, in sooth a *single* lady,
The monster Scandal well might gobble her,
If in a solitary glen
She was seen talking to a Cobbler.

'Tis true that he was very little,
And age upon his face did linger;
But there's much mischief, it is said,
Even in the devil's little finger.

And years don't always virtue bring,
But he was very, *very* old,
And very, very, *ve—ry* little;
In short, the truth may's well be told:

He was not more than two feet high,
With three-cock'd hat, red inexpressible,
Which, lucky dog, was all his own,
Seeing he had, at home, no Jezebel.

A coat to match, and a flapp'd vest,
Over his body—somewhat logy,—
At once, to cut description short,
He was just like a cut-down fogy.[2]

She saw he was a Leprechaun,
And at the drams he swill'd galore of,
As he was of the "world of spirits,"
Her wonder gradually wore off.

He was a spirit himself—'twas but
A kindred link, in social feeling,

With other spirit that he wove,
And so from *weaving* went to *reeling*.

But to my tale:—The Genius now
Thought she might make her fortune featly,
If she could catch the Leprechaun,
And make him hand the hundreds neatly.

You'll wonder that a genius, thus,
The filthy lust of gold could lure;
But pray remember, ere you blame,
That geniuses are always poor.

And here, the fate I might lament
Of Irish genius in particular,
Whose shaft of Hope is sadly bent
From its original perpendicular.

The deadly Demon of Decay
Has had a fatal sweeping rap at all;
Not only is the column bent,
But where the d—l is our capital?

Little is left——and what remains
How few there are that will "*embark*" it,
Except in steam-packets, to feed
The interest of a foreign market

But this is foreign to my tale,
And bordering upon political
Economy—on which I don't
Intend to become analytical.

But it accounts the further, why
The nymph, of whom my story's told,
Should strive, her tatter'd robe of green
To 'broider with the fairy's gold.

She stole upon him—but the sprite
Was up to trap—not lurking blindly—
And, as he finish'd a heel-tap,
Look'd up, and said, "Good morrow kindly."

Whether the heel-tap of his glass
It was, or the heel-tap of leather
He finished, I don't know,—but it
Was either—or p'rhaps both together.

"Good morrow," said the Genius, though
She wish'd he had not been so circum-
Spect,—for she thought the lad to clutch,
Altho' she did not mean to Burk him.

She ask'd politely after's health,
And, touching next upon the news,
Inquir'd what 'twas he work'd upon;
He said, "A pair of dead man's shoes."

"A dead man's shoes?" she said;—"why he
Won't want them!"—With a devilish air,
"No," said the sprite; "but I can get
What price I fix on, from his heir."

"Well, that's more sensible," said she,
"Than making brogues for living folk,

For while *I*'m to the fore, indeed,
That would be an exceeding joke."

"*You?*" said the Leprechaun; "I'd beat
All women cobblers put together;
You ladies may have finer *souls*,
But match me at an upper-leather!"

"For cobbler's duty I will yield
To no brogue-maker in the nation;
My work is *super*, ma'am;"—Said she,
"Indeed 'tis super—erogation.

"Give o'er thy toil, thou senseless sprite;
Thy labour's vain. You ought to see
'Tis useless making brogues for those
Whose *brogues* are ready-made by me.

"Your brogues are good, I don't deny;
But though you made them ne'er so stout,
They can't endure as long as mine,
For those I give will ne'er wear out.

"Take up your awl, good man, and trudge;
And as for bragging—*Voce Sotto*,
Your *upper*-leathers *down* must go,
And give up mending *heels* in *toe toe*.

"Take up your awl, I say, and go."
She hoped he'd turn, and she could catch him;
But he'd a trick worth two o' that,
For, as to tricking, who could match him?

"May be you'd give it me," says he;
"'Tis there, behind you, on the stone."
She turn'd—and *his awl* was not there,—
When she look'd back—*her all* was gone.

1. "Stitching your wig" means getting tipsy.
2. The slang name for a pensioner of the Royal Hospital in Ireland. The name will soon be obsolete, as the establishment is to be broken up, and transferred to Chelsea.

# THE SPANISH BOAR AND THE IRISH BULL

## A ZOOLOGICAL PUZZLE

HITHERTO IT HAS BEEN BELIEVED, that no animals could be more distinct, than the two whose names from the heading of this chapter. But I will show, that in the case I am about to adduce, the Irish Bull has been produced in a great state of perfection from the Spanish Boar. It will be objected, perhaps, by the learned, that there was a *cross* in the *female* line, on one side, and I do not deny it; but still, when the facts come to be developed, as I hope they shall be, in a clear and satisfactory manner, in the following pages, I am sure there will not be found any zoologist, either of the *Jardin des Plantes*, the Regent's Park, the Surrey, or the Dublin Gardens, that will not acknowledge the case I have to lay before them as, at least, *very extraordinary*.

I was for a long time undecided as to the mode in which I should treat this curious affair. To do so, scientifically is beyond my power—therefore the next best way I had of doing it, was to put it some what into the shape of a memoir. And here lay another difficulty, for the rage has been so great for autobiographies, that I fancied my memoir must be put before the world in this shape, and neither of my personages were felicitous subjects for such a mode of treatment. The Bull would prove, I fear, as unprofitable a hero in an autobiography as in a china shop, where, in the true spirit of an autobiographer, he proverbially "has it all his own way." And as for the Boar, the fact is, that so many *bores* have turned autobiographers of late, I did not like running the risk of surfeiting the public, therefore I decided, as the safest course, to speak in the third person of my principals, and the first I shall treat of, is the Boar.

The humblest biographer will scarcely commence with less than stating that his hero has been descended from a *good* family: now my hero being a Spaniard, a merely good family would not be enough, he must, in right of his national pride, come from a great one, and I can safely assert that mine was one of a very great family—there were sixteen of them at a litter. With my hero, the season of youth, which, amongst the swinish race, is proverbially that of beaty also, rapidly passed away, and he increased in age, ugliness, and devilment, in more than the usual ratio, until his pranks in the woods were suddenly put a stop to, by his being taken, one fine day, in a toil, and carried a prisoner into the town of Bilboa.

It chanced, that at the period of his capture, the captain of a ship bound for Dublin, then lying in the port, was very anxious to take home with him some rarity from "foreign parts" as a present to a lady in the aforesaid city of Dublin, from whom he had received some civility. It happened also, that the entry of the Boar into Bilboa had created a prodigious sensation amongst the worthy townsfolk, and was quite a godsend to the wonder-mongers. Now the captain heard the news amongst some gossip, just at the time he was debating in his own mind, whether he should take home some hanks of onions or a Spanish guitar for his intended present, and the bright thought struck him, that if he could only procure this wonderful savage of the woods, of whom report spoke so prodigiously, that it would be the most acceptable offering he could make to his fair friend, and he accordingly set to work to obtain the bristly curiosity, and succeeded in his negotiation. It was agreed that the Boar should remain ashore until the ship was ready for sea, in the possession of his captor, who undertook to lodge the curiosity safely on board, whenever required, but the captain, having occasion to sail suddenly, was unable to send timely notice to the Spaniard, who happened not to be at home when the captain, in person went to demand his Boar.

This was unfortunate, but as the occasion was urgent, and the Irishman could not possibly wait, he was obliged to endeavour to get his pet pig to the ship as well as he could without the assistance of the Spaniard, who understood all about "such small deer," and the consequence was, that the Boar was too much for the sailor, and to use the captain's own words, the headstrong brute "slipped his cable and bore right away down the town," to the infinite horror of the worthy townspeople.

"The boar! the boar!" was shouted on all sides, and according to the established rule in such cases, those in front of the danger ran before it, and those in the rear ran after it, until such a prodigious crowd was screeching at the heels of the Boar, that he was the most terrified of the party, and in his panic, he turned down the first open court he saw, off the high street, and ran for his life.

Now it happened, that of all places in the world, the spot he selected was the Exchange—and moreover it was 'Change hour, and the merchants were very solemnly engaged in the mysteries of per cent-age, when the Boar made his appearance amongst them. The Exchange, at Bilboa, happens to be surrounded by fine old trees, and in that space of time which is vulgarly called "the twinkling of an eye," the stately merchants were startled out of their solemnity and were seen clambering like so many monkeys into the trees to get out of the way of the new comer, and so universal was this arborial ascent, that in fact, our hero had the honor of producing the greatest *rise on 'Change* ever remembered in Bilboa. His first achievement in this court of commerce was to make an *endorsement* on an elderly gentleman who was not so active as some of his neighbours, and a Jew, who was next overthrown, never had such a horror of pork before. Cloaks and sombreros, dropt in the hurry of flight, were tossed in horrid sport by the intruder, and having been hunted into one of the corners of the square, he kept the assembled multitude at bay, until the arrival of the regular bull-fighters terminated the adventure, by retaking the vagrant. He had a narrow escape of his life, for had it not been for the entreaties of the captain, the matadors would have made short work with him. He was got on board at last, and put into a place of security.

When our hero arrived in the Irish metropolis, he was handed over to his new owner by the captain, much to the satisfaction of both. The lady being one of those who are delighted at having something that nobody else has, was charmed, of course, at having obtained such a rarity, and the captain blessed his stars at having got rid of the greatest nuisance ever was on board his ship.

A small enclosure at the rear of the city tenement was dedicated to the use of the Boar, and for some days, while the charm of novelty gave a zest to the inspection, Mrs—— used to sit, for hours, eyeing the foreigner with infinite delight, through a hole cut in a strongly barricaded door that shut in the wonder. In those cases, as Campbell says,

> "'Tis distance lends enchantment to the view."

And she used to issue cards of invitation to her friends, to come and see the *only* wild boar in Ireland. This was a great triumph, but alas! for all sublunary enjoyments, they fade but too fast, and when the first blush of novelty had faded, and that the celebrity attached to being a boar-owner had become hacknied, Mrs—— began to think this acquisition of a wild pig no such enviable matter, and she would rather have seen him hanging to the rafters of her kitchen in ham and flitch, than parading up and down her premises;—besides, the yard which he occupied was rendered useless for any other purpose than a "parlour for the pig," for the unmannerly gentleman had taken military possession of his domain, and no one in the establishment dared approach him; to such a degree had this terror arrived, that, at last, his prog was thrown to him over the wall, and serious thoughts were entertained by his owner of making "swift conveyance of her dear" wild boar, when she was relieved from further dire intents upon our hero, by the following occurrence:

A distinguished member of the Dublin Zoological Society waited upon Mrs—— as she sat at breakfast one morning, and requested permission to see "her Boar." This would have been a great delight a fortnight before: to have a member of the Zoological Society soliciting the honor of seeing *her* Boar, but the truth was, that Don Pig had rendered himself so intolerable, that nothing could compensate for the nuisance, and this additional offering to her vanity as a wonder-proprietor, came too late to be valued. Still she affected a tone of triumph, and led the zoological professor to the treat he sought for, and pointing with dignity to the loophole cut in the door, she said, "There, sir."

After the professor, in silent wonder, had feasted his eyes for some time on the barbarian through this safety valve, he exclaimed, "What a noble specimen!—The finest boar I ever saw!"

"Isn't he a lovely creature?" said Mrs——.

"Charming, madam."—

"And his tail, doctor!"

"Has the true wild curl, madam.—Oh, madam, you surely do not mean to keep this fine creature all to yourself;—you really ought to present him to the Society."

"How could you think of asking me to part with my pet, doctor?"

"I'm sure your own public spirit, madam, would suggest the sacrifice;—and of course a very handsome vote of thanks from the Society, as well as the gift securing to you all the privileges of a member.—"

Here was something to be gained, so instead of Mrs—— giving her lodger a dose of prussic acid, or something of that sort, which she contemplated, she made a present of him to the Zoological Society, and the professor took his leave, in great delight at having secured so fine an animal, but not half so happy as the lady was in getting rid of him.

The next day the proper authorities secured the bristly don, and he was consigned to the cart of the Zoological Society to be carried forthwith to the Phœnix Park, where the Gardens of that learned body are situated. The driver of the cart, who, it happened, was quite ignorant of the pains it had cost to place his inside passenger in his seat, was passing up Barrack Street, when he was accosted by a friend on the flags, with, "Why then blur-an-agers Mike, is that you"?—"By gor it's myself, and no one else," says Mike—"and how is yourself?" "Bravely!" says Jim; "and it's myself is glad to see you lookin' so clane and hearty Mikee dear, and well off to all appearance."—"By dad I'm as happy as the day's long," says Mike, "and has an iligant place, and divil a thing to do good, bad, or indifferent, but to dhrive about this cart from morning till night, excep'n when I may take a turn at feedin' the bastes."—"Why, have you more horses nor the one you're dhriving to mind?" says Jim.

"Oh, they're not horses at all," says Mike, "but *un*nathral bastes, you see, that they keep up in the Park beyant."

"And what would they be at all?" says Jim.

"Och, the quarest outlandish craythurs ye iver seen," says Mike, "and all belongin' to the gintleman that employs me; and indeed a pleasant life I have, dhrivin' all day;—indeed, it's a'most as good as a gintleman's, only I sit an a cart instead of being sayted in a Cabrowley."

"And what do you call them at all?" asked the inquisitive Jim.

"They call themselves the Sorrow-logical Sisiety, and indeed some o' them is black lookin' enough, but others o' them is as merry as if they worn't belongin' to a Sorrowlogical Sisiety, at all at all."

"And what is it y'r dhrivin' now?" asked Jim.

"Indeed an' it's a wild boar," says Mike.

"And is he like a nath'ral boar?" says Jim.

"Faix myself doesn't know for I never seen him, bekase while they wor ketchin' him and putting him in the cart, the masther sint me for to ordher gingerbread nuts for the monkeys."

"Oh, queen iv heaven, an' is it gingerbread nuts they eat!" says Jim in amazement.

"Throth an' it is," says Mike;—"they get gingerbread nuts, when the hazels is not in sayson; and sure I hear, in their own counthry, the gingerbread grows nath'ral."

"Blur an' ouns do you tell me so?" says Jim.

"Divil a lie in it," says Mike.

"And where would that be at all?" says Jim.

"Undher the line I hear them say."

"And where's that?" says Jim.

"Oh, thin don't you know that, you poor ignorant craythur says Mike; "sure that's in the north of Amerikay, where the Hot-in-pots lives."

"Ah you thief," says Jim, "you didn't know that yourself wanst; but you're pickin' up larnin' in your new place."

"Indeed and I always knew that," says Mike; "and sure you never seen a monkey yet that they hadn't a line for him to run up and down, accordin' to the nathur o' the beast."

"Well I give up to you as for the monkeys, but as I never seen a wild boar yet, don't be ill-nathured to an owld frind but let me have a peep at him Mike, *agrah!*"

"Throth an' I will, and welkim," says Mike; "just get up behind there, and rise the lid of the cart."

Jim did as he was desired; and the moment the lid of the cart was raised, so far from the sense of seeing being gratified in the explorer, according to his own account, "he thought the sight id lave his eyes when he seen all as one as two coals o' fire looking at him, and the unnath'ral brustly divil making a dart at him, that it was the marcy o' hivin didn't take the life iv him."

Jim was sent heels over head into the mud, by the Boar brushing by him in plunging out of the cart, and preferring the "pedestrian to the vehicular mode," as Domine Sampson says, the foreigner, again in freedom, charged down Barrack Street in all the glory of liberty regained. Now Barrack Street as its name implies, being in the neighbourhood of the garrison, it may be supposed is much more populous than the street of Bilboa, where the Boar made his first appearance in public; and in fulfilment of the adage, "The more the merrier," the consternation was in proportion to the numbers engaged. Apple-stands, stalls of gilt gingerbread, baskets of oysters, and still more unlucky eggs (for the Boar, like many, was one of those ignorant people who don't know the difference between an egg and an oyster), were upset with the utmost impartiality; and ere he had arrived at Queen's Bridge, full five hundred pursuers, with ten times the number of all sorts of the most elaborate curses upon him, were at his heels. Were I to give a "full and account" of the chase, the far-famed Kilruddery hunt would be nothing to it; suffice it to say, he never cried "stop" until he arrived at the Meath Hospital, a run of about a mile and a half. There, his flank being turned he was driven into a court, where he held his pursuers at bay for some time, as in the Bilboa affair, until a Paddy, more experienced than his neighbours in the taming of unruly cattle, flung his frize coat over the head of the fugitive, and finally with some help, secured him.

I shall not enter into the particulars of how he was, at last, installed in the gardens,—of how the zoologists triumphed in their new acquisition,—of the vote of thanks passed to Mrs——for her *liberality* in getting rid of a nuisance,—nor of the admiration which he excited in the visiters of the garden, until his demolition of three breadths of a silk gown, and his eating a reticule containing a bunch of keys belonging to a worthy burgess's wife who approached too near the piggery, rendered future admirers more cautious. Indeed, at length, the gentleman became so unruly, that a large placard, readable a mile and a half off, bearing the one significant word, DANGEROUS, was put up over his domicile. The intractability of the beast amounted to such a pitch, that the gallantry universally existing, even in the brute species, from the male to the female, was not to be found in our hero; for a tame female of his kind was introduced into his den, with a view to improving the race of pigs in Ireland, and, as one of the professors (an amateur in pigs) declared, for the purpose of enabling the Hibernian market to compete in some time with Westphalia, in the article of ham—of which the projector of this scheme was particularly fond; but the lady that it as intended should have the honour of introducing the aristocratic Spanish blood into the race of *Paddy* pigs, was so worried by her intended lord and master, that she was obliged to be withdrawn, and as it has frequently happened before, to the mortification of matchmakers—the affair was broken off.

In the mean time, the Boar became more and more mischievous. It was then that Mrs——was waited upon again by the zoologist, who wheedled her out of her darling, and was requested to take back her gift; but Mrs——knew a trick worth two of that, and said she had been so convinced by the professor's former arguments, that the garden was the only place for him, she could not think of depriving the public of such an inestimable benefit.

The professor hinted a second vote of thanks; but it would not do, and Mrs——declared she was perfectly content with the first.

So the Society's bad bargain remained on their hands, and the Westphalia project failed.

Why it did so, was never cleared up to the satisfaction of the learned; but Mike, who sometimes "took a turn at feedin' the bastes," had his own little solution of the mystery—very *unscientific*, I dare say, but appearing quite natural to such poor ignorant creatures as his confidential friends, to whom he revealed it under the seal of solemn secrecy, they being all "book-sworn never to tell it to man or mortyal," for fear of Mike losing his place. But Mike darkly insinuates to these his companions, with as many queer grimaces as one of his own monkeys, and a knowing wink, and a tone almost sufficiently soft for a love secret—that, "by the powdhers o' war, accordin' to his simple idays, the divil a bit of the *Boar* but's a *Sow*."

So much, gentle reader, for Spanish *boars* and Irish *bulls*.

# LITTLE FAIRLY

> The world was very guilty of such a ballad some three ages since; but, I think, now 'tis not to be found—
> I will have the subject newly writ o'er, that I may example my digression by some mighty precedent.
>
> LOVE'S LABOUR'S LOST.

THE WORDS GREAT AND LITTLE are sometimes contradictory terms to their own meaning. This is stating the case rather confusedly, but is I am an Irishman, and writing an Irish story, it is the more in character. I might do perhaps, like a very clever and agreeable friend of mine, who, when he deals in some extravagance which you don't quite understand, says, "Well, you know what I mean," But I will not take that for granted, so what I mean is this—that your great man, as far as size is concerned, is often a nobody; and your little man is often a *great* man. Nature, as far as the human race is concerned, is at variance with Art, which generally couples greatness with size. The pyramids, the temple of Jupiter Olympius, St Peter's, and St Paul's, are vast in their dimensions, and the heroes of Painting and Sculpture are always on a grand scale. In Language, the *diminutive* is indicative of *endearment*—in Nature, it appears to me, it is the type of distinction. Alexander, Cæsar, Napoleon, Wellington, &c. &c. (for I have not room to detail) are instances. But do we not hear every day that "such-a-body is a big booby," while "*a clever little fellow*" has almost passed into a proverb. The poets have been more true to nature than painters, in this particular, and in her own divine art, her happiest votaries have been living evidences of her predilection to "packing her choicest goods in small parcels." Pope was "a crooked little thing that asked questions," and in our own days, our own "little Moore" is a glorious testimony to the fact. The works of fiction abound with instances, that the author does not consider it necessary his hero shall be an eligible candidate for the "grenadier corps;" the earlier works of fiction in particular: Fairy tales, universally, dedicate some *giant* to destruction at the hands of some "clever little fellow." "Tom Thumb," "Jack and the Bean Stalk," and fifty other such for instance, and I am now going to add another to the list, a brilliant example I trust, of the unfailing rule, that your little man is always a *great* man.

If any gentleman six feet two inches high, gets angry at reading this, I beg him to remember that I am a little man myself, and if he be a person of sense (which is supposing a great deal), he will pardon, from his own feeling of indignation at this *exposé* of Patagonian inferiority, the consequent triumph on my part, of Lilliputian distinction. If however, his inches get the better of him, and he should call me out, I beg of him to remember again, that I have the advantage of him there too, in being a little man. There is a proverb also, that "*little* said is soon mended," and with all my preaching, I fear I have been forgetting the wholesome adage. So I shall conclude this little introduction, which I only thought a becoming flourish of trumpets for introducing my hero, by placing *Little Fairly* before my readers, and I hope they will not think, in the words of another adage, that I have given them *great* cry and *little* wool.

You see owld Fairly was a mighty dacent man that lived, as the story goes, out over the back o' the hills beyant there, and was a thrivin' man ever afther he married little Shan Ruadh's[1] daughther, and she was little, like her father before her, a dawnshee craythur, but mighty cute, and industhered a power always, and a fine wife she was to a sthrivin' man, up early and down late, and shure if she, was doin' nothin' else, the bit iv a stocking was never out iv her hand, and the knittin' needles goin' like mad. Well, sure they thruv like a flag or a bulrush, and the snuggest cabin in the counthry side was owld Fairly's. And, in due coorse she brought him a son, throth she lost no time about it either, for she was never given to loitherin', and he was the picthur o' the mother, the little ottomy that he was, as slim as a ferret and as red as a fox, but a hardy craythur. Well, owld Fairly didn't like the thoughts of havin' sitch a bit iv a brat for a son, and besides he thought he got on so well and prospered in the world with one wife, that by gor, he detarmined to improve his luck and get another. So with that, he ups and goes to one Doody, who had a big daughter—a whopper, by my sowl, throth she was the full of a door, and was called by the neighbours *garran more*[2], for in throth she was a garran, the dirty dhrop was in her, a nasty stag that never done a good turn for any one but herself; the long-sided jack that she was, but her father had a power o' money, and above a hundher head o' cattle, and divil a chick nor child he had but herself, so that she was a great catch for whoever could get her, as far as the fortin' wint; but throth the boys did not like the looks iv her, and let herself and her fortin' alone. Well, as I was sayin', owld Fairly ups and he goes to Doody and puts his *comether* an the girl, an faix she was glad to be ax'd, and so matthers was soon settled, and the ind of it was they wor married.

Now maybe it's axin' you'd be, how he could marry two wives at wanst; but I towld you before, it was long ago, in the good owld ancient times, whin a man could have plinty of every thing. So home he brought the dirty garran, and sorra long was she in the place whin she began to breed, (arrah, lave off and don't be laughin' now; I don't mane that at all,) whin she began to breed *ructions* in the fam'ly, and to kick up *antagions* from mornin' till night, and *put betune* owld Fairly and his first wife. Well, she had a son of her own soon, and he was a big boss iv a divil, like his mother—a great fat lob that had no life in him at all; and while the little daunshee craythur would laugh in your face and play wid you if you cherrup'd to him, or would amuse himself the craythur, crawlin' about the flure an playin' wid the sthraws, and atein' the gravel, the jewel,—the other bosthoon was roarin' from mornin' till night, barrin' he was crammed wid stirabout and dhrownded a'most wid milk. Well, up they grew, and the big chap turned out a *gommoch*, and the little chap was as knowin' as a jailor; and though the big mother was always puttin' up her lob to malthrate and abuse little Fairly, the dickins a one but the little chap used to sarcumvint him, and gev him no pace, but led him the life iv a dog wid the cunnin' thricks he played an him. Now, while all the neighbours a'most loved the ground that little Fairly throd on, they cudn't abide the garran more's foal, good, bad, or indifferent, and many's the sly *malavoguein'* he got behind a hedge, from one or another, when his mother or father wasn't near to purtect him, for owld Fairly was as great a fool about him as the mother, and would give him his eyes a'most to play marvels, while he didn't care three *thraneens* for the darlint little chap. And 'twas the one thing as long as he lived; and at last he fell sick, and sure many thought it was a judgment an him for his unnathrel doin's to his own flesh and blood, and the sayin' through the parish was, from one and all, "There's owld Fairly is obleeged *to take to his bed with the weight of his sins*." And sure enough off o' that same bed he never riz, but grew weaker and weaker every day, and sint for the priest to make his sowl, the wicked owld sinner, God forgive me for sayin' the word, and sure the priest done whatever he could for him; but afther the priest wint away he called his two wives beside his bed, and the two sons, and says he, "I'm goin' to lave yiz now," says he, "and sorry I am," says he, "for I'd rather stay in owld Ireland than go any where else," says he, "for a raison I have—heigh! heigh! heigh!—Oh, murther, this cough is smotherin' me, so it is. Oh, wurra! wurra! but it's sick and sore I am. Well, come here yiz both," says he to the women, "you wor good wives both o' ye; I have nothin' to say agin it—(Molly, don't forget the whate is to be winny'd the first fine day)—and ready you wor to make and to mind—(Judy, there's a hole in the foot of my left stockin'), and——"

"Don't be thinkin' o' your footin' here," says little Judy, the knowledgable craythur, as she was, "but endayvour to make your footin' in heaven," says she, "mavourneen."

"Don't put in your prate 'till you're ax'd," says the owld savage, no ways obleeged that his trusty little owld woman was wantin' to give him a helpin' hand tow'rds puttin' his poor sinful sowl in the way o' glory.

"Lord look down an you!" says she.

"Tuck the blanket round my feet," says he, "for I'm gettin' very cowld."

So the big owld hag of a wife tucked the blankets round him.

"Ah, you were always a comfort to me," says owld Fairly.

"Well, remember my son for that same," says she, "for it's time I think you'd be dividin' what you have bechuxt uz," says she.

"Well, I suppose I must do it at last," says the owld chap, "though, hegh! hegh! hegh! Oh this thievin' cough—though it's hard to be obleeged to lave one's hard airnins and comforts this a-way," says he, the unfort'nate owld thief, thinkin' o' this world instead of his own poor sinful sowl.

"Come here big Fairly," says he, "my own bully boy, that's not a starved poor ferret, but worth while lookin' at. I lave you this house," says he.

"Ha!" says the big owld sthrap, makin' a face over the bed at the poor little woman that was cryin' the craythur, although the owld villian was usin' her so bad.

"And I lave you all my farms," says he.

"Ha!" says the big owld sthreel again.

"And my farmin' *ingraydients*," says he.

"Ha!" says she again, takin' a pinch o' snuff.

"And *all* my cattle," says he.

"Did you hear that, ma'am?" says the garran more, stickin' her arms a kimbo, and lookin' as if she was goin' to bate the woman.

"All my cattle," says the owld fellow, "every head," says he, "barrin' one, and that one is for that poor scaldcrow there," says he, "little Fairly."

"And is it only one you lave my poor boy?" says the poor little woman.

"If you say much," says the owld dyin' vagabone, "the divil resave the taste of any thing I'll lave him or you," says he.

"Don't say divil, darlin'."

"Howld your prate I tell you, and listen to me. I say, you little Fairly."

"Well, daddy," says the little chap.

"Go over to that corner cupboard," says he, "and in the top shelf," says he, "in the bottom of a crack'd taypot, you'll find a piece of an owld rag, and bring it here to me."

With that little Fairly went to do as he was bid, but he could not reach up so high as the corner cupboard, and he run into the next room for a stool to stand upon to come at the crack'd taypot, and he got the owld piece iv a rag and brought it to his father.

"Open it," says the father.

"I have it open now," says little Fairly.

"What's in it?" says the owld boy.

"Six shillin's in silver, and three farthin's," says little Fairly.

"That was your mother's fortune," says the father, "and I'm goin' to behave like the hoighth of a gentleman, as I am," says he; "I'll give you your mother's fortune," says he, "and I hope you won't squandher it," says he, "the way that every blackguard now thinks he has a right to squandher any decent man's money he is the heir to," says he, "but be careful of it," says he, "as I was, for I never touched a rap iv it, but let it lie gotherin' in that taypot, ever since the day I got it from Shan Ruadh, the day we sthruck the bargain about Judy, over beyant at the 'Cat and Bagbipes,' comin' from the fair; and I lave you that *six* shillings, and *five* stone o' mouldy oats that's no use to me, and *four* broken plates, and that *three*-legged stool you stood upon to get at the cupboard, you poor *nharrough* that you are, and the *two* spoons without handles, and the *one* cow that's gone back of her milk."

"What use is the cow daddy," says little Fairly, "widout land to feed her an?"

"Maybe it's land you want, you pinkeen," says the big brother.

"Right my bully boy," says the mother, "stand up for your own."

"Well, well," says the owld chap, "I tell you what, big Fairly," says he, "you may as well do a dacent turn for the little chap, and give him grass for his cow. I lave you all the land," says he, "but you'll never miss grass for one cow," says he, "and you'll have the satisfaction of bein' bountiful to your little brother, bad cess to him for a starved hound as he is."

But, to make a long story short, the owld chap soon had the puff out iv him; and whin the wake was over, and that they put him out to grass—laid him asleep, snug, with a *daisy quilt over him*—throth that minit the poor little woman and her *little offsprig* was turned out body and bones, and forced to seek shelter any way they could.

Well, little Fairly was a cute chap, and so he made a little snug place out of the back iv a ditch, and wid moss and rishes and laves and brambles, made his ould mother snug enough, antil he got a little mud cabin built for her, and the cow gev them milk, and the craythurs got on purty well, antil the big dirty vagabone of a brother began to grudge the cow the bit o' grass, and he ups and says he to little Fairly one day, "What's the raison," says he, "your cow does be threspassin' an my fields?" say he.

"Sure and wasn't it the last dyin' words o' my father to you," says little Fairly, "that you would let me have grass for my cow?"

"I don't remember it," says big Fairly—the dirty naygur, who was put up to it all, by the garran more, his mother.

"Yiv a short memory," says little Fairly.

"Yis, but I've a long stick," says the big chap, shakin' it at him at the same time, "and I'd rekimmind you to keep a civil tongue in your head," says he.

"You're mighty ready to bate your little brother, but would you fight your match?" says little Fairly.

"Match or no match," says big Fairly, "I'll brake your bones if you give me more o' your prate," says he; "and I tell you again, don't let your cow be threspassin' an my land, or I warn you that you'll be sorry," and off he wint.

"Well, little Fairly kept never mindin' him, and brought his cow to graze every day on big Fairly's land; and the big fellow used to come and *hish* her off the land, but the cow was as little and cute as her masther—she was a Kerry cow, and there's a power o' cuteness comes out o' Kerry. Well, as I was sayin', the cow used to go off as *quite* as a lamb; but the minit the big bosthoon used to turn his back, *whoo!* my jewel, she used to leap the ditch as clever as a hunther, and back wid her again to graze, and faix good use she made of her time, for she got brave and hearty, and gev a power o' milk, though she was goin' back of it shortly before, but there was a blessin' over Fairly, and all belongin' to him, and all that he put his hand to thruv with him. Well, now I must tell you what big Fairly done—and the dirty turn it was; but the dirt was in him ever and always, and kind mother it was for him. Well, what did he do but he dug big pits all through the field where little Fairly's cow used to graze, and he covers them up with branches o' threes and sods, makin' it look fair and even, and all as one as the rest o' the field, and with that he goes to little Fairly, and says he, "I tould you before," says he, "not to be sendin' your little blackguard cow to threspass on my fields," says he, "and mind I tell you now, that it won't be good for her health to let go there again, for I tell you she'll come to harm, and it's dead she'll be before long."

"Well, she may as well die one way as another," says little Fairly, "for sure if she doesn't get grass she must die, and I tell you again, divil an off your land I'll take my cow."

"Can't you let your dirty cow graze along the road side?" says big Fairly.

"Why then do you think," says little Fairly, answering him mighty smart, "do you think I have so little respect for my father's cow as to turn her out a beggar an the road to get her dinner off the common highway? throth I'll do no sitch thing."

"Well, you'll soon see the end iv it," says big Fairly, and off he wint in great delight, thinkin' how poor little Fairly's cow would be killed. And now wasn't he the dirty, threacherous, black-hearted villain, to take advantage of a poor cow, and lay a thrap for the dumb baste?—but whin the dirty dhrop is in, it must come out. Well, poor Fairly sent his cow to graze next mornin', but the poor little darlin' craythur fell into one o' the pits and was kilt; and when little Fairly kem for her in the evenin' there she was cowld and stiff, and all he had to do now was to sing *drimmin dhu dheelish* over her, and dhrag her home as well as he could, wid the help of some neighbours that pitied the craythur, and cursed the big bosthoon that done such a threacherous turn.

Well, little Fairly was the fellow to put the best face upon every thing; and so, instead of givin' in to fret, and makin' lamentations that would do him no good, by dad he began to think how he could make the best of what happened, and the little craythur sharpened a knife immediantly and began to shkin the cow, "and anyhow," says he, "the cow is good mate, and my ould mother and me 'ill have beef for the winther."

"Thrue for you little Fairly," said one of the neighbours waas helpin' him, "and besides, the hide 'ill be good to make soles for your brogues for many a long day."

"Oh, I'll do betther with the hide nor that," says little Fairly.

"Why what better can you do nor that wid it?" says the neighbour.

"Oh, I know myself," says little Fairly, for he was as cute as a fox as I said before, and wouldn't tell his saycrets to a stone wall, let alone a companion. And what do you think he done with the hide? Guess now—throth I'd let you guess from this to Christmas, and you'd never come inside it. Faix it was the complatest thing ever you heerd. What would you think but he tuk the hide and cut six little holes an partic'lar places he knew av himself, and thin he goes and he gets his mother's fortin, the six shillin's I tould you about, and he hides the six shillin's in the six holes, and away he wint to a fair was convenient, about three days afther, where there was a great sight o' people, and a power o' sellin' and buyin', and dhrinkin' and fightin', by course, *and why nat?*

Well, Fairly ups and he goes right into the very heart o' the fair, an' he spread out his hide to the greatest advantage, and he began to cry out (and by the same token, though he was little he had a mighty sharp voice, and could be hard farther nor a bigger man), well he began to cry out, "Who wants to buy a hide?—the *rale* hide—the ould original goolden bull's hide that kem from furrin parts,—who wants to make their fortin' now?"

"What do you ax for your hide?" says a man to him.

"Oh, I only want a thrifle for it," says Fairly, seein' I'm disthressed for money, at this present writin," says he, "and by fair or foul manes I must rise the money," says he, "at wanst, for if I could wait, it's not the thrifle I'm axin now I'd take for the hide."

"By gor you talk," says the man, "as if the hide was worth the King's ransom, and I'm thinkin' you must have a great want of a few shillin's," says he, "whin the hide is all you have to the fore, to dipind an."

"Oh, that's all *you* know about it," says Fairly, "shillin's indeed! by gor it's handfuls o' money the hide is worth. Who'll buy a hide—the rale goolden bull's hide!!!"

"What do you ax for your hide?" says another.

"Only a hundher guineas," says little Fairly.

"A hundher what?" says the man.

"A hundher guineas," says Fairly.

"Is it takin' lave of your siven small sinses you are?" says the man.

"Why thin indeed I b'lieve I am takin' lave o' my sinses sure enough," says Fairly, "to sell my hide so chape."

"Chape," says the man, "arrah thin listen to the little mad vagabone," says he to the crowd that was gother about by this time, "listen to him askin' a hundher guineas for a hide."

"Aye," says Fairly, "and the well laid out money it'ill be to whoever has the luck to buy it. This is none o' your common hides—it's the goolden bull's hide,—the Pope's goolden bull's hide, that kem from furrin parts, and it's a fortune to whoever 'ill have patience to bate his money out iv it."

"How do you mane?" says a snug ould chap, that was always poachin' about for bargains—"I never heard of batin' money out of a hide," says he.

"Well, then, I'll show you," says Fairly, "and only I'm disthressed for a hundher guineas, that I must have before Monday next," says he, "I wouldn't part wid this hide; for every day in the week you may thrash a fistful o' shillin's out iv it, if you take pains, as you may see." And wid that, my jew'l, he ups wid a cudgel he had in his hand, and he began leatherin' away at the hide; and he hits it *in the place he knew himself*, and out jump'd one o' the shillin's he hid there. "Hurroo!" says little Fairly, "darlint you wor, you never desaived me yet!!" and away he thrashed agin, and out jumped another shillin'. "That's your sort!" says Fairly, "the devil a sitch wages any o' yiz ever got for thrashin' as this"—and then another whack, and away wid another shillin'.

"Stop, stop!" says the ould cravin' chap, "I'll give you the money for the hide," says he, "if you'll let me see can I bate money out iv it." And wid that he began to thrash the hide, and, by course, another shillin' jumped out.

"Oh! its yourself has the rale twist in your elbow for it," says Fairly; "and I see by that same, that you're above the common, and desarvin' of my favour."

Well, my dear, at the word "*desarvin' o' my favour*," the people that was gother round, (for by this time all the fair a'most was there), began to look into the rights o' the thing, and, one and all, they agreed that little Fairly was one o' the '*good people*;' for if he wasn't a fairy, how could he do the like? and, besides, he was sitch a dawnshee craythur they thought what else could he be? and says they to themselves, "That ould divil, Mulligan, it's the likes iv him id have the luck iv it; and let alone all his gains in *this* world, and his scrapin and screwin, and it's the fairies themselves must come to help him, as if he wasn't rich enough before." Well, the ould chap paid down a hundher guineas in hard goold to little Fairly, and off he wint wid his bargain.

"The divil do you good wid it," says one, grudgin' it to him.

"What business has he wid a hide?" says another, jealous of the old fellow's luck.

"Why nat?" says another, "sure he'd shkin a flint any day, and why wouldn't he shkin a cow?"

Well, the owld codger wint home as plased as Punch wid his bargain; and indeed little Fairly had no raison not to be satisfied, for in throth, he got a good price for the hide, considherin' the markets wasn't so high thin as they are now, by rayson of the staymers, that makes *gintlemin av the pigs*, sendin' them an their thravels to furrin parts, so that a rasher o' bacon in poor Ireland is gettin' scarce even on a Aisther Sunday.[3]

You may be sure the poor owld mother of little Fairly was proud enough whin she seen him tumble out the hard goold an the table forninst her, and "my darlint you wor," says she, "an' how did you come by that sight o' goold?"

"I'll tell you another time," says little Fairly, "but you must set off to my brother's now, and ax him to lind me the loan av his scales."

"Why, what do you want wid a scales, honey?" says the owld mother.

"Oh! I'll tell you *that* another time too," says little Fairly; "but be aff now, and don't let the grass grow undher your feet."

Well, off wint the owld woman, and may be you'd want to know yourself what it was Fairly wanted wid the scales. Why, thin, he only wanted thim just for to make big Fairly curious about the matther that he might play him a thrick, as you'll see by-an-by.

Well, the little owld woman wasn't long in bringin' back the scales, and whin she gave them to little Fairly, "There, now," says he, "sit down beside the fire, and there's a new pipe for you and a quarther o' tobaccy, that I brought home for you from the fair, and do you make yourself comfortable," says he, "till I come back;" and out he wint and sat down behind a ditch, to watch if big Fairly was comin' to the house, for he thought the curosity o' the big gommoch and the garran more would make them come down to spy about the place, and see what he wanted wid the scales; and, sure enough, he wasn't there long when he seen them both crassin' a stile hardby, and in he jumped into the gripe o' the ditch, and run along under the shelter o' the back av it, and whipped into the house, and spread all his goold out an the table, and began to weigh it in the scales.

But he wasn't well in, whin the cord o' the latch was dhrawn, and in marched big Fairly, and the garran more, his mother, without "by your lave," or "God save you," for they had no breedin' at all[4]. Well, my jewel, the minit they clapped their eyes an the goold, you'd think the sight id lave their eyes; and indeed not only their eyes, let alone, but their tongues in their heads was no use to thim, for the divil a word either o' them could spake for beyant a good five minutes. So, all that time little Fairly kept never mindin' them, but wint an a weighin' the goold, as busy as a nailor, and at last, when the big brute kem to his speech, "Why thin," says he, "what's that I see you doin'?" says he.

"Oh, it's only divartin' myself I am," says little Fairly, "thryin' what woight o' goold I got for my goods at the fair," says he.

"Your goods indeed," says the big chap, "I suppose you robbed some honest man an the road, you little vagabone," says he.

"Oh, I'm too little to rob any one," says little Fairly. "I'm not a fine big able fellow, *like you*, to *do that same*." "Thin how did you come by the goold?" says the big savage. "I towld you before, by sellin' my goods," says the little fellow. "Why, what goods have *you*, you poor unsignified little brat?" says big Fairly, "you never had any thing but your poor beggarly cow, and she's dead."

"Throth then, she is dead; and more by token, 'twas yourself done for her complate, anyhow; and I'm behoulden to you for that same the longest day I have to live, for it was the makin' o' me. You wor ever and always *the good brother to me*; and never more than whin you killed my cow, for it's the makin' o' me. The divil a rap you see here I'd have had if my cow was alive, for I wint to the fair to sell her hide, brakin' my heart to think that it was only a poor hide I had to sell, and wishin' it was a cow was to the fore; but, my dear, whin I got there, there was no ind to the demand for hides, and the divil a one, good, bad, or indifferent, was there but my own, and there was any money for hides, and so I got a hundher guineas for it, and there they are."

"Why thin do you tell me so?" says the big chap. "Divil a lie in it," says little Fairly—"I got a hundher guineas for the hide. Oh, I wish I had another cow for you to kill for me,—throth would I!

"Come home mother," says big Fairly without sayin' another word, and away he wint home, and what do you think he done but he killed every individyal cow he had, and, "By gor," says he, "it's the rich man I'll be when I get a hundher guineas apiece for all their hides," and accordingly off he wint to the next fair, hardby, and he brought a car load o' hides, and began to call out in the fair, "Who wants the hides?—here's the chape hides—only a hundher guineas apiece!"

"Oh do you hear that vagabone that has the assurance to come chatin' the country again?" says some people that was convaynient, and that heerd o' the doin's at the other fair, and how the man was chated by a *sleeveen* vagabone—"and think of him, to have the impudence to come *here*, so nigh the place to take in *uz* now! But we'll be even wid him," says they; and so they went up to him, and says they to the thievin' rogue, "Honest man," says they, "what's that you have to sell?"

"Hides," says he.

"What do you ax for them?" says they.

"A hundher and ten guineas apiece," says he—for he was a greedy crathur, and thought he never could have enough.

"Why you riz the price on them since the last time," says they.

"Oh these are better," says big Fairly; "but I don't mind if I sell them for a hundher apiece, if you give me the money down," says he.

"*You shall be ped an the spot*," says they—and with that they fell on him, and thrash'd him like a *shafe*, till they didn't lave a *spark* o' sinse in him, and then they left him sayin', "*Are you ped now, my boy?*—faix you'll be a warnin' to all rogues for the futhur, how they come to fairs, chatin' honest min out o' their money, wid cock-and-bull stories about their hides;—but in throth I think your own hide isn't much the better of the tannin' it got to-day—faix an it was the rale *oak bark* was put to it, and that's the finest tan stuff in the world, and I think it'ill sarve you for the rest o' your life."—And with that they left him for dead.

But you may remark its hardher to kill a dirty noxious craythur than any thing good,—and so by big Fairly—he conthrived to get home, and his vagabone mother sawdhered him up afther a manner, and the minit he was come to his sthrenth at all, he detarmint to be revenged on little Fairly for what he had done, and so off he set to catch him while he'd be at brekquest, and he bowlted into the cabin wid a murtherin' shillely in his fist—and "Oh," says he, "you little mischievious miscrayant," says he, "what made you ruinate me by makin' me kill my cows?" says he.

"Sure I din't bid you kill your cows," says little Fairly—and that was all thrue, for you see, *there* was the cuteness o' the little chap, for he didn't *bid* him kill them sure enough, but he *let an* in that manner, that deludhered the big fool, and sure divil mind him.

"Yes you did bid me," says big Fairly, "or all as one as bid me, and I haven't a cow left, and my bones is bruk all along o' your little jackeen *manyeuvers*, you onlooky sprat that you are, but by this and that I'll have my revinge o' you now," and with that he fell an him and was goin' to murther poor little Fairly, only he run undher a stool, and kept tiggin' about from one place to th' other, that the big botch couldn't get a right offer at him at all at all, and at last the little owld mother got up to put a stop to the ruction, but if she did, my jew'l, it was the unlooky minit for her, for by dad she kem in for a chance tap o' the cudgel that big Fairly was weltin' away with, and you know there's an owld sayin, "a chance shot may kill the divil," and why not an owld woman?

Well, that put an end to the *skrimmage*, for the phillilew that little Fairly set up whin he seen his ould mother kilt, would ha' waked the dead, and the big chap got frekened himself, and says little Fairly, "By gor, if there's law to be had," says he, "and I think *I have* a chance o' justice, *now that I have money to spare*, and, if there's law in the land, I'll have you in the body o' the jail afore to-morrow," says he; and wid that the big chap got cowed, and wint off like a dog without his tail, and so poor little Fairly escaped bein' murthered that offer, and was left to cry over his mother, an' indeed the craythur was sorry enough, and he brought in the neighbours and gev the ould woman a dacent wake, and there was few pleasanther evenin's that night in the county than the same wake, for Fairly was mighty fond of his mother, and faix he done the thing ginteely by her, and good raison he had, for she was the good mother to him while she was alive, and by dad, by his own cuteness, he conthrived she should be the useful mother to him afther she was dead too. For what do you think he done? Oh! by the Piper o' Blessintown you'd never guess, if you wor guessin' from this to Saint Tib's eve, and that falls neither before nor afther Christmas we all know. Well, there's no use guessin', so I must tell you. You see the ould mother was a nurse to the Squire that lived hard by, and so, by coorse, she had a footin' in the house any day in the week she pleased, and used often to go over to see the Squire's childhre, for she was so fond o' them a'most as if she nursed *thim* too; and so what does Fairly do but he carried over the ould mother stiff as she was, and dhressed in her best, and he stole in, *unknownst*, into the Squire's garden, and he propped up the dead ould woman stan'in hardby a well was in the gardin, wid her face forninst the gate, and her back to the well, and wid that he wint into the house, and made out the childhre, and says he, "God save you, Masther Tommy," says he, "God save you, Masther Jimmy, Miss Matty, and Miss Molshee," says he, "an' I'm glad to see you well, and sure there's the old Mammy nurse come to see yiz, childhre," says he, "and she's down by the well in the garden, and she has gingerbread for yiz," says he, "and whoever o' yiz runs to her first 'ill get the most gingerbread; and I'd rekimmind yiz to lose no time but run a race and sthrive who'll win the gingerbread." Well, my dear, to be sure off set the young imps runnin' and screechin', "Here I am, mammy nurse, here I am," and they wor brakin' their necks a'most, to see who'd be there first, and wid that, they run wid sitch *voylence*, that the first o' thim run whack up agin the poor ould woman's corps, and threwn it over plump into the middle o' the well. To be sure the childhre was frekened, as well they might, and back agin they ran as fast as they kem, roarin' murdher, and they riz the house in no time, and little Fairly was among the first to go see what was the matther, (by the way) and he set up a *hullagone* my jewel that ud split the heart of a stone; and out kem the Squire and his wife, and "What's the matther?" says they. "Is it what's the matther?" says Fairly, "don't yiz see my lovely ould mother is dhrowned by these devil's imps o' childhre?" says he, "oh Masther Jimmy, is that the way you thrated the poor ould mammy nurse, to go dhrownd her like a *rot* afther that manner?" "Oh, the childhre didn't intind it," said the Squire. "I'm sorry for your mother, Fairly, but——"

"But what?" says little Fairly, "sorry—in throth and I'll make you sorry, for I'll rise the counthry or I'll get justice for sitch an unnath'ral murther; and whoever done it must go to jail, if it was even Miss Molshee herself."

Well the Squire did not like the matther to go to that, and so says he, "Oh, I'll make it worth your while to say nothing about it Fairly, and here's twenty goolden guineas for you," says he.

Why thin do you think me such a poor-blooded craythur, as to sell my darlin' ould mother's life for twenty guineas? No in throth, tho' if you wor to make it fifty I might be talkin' to you."

Well, the Squire thought it was a dear mornin's work, and that he had very little for his money in a dead ould woman, but sooner than have the childhre get into throuble and have the matther made *a blowin' horn* of, he gev him the fifty guineas, and the ould mother was dhried and waked over agin, so that she had greather respect ped to her than a Lord or a Lady. So you see what cleverness and a *janius* for cuteness does.

Well, away he whit home afther the ould woman was buried wid his fifty guineas snug in his pocket, and so he wint to big Fairly's to ax for the loan of the scales once more, and the brother ax'd him for what? "Oh, it's only a small thrifle more o' goold I have," says the little chap, "that I want to weigh."

"Is it *more* goold?" says big Fairly, "why it's a folly to talk, but you must be either a robber or a coiner to come by money so fast."

"Oh, this is only a thrifle I kem by at the death o' my mother," say little Fairly.

"Why bad luck to the rap *she* had to lave you, any way," says the big chap.

"I didn't say she left me a fortin," says little Fairly.

"You said you kem by the money by your mother's death," says the big brother.

"Well, an' that's thrue," says the little fellow, "an' I'll tell you how it was. You see, afther you killed her, I thought I might as well make the most I could of her, and says I to myself, faix and I had great good luck wid the cow he killed for me, and why wouldn't I get more for my mother nor a cow? and so away I wint to the town and I offered her to the docthor there, and he was greatly taken wid her, and by dad he wouldn't let me lave the house without sellin' her to him, and faix he gev me fifty guineas for her."

"Is it fifty guineas for a corps?"

"It's thruth I'm tellin' you, and was much obleeged into the bargain, and the raison is you see, that there's no sitch thing to be had for love or money, as a dead ould woman—there's no killin' them at all at all, so that a dead ould woman is quite a curosity."

"Well, there's the scales for you," says big Fairly, and away the little chap wint to weigh his goold (as he let on) as he did before. But what would you think, my dear—throth you'll hardly b'lieve me whin I tell you. Little Fairly hadn't well turned his back whin the big savage wint into the house where his ould mother was and tuck up a rapin' hook, and kilt her an the spot—divil a lie in it. Oh, no wondher you look cruked at the thoughts of it; but it's morially thrue,—faix he cut the life out iv her, and he detarmined to turn in his harvist for that same, as soon as he could, and so away he wint to the docthor in the town hard by, where little Fairly towld him he sowld *his* mother, and he knocked at the door and walked into the hall with a sack on his shouldher, and settin' down the sack, he said he wanted to spake to the docthor. Well, when the docthor kem, and heerd the vagabone talkin' of fifty guineas for an owld woman, he began to laugh at him; but whin he opened the sack and seen how the poor owld craythur was murthered, he set up a shout. "Oh, you vagabone," says he, "you sack-im up villain," says he, "you've Burked the woman," says he, "and now you come to *rape* the fruits o' your *murdher*." Well, the minit big Fairly heerd the word murdher, and *rapin'* the reward, he thought the docthor was up to the way of it, and he got frekened, and with that the docthor opened the hall-door and called the watch, but Fairly bruk loose from him, and ran away home; and when once he was gone, *the docthor thought there would be no use in rising a ruction* about it, and so he shut the door and never minded the police. Big Fairly to be sure, was so frekened, he never cried stop, antil he got clean outside the town, and with that, he first place he wint to was little Fairly's house, and, burstin' in the door, he said, in a tarin' passion, "What work is this you have been at now, you onlooky miscrayint?" says he.

"I haven't been at any work," says little Fairly, "See, yourself," says he, "*my sleeves is new*," says he, howldin' out the cuffs av his coat to him at the same time, to show him.

"Don't think to put me aff that-a-way with your little kimmeens, and your divartin' capers," says the big chap, "for I tell you I'm in airnest, and it's no jokin' matther it 'ill be to you, for, by this an' that, I'll have the life o' you, you little *spidhogue* of an abortion as you are, you made me kill my cows. Don't say a word, for you know it's thrue."

"I never made you kill your cows," says little Fairly, no ways danted by the fierce looks o' the big bosthoon.

"Whisht! you vagabone!" says the big chap. "You didn't bid me do it out o' the face, in plain words, but you made me sinsible."

"*Faix, an that was doin' a wondher*," says little Fairly, who couldn't help havin' the laugh at him though he was sore afeard.

"Bad luck to you you little sneerin' vagabone," says the big chap again, "I know what you mane you long-headed schkamer, that you are; but by my sowl, your capers 'ill soon be cut short, as you'll see to your host. But before I kill you, I'll show you to your face, the villian that you are, and it is no use your endayvourin' to consale your bad manners to me, for if you had a veil as thick as the shield of A—jax, which was made o' siv'n bull hides, it would not sarve for to cover the half o' your inni—quitties[5]."

"Whoo! that's the ould schoolmasther's speech you're puttin' an us now," says little Fairly, "and faith it's the only thing you iver larned, I b'lieve, from him."

"Yis, I larned how fine a thing it is to bate a little chap less than myself, and you'll see with a blessin', how good a scholar I am at that same; and you desarve it, for I towld you just now before you intherrupted me, how you made me kill all my cows, (and that was the sore loss,) and afther that whin you could do no more, you made me kill my mother, and divil a good it done me, but nigh hand got me into the watch-house; and so now I'm detarmint you won't play me any more thricks, for I'll hide you, snug, in the deepest bog-hole in the Bog of Allen, and if you throuble me afther that, faix I think it 'ill be the wondher;" and, with that he made a grab at the little chap, and while you'd be sayin' "thrap stick," he cotch him, and put him body and bones into a sack, and he threwn the sack over the back of a horse was at the door, and away he wint in a tarin' rage, straight for the Bog of Allen. Well, to be sure, he couldn't help stoppin' at a public-house, by the road-side, *for he was dhry with the rage*; an he tuk the sack where little Fairly was tied up, and he lifted it aff o' the horse, an' put it standin' up beside the door goin' into the public-house; an he wasn't well gone in, whin a farmer was comin' by too, and he was as dhry wid the dust, as ever big Fairly was with the rage, (an' indeed it's wondherful how aisy it is to make a man dhry;) and so, as he was goin' by he sthruck agin the sack that little Fairly was in, and little Fairly gev a groan that you'd think kem from the grave; and says he (from inside o' the sack), "God forgive you," says he.

"Who's there?" says the farmer startin', and no wondher.

"It's me," says little Fairly, "and may the Lord forgive you," says he, "for you have disturbed me, and I *half-way to heaven*."

"Why who are you at all?" says the farmer. "Are you a man?" says he.

"I am a man, now," says little Fairly, "though if you didn't disturb me I'd have been an angel of glory in less than no time," says he.

"How do you make that out, honest man?" says the farmer.

"I can't explain it to you," says little Fairly, "*for it's a mysthery*; but what I tell you is thruth," says he, "and I tell you that whoever is in this sack at this present," says he, "is as good as half way to heav'n, and indeed I thought I was there a'most, only you sthruck agin me, an disturbed me."

"An do you mar for to say," says the farmer, "that whoiver is in that sack will go to heaven?"

"Faix they are on their road there at all events," says little Fairly, "and if they lose their way, it's their own fault."

"Oh thin," says the farmer, "may be you'd let me get into the sack along wid you, for to go to heaven too."

"Oh, the horse that's to bring us *doesn't carry double*," says little Fairly.

"Well, will you let me get into the sack instead iv you?" says the farmer.

"Why thin, do you think I'd let any one take sitch a dirty advantage o' me as to go to heaven afore me?" says little Fairly.

"Oh, I'll make it worth your while," says the farmer.

"Why thin, will you ontie the sack," says little Fairly, "and just let me see who it is that has the impidince to ax me to do the like." And with that, the farmer ontied the sack, and little Fairly popped out his head. "Why thin, do you think," says he, "that a hangin'-bone lookin' thief *like you*, has a right to go to heaven afore me?"

"Oh," says the farmer, "I've been a wicked sinner in my time, and I havn't much longer to live; and to tell you the thruth, I'd be glad to get to heaven in that sack, if it's thrue what you tell me."

"Why," says little Fairly, "don't you know it is by *sackcloth and ashes* that the faithful see the light o' glory?"

"Thrue for you indeed," says the farmer. "Oh murther, let me get in there, and I'll make it worth your while."

"How do you make that out?" says little Fairly.

"Why, I'll give you five hundher guineas," says the farmer, "and I think that's a power o' money."

"But what's a power o' money compared to heaven?" says little Fairly; "and do you think I'd sell my sowl for five hundher guineas?"

"Well, there's five hundher more in an owld stockin' in the oak box, in the cabin by the crass-roads, at Dhrumsnookie, for I am owld Tims o' Dhrumsnookie, and you'll inherit all I have, if you consint."

"But what's a thousand guineas compared to heaven?" says little Fairly.

"Well, do you see all them heads o' cattle there?" says the farmer. "I have just dhruv them here from Ballinasloe," says he, "and every head o' cattle you see here, shall be your's also, if you let me into that sack that I may go to heaven instead o' you."

"Oh think o' my poor little sowl!" says Fairly.

"Tut man," says the farmer, "I've twice as big a sowl as you; and besides I'm owld, and you're young, and I have no time to spare, and you may get absolution aisy, and make your pace in good time."

"Well," says little Fairly, "I feel for you," says he, "an' I'm half inclined to let you overpersuade me to have your will o'me."

"That's a jewel," says the farmer.

"But make haste," says little Fairly, "for I don't know how soon you might get a refusal."

"Let me in at wanst," says the farmer. So, my dear Fairly got out, and the farmer got in, and the little chap tied him up; and says he to the farmer, "There will be great *norations* made agin you, all the way you're goin' along; and you'll hear o' your sins over and over agin, and you'll hear o' things you never done at all," says little Fairly, "but never say a word, or you won't go where I was goin'. Oh! why did let you persuade me?"

"Lord reward you!" says the poor farmer.

"And your conscience will be sthreckin' you all the time," says little Fairly; "and you'll think a'most it's a stick is sthrekin' you, but you mustn't let an, nor say a word, hut pray *inwardly* in the sack."

"I'll not forget," says the farmer.

"Oh! you'll be reminded of it," says Fairly, "for you've a bad conscience I know; and the seven deadly sins will be goin' your road, and keepin' you company, and every now and then they'll be *puttin' their comether* an you, and callin' you 'brother,' but don't let on to know them at all, for they'll be mislaydin' you, and just do you keep quite (quiet) and *you'll see the ind iv it.*" Well, just at that minit little Fairly heerd big Fairly comin', and away he run and hid inside iv a churn was dhryin' at the ind o' the house; and big Fairly lifted the sack was standin' at the door, and feelin' it more weighty nor it was before, he said, "Throth, I think you're growin' heavy with grief; but here goes any how," and, with that he hoist it up on the horse's back, an' away he wint to the bog iv Allen.

Now you see, big Fairly, like every blackguard that has the bad blood in him, the minit he had the sup o' dhrink in, the dirty turn kem out: and so, as he wint along he began to wollop the poor baste, and the sack where his little brother was (as he thought, the big fool), and to gibe, and jeer him for his divarshin. But the poor farmer did as little Fairly towld him, an' never a word he said at all, though he could not help roaring out every now and thin, whin he felt the soft ind of big Fairly's shillelah across his backbone; and sure the poor fool thought it was his bad conscience and the seven deadly sins was tazin' him; but he wouldn't answer a word for all that, though the big savage was *aggravatin'* him every fut o' the road antil they kem to the bog; and whin he had him there, faix he wasn't long in choosin' a bog hold for him—and, my jew'l, in he popped the poor farmer neck and heels, sack and all; and as the soft bog stuff and muddy wather closed over him, "I wish you a safe journey to the bottom, young man," says the big brute, grinnin' like a cat at a cheese, "and as clever a chap as you are, I don't think you'll come back out o' that in a hurry; and it's throubled I was wid you long enough, you little go-the-round schkamer, but I'll have a quiet life for the futhur." And wid that he got up an his horse, and away he wint home; but he had not gone over a mile, or there-away, whin who should he see but little Fairly mounted on the farmer's horse, dhrivin' the biggest dhrove o' black cattle you ever seen; and by dad, big Fairly grewn as white as a sheet whin he clapt his eyes an him, for he thought it was not himself at all was in it, but his ghost; and he was goin' to turn and gallop off, whin little Fairly called out to him to stay, for that he wanted to speak to him. So whin he seen it was himself, he wondhered to be sure, and small blame to him—and says he, "Well, as cute as I knew you wor, by gor, this last turn o' your's bates Bannagher—and how the divil are you here at all, whin I thought you wor cuttin' turf wid your sharp little nose, in the bog of Allen? for I'll take my affidowndavy, I put you into the deepest hole in it, head foremost, not half an hour agon."

"Throth you did sure enough," says little Fairly, "and you wor ever and always the good brother to me, as I often said before, but by dad you never done rightly for me antil to-day, but you made me up now in airnest."

"How do you mane?" says big Fairly.

"Why, do you see all this cattle here I'm dhrivin'?" says little Fairly.

"Yes I do, and whose cattle are they?"

"They're all my own—every head o' them."

"An' how did you come by them?"

"Why you see, when you threwn me into the boghole, I felt it mighty cowld at first, and it was mortial dark, and I felt myself goin' down and down, that I thought I'd never stop sinking, and wondhered if there was any bottom to it at all, and at last I began to feel it growin' warm, and pleasant, and light, and whin I kem to the bottom there was the loveliest green field you ever clapped your eyes on, and thousands upon thousands o' cattle feedin', and the grass so heavy that they wor up to their ears in it—it's thruth I'm tellin' you—O divil sitch meadows I ever seen, and when I kem to myself, for indeed I was rather surprised, and thought it was dhramin' I was—whin I kem to myself, I was welkim'd by a very ginteel spoken little man, the dawnshiest craythur you ever seen, by dad I'd have made six iv him myself, and says he, 'You're welkim to the undher story o' the Bog iv Allen, Fairly.' 'Thank you kindly, sir, says I.—'And how is all wid you?' says he.—'Hearty indeed,' says I. 'And what brought you here?' says he.—'My big brother,' says I. 'That was very good iv him,' says he.—'Thrue for you, sir,' says I. 'He is always doin' me a good turn,' says I. 'Oh then he never done you half so good a turn as this,' says he; 'for you'll be the richest man in Ireland soon.' 'Thank you sir,' says I; 'but I don't see how.' 'Do you see all them cattle grazin' there?' says he. 'To be sure I do,' says I. 'Well,' says he, 'take as many o' them as your heart desires, and bring them home wid you.' 'Why sure,' says I, 'how could I get back myself, up out of the boghole, let alone dhraggin' bullocks afther me?' 'Oh,' says he, 'the way is aisy enough, for you have nothin' to do but dhrive them out the back way over there,' says he, pointin' to a gate. And sure enough, my darlint, I got all the bastes you see here, and dhruv them out, and here

I am goin' home wid 'em, and maybe I won't be the rich man—av coorse I gev the best o' thanks to the little owld man, and gev him the hoighth o' good language for his behavor. And with that says he, 'You may come back again, and take the rest o' them,' says he—and faix sure enough I'll go back the minit I get these bastes home, and have another turn out o' the boghole."

"Faix and I'll be beforehand wid you," says big Fairly.

"Oh but you shan't," says little Fairly; "it was I discovered the place, and why shouldn't I have the good iv it?"

"You greedy little hound," says the big fellow, "I'll have my share o' them as well as you." And with that he turned about his horse, and away he galloped to the boghole, and the little fellow galloped afther him, purtendin' to be in a desperate fright afeard the other would get there first, and he cried 'Stop the robber,' afther him, and whin he came to the soft place in the bog they both lit, and little Fairly got before the big fellow, and purtended to be makin' for the boghole in a powerful hurry, cryin' out as he passed him, "I'll win the day! I'll win the day!" and the big fellow pulled fut afther him as hard as he could, and hardly a puff left in him he run to that degree, and he was afeared that little Fairly would bate him and get all the cattle, and he was wishin' for a gun that he might shoot him, whin the cute little divil, just as he kem close to the edge o' the hoghole, *let an* that his fut slipped and he fell down, cryin' out, "Fair play! fair play!—wait till I rise!" but the words wasn't well out of his mouth when the big fellow kem up. "Oh, the divil a wait," says he, and he made one desperate dart at the and jumped into the middle of it. "Hurroo!" says little Fairly, gettin' an his legs agin and runnin' over to the edge o' the boghole, and just as he seen the great splaw feet o' the big savage sinkin' into the sludge, he called afther him, and says he, "I say, big Fairly, don't take all the cattle, but lave a thrifle for me. *I'll wait however, till you come back*," says the little rogue laughin' at his own cute conthrivance, "and I think now I'll lade a quiet life," says he; and with that he wint home, and from that day out he grewn richer and richer every day, and was the greatest man in the whole counthry side; and all the neighbours gev in to him that he was the most knowledgable man in thim parts, but they all thought it was quare that his name should be *Fairly*, for it was agreed one and all, *that he was the biggest rogue out*,—barrin' Balfe, the robber.

1. Red John.
2. Big horse.
3. On Easter Sunday, in Ireland, whoever is not proscribed by the dire edicts of poverty, from the indulgence, has a morsel of meat on Easter Sunday, as a *bonne bouche* after the severe fasting in Lent, enjoined by the Roman Catholic Church.
4. Good manners.
5. A lady assured me of this as the genuine speech of a hedge schoolmaster.

# JUDY OF ROUNDWOOD[1]

Here will be an old abusing of God's patience and the King's English

SHAKSPEARE.

THERE IS A LITTLE STRAGGLING village in Wicklow, named Roundwood, which is a sort of outpost to the many beauties of that romantic and lovely county, and consequently, often made a stopping place by those ramblers who can steal a day or two from toil and care, and have the dust of Dublin blown from about them by the mountain breezes of the alpine county I have named. I, for one, confess the enormity of having eaten eggs and bacon in the little inn of Roundwood, served to me by the hand of Judy;—her surname has never reached me, for as the Italians called many of their celebrated painters after the towns or cities that gave them birth, so Judy has been named, "Judy of Roundwood."

Her principal peculiarity was stinting every word she could of its fair proportion, whether from any spite she had against the alphabet, or from wishing to clear her sex from the charge of overwordiness, I know not; but Judy talked shorthand, if an Irishman may be allowed the phrase. Her merits in this particular cannot be appreciated in modern times, but Judy would have been a darling among the Spartans.

At the door of the inn, which owed much of its custom to this original, Judy would salute the weary traveller with a low courtesy, crossing her hands before her upon her chequered apron, and say, "Consola to the gent"—meaning thereby consolation to the gentleman—Judy considering refreshment the greatest *consola*—the *gents* could have. Whisky she called by the poetical name of "Temptation"—abbreviated of course to "*Timpta*."—Dublin was either familiarly *Dub*;—or *dubbed* with the more high sounding title of *Metrop*—and being also given to rhyming, whenever a tag was to be made, she jumped at it.

When first I visited Judy in company with a friend who was equally anxious with myself to draw her out, we affected not to comprehend the meaning of all her abbreviations, with a view to force her upon an explanation; and she said—"You see, sir, Ju deals in *abrevia*—because that is the *perfec* of the *English lang.*—*din*, for dinner; *brek*, for breakfast; *rel*, for relish. Ju's *conversa* is *allegor*. I calls the dinner *satisfac*, and the drop o' comfort the *timpta*; and this little *apart* where we give *consola* to the *gents*, I call the bower of *hap*."

After having had some rustic refreshment, we ordered whisky, and when Judy brought it to us, her look and manner were highly amusing. With a stealthy step and an air of mock mystery she stole across the room towards us, and withdrawing her apron with one hand, from over the measure of spirits she held in the other, she said—"Ju was only throwing an *obscu* over the *opportu*." We then noticed to her some verses that were written on the walls of the apartment in her praise. "That's the rayson I call it the bower of *hap*," said she; "but sure I'm not such an *ignora* as to believe all the *flat* of the *cits*. Good bye, dear; yiz are gay gents goin' round the world for sport; may you never be wretched; may you share in the wisdom of *Sol*; may you never have to climb the rocks of *dif*; or be cast on the quicksands of *adver*, or stray from the paths of *vir*."

But perhaps the best thing I can do to put Judy more completely *en evidence* is, to give a conversation in her own style; that will serve, as Judy herself would say, as the best *exemplifica*.

*Consola* to the gents; happy to see you, dear! Walk in—you can sit in the bower of *hap*. If you want your *brek*, it's a good one you may *expec*; if you want your *din*, this is the place to walk *in*; and Ju will give you the *opportu*, the *consola*, and the *materia*, and the *timpta*; and if you only want a *rel*, ring the *bell*. That's what I said the other day to O'Toole; the ignorant people calls him, Mr O'Toole, but he's not *Misther* O'Toole, but O'Toole, bein' descinded from King O'Toole of these parts. Good morrow, Judy, says he.—Thank you, kindly, sir, says I. Here's a gent that is come to see you, says he, (for there was an artless sprisan along wid him). Kindly welkim, sir, says I.—You'll do all you can for us, says he.—Sir, says I, *Fidel* is my *mot*—Ju's mot—The furriners calls it *Judy's mot*—that's French, sir;—but, as I said, *fidel* is my mot:

Submissive to my supayriors,
Condescending to my infayriors,
Faithful to my frinds,
Charitable to my inimies.

You had a great party here the other day, as I'm towld, says he.—Yis, sir, says I.—Who wor they? says he.—Indeed, says I, they did not indulge me with much *communica*; so I could not come to a *conclu*;—but though I could not be *pos*, I had my *suspish*.—And who wor they? says he.—They were no less than Sir *Wal* and Miss *Edge*.—Who are *they*? says O'Toole's friend, for he was mighty artless.—Why, then, don't you know Sir *Wal*, says I,—and Miss *Edge*?—I hope you admire my *abrevia*, says I.—Certainly, says O'Toole, who was plased with me about my *obscu*, for the *bothera* of the innocent gent, and he could hardly help laughin' at him, and to hide his laughin' he took a pinch o' snuff: and he, bein' a rale *gintlernan*, av coorse liked the *blackguard*[2]; and so takin' out his box, he said, like a rale gintleman, Judy, says he, will you have a pinch?—Thank you, sir, says I, for the *condescen*,—and with that his friend, not likin' to be worse nor another, said, Maybe you'll take a pinch from me, says he—handin' me a box of the dirty soft wet thrash them furrinners takes, sure there's no good in any thing or anybody that isn't always *dhry*, as I says to the *gents* from *Dub*, when I keeps continually bringin' them the whisky and the hot wather.—Well, to come back to my story, the two handed me their boxes—and so O'Toole said, says he, Which will you have, Judy?—take whatever you plaze;—which do you like, the common snuff, or the scented snuff?—Sir, says I—making a low curtshee for the *civil*—I give the *com* the *pref*.—But I was forgettin' about Sir *Wal* and Miss *Edge*. Sure, they kem here to take the *opportu* to see *Ju*, to incrase their *admira* for the beauties of *na*—in the county *Wick* in *partic*—and so when they arrived in

A post chay
From "Quin Bray,"

I was ready to give *consola* to the gents; and they asked for *brek*.—What do you *expec*? says I.

Coffee, says he.
Cushlamachree,

says I, there's no sitch thing here, at all at all. There is neither coffee tay, nor chocolaritee tay; but there is the best of Bohay, says I.—Have you no green? says he.—Plenty in the fields, says I. But no where else?—But I'll make up for the *defish*. How? says he.—I'll give you a *rel*,—says I.—What's that? says he.—A *rash*, says I.—I don't know what you mane, says he,—so I was obleeged to explain:—A relish, or a rasher, says I; for the *artif* of my *abrevia* was beyond his *conjec*.—Bring it in at wanst, says he.—So, no sooner said than done—but you see I was obleeged to bring in the rasher an a cracked plate—and very well I had it—for Roundwood was mighty throng that mornin'—loads of gents—barrowfuls o' gents from *Dub* to see *Ju*—coming into the county *Wick* with a short *stick* to enjoy the *admira* of the beauties of *na*—Well, as I said, I brought in the *rash* an a cracked plate, and Sir Wal was *indig*; and, says he, How dar you bring the like to a dacent man?—And what do you think I said? says I, the *necess* is my *apol*. I thought he'd split himself wid the laughin'—So with that he wint to reading the po'thry an the walls; and at last he kem to one that a young *vag*—from the *Col*—the *Univer*—*Trin. Coll. Dub*, wrote an me,—and I put my hand over it;—Don't read that, sir, says I—for I purtended not to know who he was, though I knew very well all the time:—don't read that, says I.—Why? says he.—Because, says I, 'twas written by a *vulga*, and 'twould shock your *sinsibil*, if any thing came under your *contempla* bordering on the *indel*.

Then, says Miss Edge, that's very proper of you, Ju, says she.—Yis, ma'am, says I. I was always a *Dia*; for I have had a good *educa*.

How could *you* have a good education? says *Sir Wal*.

Bekase the gintlemin o' larnin comes to see Ju; and where would I larn *educa*, says I, if not from them?

Why what gintlemen o' larnin' comes here? says *Sir Wal*.

*More than owns to it, says I.*—lookin' mighty signified at him.

Indeed! says he.—Yis, says I—and one o' the gintlemin was no *gintleman*, he was only a *vag*; for he put me in a *mag*;—but in gineral they are the rale quolity, and I know a power o' them.

Name one, says he.

T. M. says I.

Who's T. M.? says he.

You're mighty ignorant, says I to *Sir Wal*. Wasn't that a good thing to say to him? I thought *Miss Edge* and he would die with the laughin.'

Well, but who is T. M.? says he.

Tom Moore, says I, the glory of Ireland, says I, crassin' myself.

Oh, Moore the poet, says *Sir Wal*.

By dad he's no poet at all, says I; but a rale gintleman; for he gev me half a crown.

Well, I thought the both o' them would die with the laughin'; and so when they wor goin', says I to the lady, Good mornin' and many thanks to you, ma'am, says I, for your *condescen*—long may you reign, says I, Miss *Edge*. Well, she looked mightily susprised at me; for you see I had a *conjec* who they wor from the sarvants, by a way o' my own.

You've taken the *worth* out of my name, Judy, says she, mighty goodnathured.

Throth then, that's more nor I could do, ma'am, says I; for there's more worth in the half o' your name than in the whole o' mine, though I *am* Judy O'Roundwood.

Well, with that *Sir Wal* laughed out; and, says he, How did you find the lady out? says he.

Only by *supposish*, says I; for I wouldn't be guilty of *infidel* to the sarvants who let on to me.

Then I suppose you found out who *I* am too, says *Sir Wal*.

No indeed sir, says I, how could I *know* the Great *Un*?

Oh, I wish you seen the look he gave when I said that!

1. This sketch was originally written for Mr J. Russel, who gave it, with an admirable personation of Judy, in his very clever entertainment of "The Standard Actor."
2. Lundy Foot's celebrated snuff.

THE END

## Also available in the Nonsuch Classics series

| | | |
|---|---|---|
| Balzac, Honoré de | *At the Sign of the Cat and Racket* | 1 84588 051 X |
| Balzac, Honoré de | *The Seamy Side of History* | 1 84588 052 8 |
| Beckford, William | *Vathek* | 1 84588 060 9 |
| Bede, Cuthbert , B.A. | *Mr Verdant Green* | 1 84588 197 4 |
| Caldwell, Anne Marsh | *Chronicles of Dartmoor* | 1 84588 071 4 |
| Caldwell, Anne Marsh | *Two Old Men's Tales* | 1 84588 081 1 |
| Clarke, William | *Three Courses and a Dessert* | 1 84588 072 2 |
| Clarke, Marcus | *For the Term of His Natural Life* | 1 84588 082 X |
| Clarke, Percy | *Three Diggers* | 1 84588 084 6 |
| Cooper, James Fenimore | *The Spy* | 1 84588 055 2 |
| Craik, Dinah | *John Halifax, Gentleman* | 1 84588 027 7 |
| Dickens, Charles | *Christmas Books* | 1 84588 195 8 |
| Galsworthy, John | *The Apple Tree* | 1 84588 013 7 |
| Galsworthy, John | *A Long-Ago Affair* | 1 84588 105 2 |
| Galsworthy, John | *The White Monkey* | 1 84588 058 7 |
| Gosse, Edmund | *Father and Son* | 1 84588 018 8 |
| Haliburton, Thomas Chandler | *The Attaché* | 1 84588 049 8 |
| Haliburton, Thomas Chandler | *The Clockmaker* | 1 84588 050 1 |
| Hardy, Thomas | *Desperate Remedies* | 1 84588 099 4 |
| Howells, William Dean | *Suburban Sketches* | 1 84588 083 8 |
| Poe, Edgar Allan | *Tales* | 1 84588 036 6 |
| Radcliffe, Ann | *The Romance of the Forest* | 1 84588 073 0 |
| Surtees, Robert S. | *"Ask Mamma"* | 1 84588 002 1 |
| Trollope, Anthony | *The Vicar of Bullhampton* | 1 84588 097 8 |
| Wilkins, Mrs William Noy | *The Slave Son* | 1 84588 086 2 |